JADE'S BROKEN BRIDGE

A NOVEL

MICHELE LEE SEFTON

tumbleweed
Spirit press

Published by: Tumbleweed Spirit Press
Cover and book design by: TreeHouse Studio
Edited by: Sharon Skinner
Author website: msefton.com

tumbleweed
Spirit press

Praise for
JADE'S BROKEN BRIDGE

"What stands out in Sefton's writing is her ability to let readers into the story without weighing them down. Despite the subject matter, including addiction, grief, and exploitation, there's an undercurrent of hope and a desire for something more... It's a coming-of-age book for readers who appreciate storytelling that doesn't flinch. With its engaging voice and heartfelt honesty, *Jade's Broken Bridge* is both a cautionary tale and a testament to the strength it takes to rebuild. A heavy story, yes, but told with just enough wit and heart to keep readers turning the page."

–San Francisco Book Review

"In her vivid and haunting debut, Sefton deftly portrays the life of a survivor. Jade is a reliable character in an unreliable world. Carefully crafted with moving prose and striking imagery, the author delivers a passionate, gritty tale of impossible choices and ultimate redemption. An impressive debut, indeed. "

–Jennifer Gooch Hummer, bestselling author, *Veridian Sterling Fakes It*

"Sefton carves out one woman's fight for survival in this moving debut, following Arizona teenager Jade, whose desperate need for money propels her into "a life of despair and addiction." ...What makes her journey unique is Sefton's skill at crafting her gradual transformation: visceral disgust at this new world, followed by a begrudging appreciation of the strength and community she discovers there, to the final wild, drugged mess it turns her into... Sefton triumphs with this riveting portrait of a broken girl desperate for the light..."

–BookLife

"In a masterful debut, Michele Lee Sefton carries readers through a woman's journey of self-discovery, unflinchingly guiding her main character from feelings of loss and, perhaps, resentment to strength and independence. Jade's path through the adult dancing world offers readers a glimpse into the shadows and a raw and honest portrait of the opportunities as well as the risks that lie there. Sefton has created a character to root for... it is impossible not to feel her struggles in your bones as you read. A deep, thoughtful and immersive read that will stay with you long after the final sentence."

–Ginger Scott, *USA Today, Wall Street Journal*
and Amazon bestselling author

"Sefton offers a gritty and introspective chronicle of one woman's descent into addiction and sex work in 1980s America. The author invites readers into a visceral, memory-laden interior landscape. Chapters move fluidly between present-tense narration and past recollections. Vivid descriptions of frozen sidewalks, smoky clubs, sticky bar floors, and the ache of unspoken shame create an immersive reading experience. ...the author maintains control over the narrative voice, even as Jade loses control over her life. A harrowing yet beautifully rendered chronicle of loss, self-destruction, and the long road to self-acceptance."

–Kirkus Reviews

"Author Michele Sefton uses vivid and poetic imagery to tell the story of Jade's descent into a world filled with loud music, flashing lights, and parties laced with "liquid courage" and an overabundance of cocaine. Jade takes the reader on a journey through her inner demons as well as her inner goddess who is trying hard to pull her life forward."

–Sandra Marinella, author, *The Story You Need to Tell*

Dedication

Jade's Broken Bridge is dedicated to those who arrive with much to offer this world and yet, feel lost and alone in it. To those who silently struggle to survive while dreaming and reaching for a better life, I feel your pain and I understand your plight. A burdened path that can lead to desperation, a dead end. I know all too well. I also know, this is not where *your* story ends. You may not see it now, but beyond the darkness there is a place for *you* to shine.

To the angels who offer hope and make a difference, sometimes with just a few sentences, thank you for your presence.

– Michele Lee

JADE'S BROKEN BRIDGE

Traveling down Grand Boulevard, it looms beside me...an abandoned building under an overpass I drive by on my way to downtown Phoenix. The building stirs up memories I would rather forget. A red stop light gives me more time to stare at the empty building. The huddle of people and trash, that now reside on the cracked black tar are transformed into a bustling scene of young women running across the crowded parking lot to beat the clock and the late fee that will surely follow if the clock wins.

I still see the men, in their work uniforms, making "one stop" before heading home, and the broad-framed bouncer surveying the parking lot from his perch on a stool near the door. The once brightly lit sign high above him is now shattered with no announcements to make. I gaze and remember... until the green light jolts me back to the present. I drive away, leaving my memories discarded like the debris and lost people who now live where my feet once stepped.

Chapter 1

a dying wish

I stood at the edge of her bed, cowering from a stench that had replaced her usual butterscotch scent. It was hard to distinguish where her frail body began and the pale sheets ended, blended as they were on the plastic-covered hospice-grade twin. She spoke without lifting her head and without moving a finger or a limb. Her faint voice moved slowly along the crumpled top sheet as it traveled toward me, her granddaughter. She forced her fading energy into light discussion and attempted pleasantries with me, the only visitor in her room. I asked her if I could bring anything the next time I visited.

Without hesitation, she whispered, "Some citrus would be nice."

The longing in her tone revealed a mind clinging to hope. The desperate thirst in her voice revealed a body that had abandoned her. Her request did not sound like a whim, or a ploy to see me again. It sounded like she had been dreaming about eating a sweet orange, and finally, someone came along to fulfill her wish. I would not be that person.

I saw the pleading in her eyes. I failed to understand the urgency. How cruel I was to evoke a longing in her and not deliver. I loved my dear grandmother, and I would have done anything for her. Later.

The winter sun was setting, and the golden rays that had danced across my grandmother's room when I first arrived were disappearing. A chill ran through me when the last sliver of sunshine slipped beyond the horizon, turning her white room a charcoal gray. I noticed a shadowy figure resting on my grandmother's chest as she labored to breathe. It began shifting into the shape of a cat. I should have tried to protect my grandmother from the cat's creepy presence, but I was mesmerized by its slinking movements. The line of cocaine I'd done in my car thirty minutes prior was making my mind a liar.

No one, including the nurse who checked on my grandmother while I stood bedside, would have noticed that she and I were both being courted by a luring spirit from the underworld. Death's messenger was closing in, inviting both of us to join him. Arms outstretched, he reached for her with his left hand, and with his right hand he was reaching for me. My outward appearance did not reflect the invitation.

My grandmother may have been comforted by my tan skin, my fit frame, and my goldilocks, but under my youthful disguise lived a truth that I was not ready to admit to anyone, including myself. A year that had begun with a desperate decision to better my financial situation had descended me into a life of despair and addiction. Maybe the dying woman sensed more of this than I realized.

Tempted, I was, to lie down next to the death scene unfolding before me, to inhale the last bit of goodness from the world, in hopes it would purify my fraying soul. One last exhale before slipping into nothingness. Tempting, it was, to join the one-woman cast of this final show.

Too weak in spirit to reject death's invitation, I did the only thing I could do and what I always do when a situation becomes too intense—I closed my eyes. If I cannot see it, it does not exist. In that moment, while sinking into the valley of my thoughts, a voice outside of myself, stronger than my own, told me what I wasn't ready to hear:

Your grandmother is fighting to live, and you are slowly killing yourself.

I began to shiver and shake. I saw myself in my grandmother's dying frame. The great awakening exited my body and made room for shame. I wasn't ready to lose my grandmother. *I wasn't ready to change.* Fighting every urge to run from the prophetic message overwhelming my senses, and from the wilting flower stretched before me, I sat on her bed and cupped her left hand between my hands. I wanted to be strong for her. I wanted to confess all I had lived through over the past year. I wanted her to tell me it would be okay and that I would find my way out of the mess I had made. I said nothing.

I began reciting a prayer that I learned from a doll my grandmother had given to me as a Christmas gift when I was eight. I remembered my grandmother sitting on the edge of our brown couch, leaning toward me while I opened the plain paper package. I pulled out a chocolate brown doll with long brown hair. She wore a pink nightgown. I hugged the doll and said "I love her" while my grandmother smiled. One press on the doll's belly and a tiny gold record played the prayer that I recited while seated on the edge of my grandmother's bed.

"Now I lay me down to sleep, I pray the Lord my soul to keep. If I shall die before I wake, I pray the Lord my soul to take."

Hearing these words, my grandmother turned toward me.

"Do you remember the doll you gave me?" I asked her. "The one that said that prayer? I loved that doll. I wish I had her now."

My grandmother responded with a smile.

I began to cry. I tried not to, but I could no longer contain the emotions I had been suppressing. Our eyes met, and in that moment, a lifetime of grandma memories flooded my brain. Me seated on the barstool, watching as she served customers at my grandparents' diner...unwrapping Easter baskets as tall as me, while my grandmother watched and smiled...eating large red radishes from her garden...her seated, tense and shivering, at the bow of my dad's bass boat, relaxing only when my dad eased the throttle and coasted to the calm shore.

Sweet memories of my childhood morphed into fractured scenes from my last year of extreme living. Drunk men on barstools entertained by my bare skin…driving past my grandmother's neighborhood in the early hours after a night of dancing…sacrificing my common sense and my soul for dollars and cents…not taking my grandmother out to lunch a single time in over a year. *Not once.* Avoiding her was easier than lying to her about my daily choices. With her, I would get no more chances to make it right. Was it too late to change my life?

I could not control the memories or the sobs that washed my grandmother's tiny wrist while letting my face rest on her fragile hand. A lifetime of memories and a year's worth of shame soaked her thin sheets.

Chapter 2

a yellow brick road, this is not

From my studio apartment balcony, I watched an army of small scattered gray clouds find each other. Many became one. Darkness swallowed the blue sky and the sun. Rain is rare in the Sonoran Desert, but that did not stop my pleading. I begged the growing entity to crack open and release a cleansing on me. I wanted to be washed away; I would settle for a balcony baptism. My legs were too tired to seek shelter for my shivering skin. On my thrift-store chair, I remained. My mind was too exhausted to care about work. I didn't even have the strength to call in.

Everything will be fine, the devil inside reassured my slouching frame. *Just get yourself to work then you can do another line*. I did not have the willpower to disagree. Another line in the parking lot would get my body through the night shift, but it would do nothing to calm my mind.

How did I end up here? A defeated woman, begging for inky rain to wash me away. A topless dancer, craving the burn of chalky lines. Anything…to escape. How did a girl with so much potential fuck up so badly?

As a young girl, I read all the fairy tales. I knew the words to "A Dream Is a Wish Your Heart Makes." I became Cinderella—mistreated, then celebrated—as I twirled and sang that song in my light blue polyester pajamas. I believed in magic, dreams, and fairy dust. For the last year, I had been surviving in a world that chews up sparkles—a dark world that did not host fairy godmothers for tea, and a Prince Charming I had yet to see. I only saw toads who licked their lips while they croaked at our spinning tricks.

Evil characters and forces in fairy tales disappear when the book is closed, but my dark world was never ending. It was full of people who take and use without regard for their actions, and where substances that easily slip from "trying" to "abusing" are plentiful. I did not belong in this chaotic world with these characters. My casting in this story was wrong. *That's what I told myself.*

One glance through my childhood scrapbooks would confirm the belief I held of my purity and potential. Those scrapbook pages contained academic achievement awards, band accomplishments, pom and dance photographs, along with black and white photos that I developed in a high school dark room, volunteer ribbons and certificates, and numerous other glued-on items that were creating a path toward a promising future.

Flipping through family photo albums would reveal more of my story. In those albums, I am the girl with large emerald eyes that reflect the pain of a fractured family. Fractures that eventually tore idealistic family photos to shreds. Fitting that my scrapbooks and hundreds of family photos are now disintegrating in a landfill—tossed there by a thief who kept things of value and threw the rest in the trash. His greedy hands destroyed the items we valued most and most of the evidence that I ever was a child. Now I was an adult needing to climb out of the garbage I buried myself in.

The dark cloud wasn't budging, and my bitter memories weren't bringing me closer to understanding. More questions were forthcoming. Why am I sitting here alone, facing a firing squad whose strength-in-numbers is growing? Where are my parents during my tortured lament? Why are they not by my side? If not in flesh, then why not in spirit? Why isn't their love an armor against anything that might harm me? Shouldn't that be the promise of every parent? I can't defeat these dark forces alone. Why should I? Alone, these crimes I did not commit.

I watched a tumbleweed roll down the street, whipped by a strengthening desert wind, taking my pointless questions with it. My eyes followed its lift and spin until it was out of vision.

My young parents' volatile relationship reached a dramatic ending when I was twelve and my brother, fourteen. Our mom, a curvy whirlwind of fury, finally had enough. She smashed the glass of a framed family portrait before storming through the house. She ripped my dad's clothes from hangers and emptied his dresser drawers. She tossed his fishing gear down from the attic, causing an explosion when toolboxes and poles smacked against concrete. She threw my dad's neat and tidy life across the lawn and with an ounce of compassion or a large dose of sarcasm, she topped off the pile with a pot and pan. A war once contained within was now on display for all to see. Peering through the heavy curtains at my dad's belongings, I wondered, *What will the neighbors think?*

Eight years had passed since that embarrassing front yard scene. I had kept the evil characters and forces at bay for as long as I could. I had heeded the First Lady's warning. "Just say no," we were told, over and over. I listened. I said, "No," at high school parties, over and over. I despised the twisted smiles and twitching skin of those who kept offering.

So much had happened since I graduated from high school two and a half years ago. *So much but nothing of value, to me.* Some might say being the first in my family to graduate from high school *was something*. Maybe it is, but I had greater goals than a high school diploma. If my life had gone according to my childhood dreams, I would be well into a journalism program at a choice university. I received my share of attractive university brochures as a junior in high school. I read every page and dreamed about being a student at each of the campuses that mailed me an invitation package. I dreamed. I wished. I did not talk to either of my divorced parents about these grand college goals. They were dealing with their own problems. The dream of an out-of-state university was too big. I tossed the brochures in the trash.

On my own before high school ended, I did not pursue a path toward my university dream—the one that had motivated me to do well in school. The one that had given me hope through my parents' many fights and moves. I was living a broke girl's nightmare. I did not have a boyfriend. My brother had joined the army. My parents were consumed with failing second marriages. Most of my childhood friends were busy getting on with their lives.

Many forces helped set the stage for my year of traveling down a wayward road scattered with other lost souls. *That's what I told myself.*

My Swatch Watch told me it was time to bury thoughts of a painful past and get ready for work. I gave up on my balcony baptism and dragged my worn-out self to a hot shower. That would have to do. For now. To escape this darkness, I would need to spin my own magic and save myself.

Chapter 3

amateur hour

I did not plunge into a world that left me broken and exposed, nor was I forced. A year and a half after graduating from high school, I tested the unfamiliar environment by dipping my toes in. I had been working full-time at a video store in Scottsdale and taking two classes at Mesa Community College. I did not have much food in my fridge, but I had plenty of bills on the counter. I had stretched my five dollar an hour gig as far as it could go.

When I wasn't working or studying, I was searching the help wanted ads for a financial lifeline out of my barely surviving existence. I went to a few interviews. As a nineteen-year-old with limited education or experience, I was either deemed underqualified, or the jobs were more of what I already had: not enough. When scanning the help wanted section, I kept noticing ads for "dancers." I didn't know anything about that world, but I knew they weren't looking for ballerinas. I began imagining the possibilities. What if dancing in a "gentlemen's club" was my ticket out of the financial black hole I had fallen into? After all, I knew how to dance.

I kept going to work and school and pondering a dancing escape. *Making more than five dollars an hour. Working less. Schooling more.* The temptation of having more control over my future and finances became too great. I caved. I called one of the "Adult Entertainment" ads that advertised an amateur night. The lady on the other end of the call was direct; she told me when, where, and what to wear while loud music thumped in the background.

I did not have grand expectations for my first, and possibly last, amateur dancing contest. I expected the evening to reveal what an ill-suited pair we were: a socially awkward, studious girl and the adult dancing world. I had another thought, too—a tiny belief that I could do this.

After sunset, on the 27th of October, 1988, I left my massive Tempe apartment complex and made my way into Phoenix. I did not tell my two roommates, university students and high school friends, where I was going.

Every mile I drove took me farther away from the vibrant campus sidewalks. Zip code boundary lines blurred. No longer did I see college students who walked with purposeful, yet relaxed strides. I saw women in thigh-high boots strutting slowly, perilously close to cars cruising by. One woman waved a large fan toward her face, hidden by heaps of hair. I passed men in a convenience store parking lot, talking close and exchanging items, rushed by the approaching glare of headlights. A silhouette stumbled near a large trash container in a dimly lit alley. A car horn blared when I stared too long at an elderly man crossing the sidewalk to my right, the hunch in his back further curved by the weight of his bag.

I was not afraid of traveling into the city, alone at night. My own dark shadow sat next to me, and it was more at home with other lost souls than it was with the college crowd. I was on a mission to give this help-wanted curiosity one date before rewinding myself down the city streets, back to my dreams, nestled in a college town where I felt like an outsider. Maybe there was a place in the middle of these worlds where I could find a path to me.

I sat in my car long enough to draw suspicion from the bouncer. I found courage, or borrowed it from somewhere, got out of my car, and walked up to him. He asked for an ID. Legal age verified, I stepped onto worn carpet and into a blurry scene. A wave of smoke, swirling with the vapors of strong alcohol, floating dust, cheap perfume, and stale sweat almost knocked me over. It would have been an easy task since my legs were already shaking.

Men were seated around tables. Some were alone and some were with others. They all seemed to move in slow motion, if they moved at all. It was like looking at a tacky, smoke-covered picture hanging in a dive bar.

The hazy reality also contained voluptuous women, who wore the same amount of clothing as women resting poolside, or swimming at the lake. Their movements reminded me that I was not lounging lakeside, and I was not a carefree sun goddess ruling over slow-moving mortals. I was a desperate girl trying to build a better life. I watched the women slink around the beer-covered tables, like sharks circling prey, vying for the attention of the men, not for their affection but for what they had in their back pockets.

As I leaned against the sticky bar, a woman approached me. Her charged presence devoured the energy of everyone in the room. She quickly introduced herself as the "House Mom," then motioned me to follow her down a corridor that seemed to have no end. She pointed to the "first stage," and my eyes followed the direction of her finger. I was flooded with a dizzying, nauseous feeling.

As we continued down the hallway, a struggle began brewing within me; opposing sides were choosing their weapons and lining up. Maybe angels would arrive and shelter me under their wings, but I only saw thugs and thieves. The light, and my courage, began to dim. I was another sacrificial lamb walking foolishly toward a swinging axe smudged with the blood of other desperate women.

A shrill *ting*ing pierced my brain. It sounded like the sharpening of that axe. A vision began to form in my mind, of an axe held by hands that would not rock me gently or protect me from beasts that would arrive on the splintered wings of nightmares. These hands would chop me in half without tremor, with the sole purpose of stealing the life-giving passion pumping under my youthful skin.

Thirsty creatures were circling me, their tongues wagging, catching flies and licking their slanted lips. The hue of the main room turned deep red, then black, as we walked farther down the long corridor, which seemed to be closing around me. We entered what appeared to be a storage room at the end of the hall. The waiting room—waiting to see if we were good enough to enter the dressing room, reserved for the "professional" dancers.

The House Mom skipped pleasantries and asked me my stage name. *A stage name*? I had not considered that. I told her the first thing that came to mind—Jade. She then told me to change into my costume, wait for my name to be called, then follow the girl in front of me to stage two, then three.

"Do you have pasties?" she asked.

"Yes, I was told to bring them when I called."

"Good. Any tips collected are yours to keep," she explained in a tone that made no attempt at false promises. Being a cheerleader was apparently not in her House Mom job description. There was nothing maternal about her.

"They will announce the winner at the end of the contest," she added.

I already knew that would not be me. I was out of my element and out of my mind for being here. Like an awkward teenager in gym class, I quickly changed into my pauper dance costume and slipped into my white stilettos—a recent Payless ShoeSource purchase. Buy one, get the second pair half off. The second pair, I wore into the joint, a pair of tennis shoes that would allow me to run the fuck out of here. Maybe the smoky still-life crowd would take pity on the dancing peasant and shower her with dollar bills. *Not likely*. This was not a nonprofit destination where do-gooders donated. This was a harsh place where men used their money as power and women used their skin to survive.

Call my name. Don't call my name. Call my name. Fuck my name! Fuck this!

Waiting for the axe to drop, I paced the carpet that, like the customers in the carnival room, was stained and frayed. Outdated paneling lined the walls. Rubber padding would have been more appropriate, I thought. I had to keep moving or my legs might turn to stone. Like Medusa's victims, my body would follow. No one would know that I was once a vibrant young woman with a pumping heart and sky-reaching dreams. My stone legs would feature scribbled profanity, written by other amateurs waiting for their names to be called. Women would glance, only to compare my body to theirs, never to wonder who I once was. Upon my stone arms, they would hang their cheap purses and worn-out troubles. Thin garments and worries would cover my stone head. My mind was spiraling. I kept pacing.

The end of a song sent my heart into summersaults. The silence after the last note drew me toward the crackling speaker, like a flittering moth toward its shocking death. *Will it be me*? Like in Shirley Jackson's short story, "The Lottery," I was waiting for my lucky number to be called. I would gladly step into that shocking story and accept my stone fate versus spending one more hour in this tormented state. The DJ would be my spinning savior. His voice hissed and popped its way through the exposed speaker wire that coiled its way up the '70s faux wood.

Faux was an appropriate option for a place that spotlighted silicone. Real wood could have turned that room into a pot-burning stove reducing the entire building to ashes in a matter of minutes. For the betterment of society, that did need to happen, but, like the mythical Phoenix, it would rise again, ready to lure cash-seeking women and flesh-seeking men into a world of smoky make-believe.

At last, as in the very last amateur, I finally heard my newly acquired name.

"Next up, we have Jade …"

A new name acknowledged without any paperwork or mandatory fees. One just needed to walk down the long dark corridor, slip on some stilettos, and become someone else. The new name did not erase my troubles or my faults and this glimpse into another world did not erase my old one. I dragged that bag of jagged boulders and stinking shit with me down the dark hallway. Life baggage that now felt like an oversized pair of stilettos standing on my shoulders, digging and twisting their pointy heels into my flesh.

Trapped under imaginary skin-splitting spikes and pulsating with pops and fizzles, I began to walk toward the stage. I scanned the tunnel for a trash can or any receptacle that could catch my vomit. I wanted to run back down the hall and back to my car, but that would take more courage and strength than stepping onto the flesh freakshow that began on stage one.

I did not need another reason to feel insecure and out of place, but there she was, walking toward me. A poised dancer wearing a tiny sailor costume. White fishnet thigh-highs enwrapped her toned legs, and a tiny blue skirt with red ribbing along its short hem bounced with each step. Her blue-and-white striped bra with a red bow in the front was unattached in the back, and a blue-and-white striped sailor hat completed the costume. Dirty and dull dollar bills tucked under her blue and white G-string contrasted with her sweat-covered skin, sparkling like diamonds. I resisted my urge to salute her as she brushed past. I could have used a life preserver.

I walked the five steps up to the stage and attempted to move to "Pour Some Sugar on Me," by Def Leppard. My squeaky Payless shoes were slipping off my sweaty feet and my legs felt like concrete. *What was happening to me*? I needed to pull myself together. I went into survival mode and became a fast-learning understudy. I watched other girls—women—who knew what they were doing, including smiling their way through repetitive movements. I tried to emulate their sultry slinking and skin-exposed gyrating. Awkward and uncomfortable to watch and mimic, but as a dancer, I knew how.

I wanted it to end—the torture. My penance for wanting to join the college crowd, it seemed. I could hear the end of the song approaching, just above the grinding axe noise still buzzing in my brain. I had yet to emulate one expert move—the main reason men visited topless clubs—or the two reasons, tucked temporarily under polyester triangles. I needed to take my top off, and I needed to do it without spewing chunks on the tops of balding heads attached to the bulging bodies seated beside the stage. I unhooked my bra and shared my full natural Cs with a room full of strangers. They glanced or stared, but no one became hypnotized by my glittery pasties. No one fell out of his chair. Clearly, I was the only one having a life-changing moment.

A scruffy older man sitting close to the stage, watching a view he had probably seen ten thousand times before, asked me, "Shouldn't you be home doing your homework?" Not exactly the response I had hoped for after baring my ta-tas.

He was either wiser than I would have imagined, or more cynical. I am not sure which, but he was right. I would rather have been doing that. I made it through two more songs, danced on two more stages, and then I headed back to the utility room. My walk back down the dark hallway was made heavier, not by the weight of three sweaty dollars, but by a blanket of humiliation.

They announced the "winner" of the contest while I was changing. It was not only *not* me; she was not an "amateur." *Shouldn't there be some criteria?* I was upset and disgusted and I could not leave that building fast enough. I darted to my car with my three dollar bills and my shadow, now mocking me. A quick-footed man followed me and handed me his "Club Manager" card and asked me if I would be interested in working there. His card, with a title but no name, told me that club managers with pumped biceps and slicked-back hair probably rotated through that club as often as the desperate girls in stilettos.

"No!" I blurted in his direction. "Why would I ever want to come back here? I'm leaving here with three dollars. That barely covers my gas!"

I tossed his card on the passenger seat and punched the gas in my VW Rabbit, praying it would not break down. I was grateful for the dark so that I could hide. I did not expect to see anyone I knew, but I needed to hide from myself. Despite my almost empty gas tank and full dose of shame, my night was a success. I could put this escape plan to rest and look for another way out of my mess. I threw my stilettos in the closet and crashed hard on my unmade bed. I woke up the next morning with a headache, sore feet, and a stiff back. I showered, got dressed, had a piece of dry toast, and went back to my video job.

Chapter 4

a secondhand coat

Other than the bouncer, the House Mom, a few drunk patrons, the DJ who said my stage name, and the manager who pursued me in the parking lot, the only other person who knew of my dancing attempt was Antonio, a university student who lived in the same apartment complex as me. He had long thick hair, the color of Hershey's milk chocolate, and deep-sea eyes that consumed my words when our eyes locked. A few days after my three-dollar night, I called his place and asked him if he could meet me outside, near the apartment laundry room. It took me that many days to make the call.

Stammering, I shared highlights of my "amateur" evening with him and Antonio's only response was, "People do what they need to do to survive." I shook my head to his words, which offered acknowledgment but were void of the compassion I longed for. While we were talking on the sidewalk between our apartment buildings a girl carrying a laundry basket full of clothes walked toward us. Teasing me or torturing me, Antonio asked the passing girl her opinion about topless dancing. She quickly admonished him and the idea. My heart began to beat faster, and I could feel an infusion of blood spread across my cheeks. My eyes lowered to the cracked concrete and remained there while he entertained himself.

He seemed to delight in making me uncomfortable at parties with a playful glance or a brush against my butt, but never anything like this. Antonio and I had been on one date prior to my dancing night. After a casual dinner and playful conversation, we saw each other in passing and at apartment parties. We did not have sex or a second date. A few weeks following our sidewalk conversation I learned from his roommate that Antonio's mutilated body had been found in a ditch south of the Arizona border, in Mexico. His roommate confessed that Antonio had been dealing drugs for a few years. I was nauseated by the news. I thought about Antonio's arrogant attitude and wondered if that had contributed to his horrific demise. Not that I was offered, but I did not need to see images of his beautiful body, face, and hair destroyed by a drug deal gone wrong. My imagination conjured the violence without that evidence. It seems I was not the only one "doing what I needed to do to survive."

My dancing dream was paused, not forgotten. After weeks of working myself to exhaustion and near starvation, of body and spirit, I decided to give dancing another try. I called a different dancing ad. This ad was not for an amateur night. Maybe it would reveal a path toward a self-funded university degree. If not, no harm would come in learning more.

On a day off, I scheduled a meeting with Tara, the lady on the other end of the phone call, to discuss her "dancing opportunity." We met at a café on Mill Avenue in Tempe, just blocks from Arizona State University. I was greeted by a woman not much older than me. She appeared harmless; beautiful, even. She had short black hair that was smooth and shiny, curling slightly toward her prominent porcelain cheek bones. Her hair was a contrast to my wavy, long sandy-blond hair that turned in every direction, except the direction I desired. Tara did not seem to mind our contrasts; in fact, she seemed quite pleased with my "look." She was slender, soft-spoken, and exotic looking. She was the perfect spokesperson to lure young women away from warm winter weather into a frigid frozen land. We learned a little about each other, then she proceeded to tell me about the opportunity—the reason for our meeting.

She represented a club owner from Fairbanks, Alaska, who needed young female dancers to work at his club. All travel and lodging expenses would be covered. The lodging would be in a residence in downtown Fairbanks, and if I accepted the offer, I would live with other dancers in dorm-style accommodations. I would depart Phoenix a week before Christmas, fly to Fairbanks, and then dance for eight weeks. I would work for six days straight, with Mondays off, and my workday would begin at 6 p.m. and end when the bar closed, at 3 a.m.

At the end of my contract, I would be given my return ticket for a flight home. Tara's delivery and demeanor made everything seem simple and straightforward. Too simple. I felt like she was trying to sell me on the idea of a dream vacation, not a dancing vocation. I was curious. I was desperate. She said I might even come home with several thousand dollars. That comment hushed the alarms buzzing in my brain. "Several thousand dollars." Those words tumbled in my mind and made it difficult for me to concentrate on anything else she was saying. Several thousand dollars would make it possible for me to finally escape the less challenging but more affordable community college classes and transfer to Arizona State University. Her cash carrot was so tempting. Could I do it? Did I have the courage to travel somewhere I had never been? Alone? Without a return ticket in my purse? My shaking hands told me no. I told her I would think about it. We parted ways.

She called me a few days later to check in on me and to see if I had reached a decision. I had not. I kept going to work and thinking about her invitation. I kept dreaming about sitting in lecture halls at ASU instead of slinging CDs and movies at my minimum wage job. The job that kept me busy all week but did not pay me enough to cover all my bills. My bills and stress were mounting. I kept dealing with annoying customers, who were getting more unbearable with the approaching holiday season. I hated working in retail. I hated it even more during the busiest shopping season of the year. People can be so rude and impatient.

I wondered if the men in Alaska would be an escape from the retail stress or if they would be even more demanding. I wondered if it would be worth taking a break from my community college classes and giving up my shitty known gig for the risky unknown and what my next step might be after returning home, one month before spring. Jobless and classless, what would I do until fall semester? Stressed by bills and obsessed with dreams of school it was becoming increasingly difficult to smile and say, "Have a nice day." I kept thinking. Toiling. Losing sleep. Another battle raging within. The charming club rep kept calling and checking in. She was never pushy, only polite and patient. It was the perfect strategy.

I said yes.

I decided that what I had been doing was not getting me closer to my dream of financing a four-year degree, so I might as well try something that possibly could.

I *tried* to prepare for my eight-week trip into the unknown—the situation and the weather—but both were foreign to me. How is a desert girl supposed to prepare for tundra living? I did not own a proper coat or warm boots, or anything else that would protect my skin from frostbite. I was resourceful though, and one by one, I worked my way down Tara's list of suggested items. I picked up extra shifts at work and used the "extra" cash to buy secondhand items.

To the disappointment of my kind manager, I resigned from my video clerk job. I was unsure and scared, but I also felt like I was finally doing something that might benefit me beyond the low-paying dead-end track I was on. I completed my two community college classes. I fabricated a story to my loosely involved divorced parents about getting a nanny job in California. Caught up in their own dramas, they did not ask any questions. The fact that I took care of myself, which included paying my own bills, seemed to be a relief to them. They did not know that my stack of unpaid bills was growing and that my desire to transfer to ASU was consuming me.

They did not ask about any of this. I made life easier for everyone by lying about where I would be for two months.

When the uncertainty of the approaching situation became too overwhelming, I told myself the same lie. I told my roommates just enough of what they needed to know. They knew where I was going and how to contact me, if needed. I knew they would tell a few others who would tell a few others, but I was too busy trying to survive to lose sleep over what others might think of me. They had no idea how hard my road was, nor did they care to find out. I was not exactly forthcoming with my life struggles, either.

One of my roommates, Christina, lectured me about what I was doing and that I was looking for the "easy way out." She was right; I was. I had been traveling down a difficult road, alone, since my parents' divorce, seven years prior. Her unsolicited advice was nurtured in the comfort of knowing that her portion of the monthly rent was covered by a supportive parent, while she focused on classes, learning, and a bright future. I did not have that privilege, but there was some truth to her concern, even if delivered through judgment. My choices *were* questionable. Did I really know where I was going or who the club owner was? No, I did not. I could end up anywhere, with anyone, never to be seen again. And the details of my whereabouts would be in the hands of two young women who would have spent more time saying, "I told her so," than looking for the lost girl. Lost, I was.

Chapter 5
read the fine print

When it came time to leave Phoenix, Tara picked me up and dropped me off at Sky Harbor International Airport. It was a perfect 73-degree December day in Phoenix, Arizona. The plane touched down in Seattle over two hours later. I spent the next two hours wishing I could explore the city. *Wishful thinking.* I wasn't traveling for pleasure. The next plane carried me over a sea of snow-covered mountains. It was late and dark. I gazed out the window and watched the endless white for nearly four hours. I panicked at one point, thinking that maybe my plane had gone too far, passing over the Bering Sea, headed toward Siberia. Maybe it was a trick, or a trap. I closed the window and my eyes and tried to remain calm. There wasn't a damn thing I could do, strapped in a seatbelt 35,000 feet in the air. With my eyes closed I began to explore what I might be stepping into after getting off the plane and what I might face when I return. *Maybe getting lost in Siberia would be a better choice than taking off my clothes for cash or feeling forever lost at home?*

My plane landed in Fairbanks, Alaska, 2,634 miles from Phoenix, Arizona on Friday, December 16, 1988. I was a long way from home. It was close to midnight when I departed the plane. I stepped into the small terminal and looked around for anyone who might be looking for me. No one stepped forward. I collected my borrowed suitcase and kept scanning the bundled-up strangers. No eyes caught mine; none were even trying.

"Oh, my God," I whispered. "I landed in Fairbanks, and no one is here for me."

I felt frantically alone. I remembered that the club rep had written a name and contact number on a piece of scrap paper. Beginning to perspire, despite feeling the freezing chill every time the sliding glass door opened, I rummaged through my suitcase, found the number and some change, and called the number from a payphone. The person on the other end was difficult to understand and the hum of people in the background made it hard to hear. By the time I hung up the phone, I had some assurance that someone was on their way to get me, so I waited. What else could I do? My traveling day had ended, and a new life was beginning. I did not feel the hope that sometimes accompanies a new day, but I was not going to be stranded at the Fairbanks airport with nothing to do but watch the layered crowd slumber about.

An older Asian woman walked into the small terminal, holding a sign with my name. *If anyone ever holds up my name on a small, handwritten sign again, I hope it's under more inspiring circumstances.* With my one suitcase in tow, I followed the tiny lady, who said nothing beyond "hello," into her vehicle, which she had left running. Smart. I was no expert on tundra living, but I imagined that 33 degrees below zero could quickly freeze a car and a human. Her station wagon was warm and reeked with an odor that stole my breath and reminded me of visiting my aunt and uncle's farm as a child. Small feathers decorated the worn car seat and chickens, caged, clucked behind me. Off we drove into the unknown with my eyes burning and my stomach turning.

My eight-week home was hidden behind a storefront on a city street in Fairbanks, Alaska. Bunk bed-filled rooms and a large communal restroom with a hot tub in the corner were concealed beyond the business façade.

I was shown to my bed after passing through a smoky-dark room filled with gamblers who were too fixated on their poker hands and the actions of those betting against them to notice *another* girl rushing through their space. I dropped my suitcase next to a twin mattress that had folded sheets and a pillow waiting for me. *A folded reminder that I was there to work.* Except for two occupied bunk beds, the others were empty because their sleepers were still working. I said hello to the two girls lounging on their beds. We told each other where we were from. Those brief introductions were more than I needed to know at that time. I was tired. A twin mattress never looked so inviting. I would put on my stilettos and join the ranks the following evening. Until then, I could enjoy my last night of falling asleep before 3 a.m.

The next day, I met the rest of the dance crew. All were either my age or in their early twenties, from the Phoenix area, and the club recruiter could not have selected a more diverse group of ladies. There were eight girls in the dorm, but the four I connected with the most were Jennifer, a hippie girl with tan skin and long beach hair; Gabriela, a curvy girl with beige-colored skin, wavy dark hair, and a child back home; Loren, the tallest of the group with straight, thick black hair and large lips; and Desiree, a beautiful girl with skin the color of dark honey and a ballerina body. And then there was me, Jade, the petite, green-eyed sandy blond. After breakfast, which felt more like a late lunch, we chatted. They told me more about their lives back home than their living and dancing situation in Fairbanks. I listened, but I was more interested in the conditions of the club. *I suppose I will find out soon enough.*

I spent the rest of the day waiting for the late afternoon to arrive. For the other girls, the downtime meant time to rest. For me, it meant pacing the thinly carpeted floors. I would rather pace outside in the fresh air, but it was bone-chilling cold and dimly lit at best. When the time came to get ready for our dancing shift, there was a line of girls sitting on the floor in front of the wall-size mirror, preparing hair and makeup for another night of make-believe. The blaring Paula Abdul song did nothing to calm my nerves, already firing in every direction, making my hands shake so it was almost impossible for me to apply my cheap makeup. It was a wonder everyone's hair wasn't charged from all the electricity flowing through my veins. After a loud and staccato "Let's go!" from the lady who had picked me up from the airport, we all piled into a heated SUV and were driven to the club. I was relieved to not be riding in a station wagon with live chickens caged in the back.

My first night in the Fairbanks club was a Saturday shift that began with an unexpected gift-giving exchange. I had forgotten that Christmas was just over a week away. I was wishing those around us had as well. Having just arrived, I was surprised when I was handed a box with a bracelet inside. The owner of the club had stopped in to pass out gifts on his way out of town for the holidays. I said thank you to him as he stepped down from the stage after delivering a *thanks for all you do* speech to his "dedicated staff."

"You're welcome. Welcome to Fairbanks!" His smile grew while scanning my mostly bare body from eyes to toes. I guess that meant he was pleased with his investment.

I held back from telling him, "Thank you for giving me the only Christmas gift I will get this year." He owned my body, at least for eight weeks. I did not need to reveal how alone I was in this big, wide world.

I watched him hug a few girls, then shake the bartender's hand before rushing out the door. I never wore the bracelet; it slipped from my small wrist. Festivities over, it was time to begin our shift—my first full dance shift. I could have lit this dark town up with my energy.

The expectations of the club were given to me before I began socializing and dancing. There weren't many. We were allowed—even encouraged – to drink with the men, but not too much. Our goal was to keep the liquor flowing for the club and keep the tips flowing for ourselves. The emphasis was put on the club's needs above ours. The thought of going topless when outside temperatures would freeze nipples in a matter of minutes seemed ridiculous.

There were two stages that jetted out from mirrored walls, bordered with lights. The DJ was a doppelganger for Axel Rose, and he celebrated his twin status by playing at least one Guns and Roses song every hour. I had officially entered a snow-covered twilight zone.

I began my dancing career that night, and although I was nervous and felt exposed, the club was casual, and the men were nice enough. Most customers could be put into two groups: either older, rugged mountain men or young, muscular military personnel. There was an army base nearby, so the club had its share of buzzed-top muscular patrons. Many of those young men were born into a world that did not seem to offer too many options, like my world. We were all making the best of the choices that brought us there—doing what we needed to do to survive on the Last Frontier.

Just after my shift started until the end of the night, I heard the same line multiple times, "You should have been here when the pipeline was being built. Those girls made so much money…"

I smiled politely and repeated, "That's what I've heard. Sounds amazing!" What I did not say is, "I would have been a five-year-old then, so please stopping mentioning that!"

My first night in Fairbanks blurred into the early morning hours. Because of the tundra's missing sun, the time of day was distinguished by the clock, not by a change in light outside. Both my dancing and my socializing were awkward. I sipped slowly, paced in between table dances and stage appearances, and then repeated and retraced my steps. That was my routine for the remainder of the night. I was not making "pipeline" tips, but I was making more than five dollars an hour. I was also drinking at work—a job perk that I was not aware of when I agreed to this grand adventure. A lesson learned in reading the fine print. At nineteen, I was not practiced in adult details.

My first night ended with a buzzed brain, aching feet, a freezing ass, and one hundred fifty dollars in my dancer bag. It would have taken me thirty hours of video selling to make that much money back home. My paid-in-full college tuition was off to a cold, but solid start. I had survived my first dancing shift in the land of dark skies, white mountains, and missed opportunities.

Chapter 6

rosy cheeks and blue lips

"All work and no play" makes a dancing girl a dull Jill. Maybe dancing in a club appears as play to some. Indecent interactions to others. I didn't have the luxury of worrying about what others thought, especially others who weren't paying my bills, including those in the club who weren't tipping. Most of the others were regulars, I quickly learned. We were not digging ditches or trenches for pipes, but maybe we were digging our own graves in this strange, dimly lit place.

My first Monday off would include an adventure out of our barracks. Loren, Jennifer, Desiree, and I decided to do some exploring down the icy sidewalks in downtown Fairbanks. We bundled up in layers and ventured out into the freezing cold. A strange world lay beyond the glass doors that led into our building. It was late afternoon, but it looked and felt like midnight. Coming from the land of sunshine, I would never get used to this.

It did not matter that I did not feel an ounce of Christmas cheer or holiday spirit, the town had its own agenda. The four of us, more familiar to each other with our skin revealed, were covered from head to toe; just the circles of our faces were exposed.

"I love the holiday decorations," Loren announced as we passed a garland-covered festive streetlamp.

"It's weird," Jennifer said in a monotone. "It doesn't feel like the holidays."

"I don't think so either," I added, "but this street reminds me of the movie, *It's a Wonderful Life*."

"Yes, we are the fucked-up version of that, you know, the scene where the main guy, what's his name?"

"George," I answered.

"Yeah, that guy. The scene where he's shown how fucked up things are because he wasn't around to make things better." Jennifer's words formed a cloud in front of her face.

She did have a point. The town had lost its innocence and wholesome attitude, not because George wasn't around but because of our association with it. Living with gamblers, drinkers, and smokers and dancing for dollars blurred the picturesque holiday vibe.

"Yeah, we are fucked up," Desiree joined in.

No one responded. No one else wanted to acknowledge the desperate realities of our individual situations. We let the bitter cold freeze those thoughts.

"Let's go in here," Loren blurted, in front of a store that had a cheerfully decorated holiday window display.

She was drawn to the glitter and lights. I wanted to run away from anything that reminded me of the holidays or fake cheer. I wanted to run away from the laughing Santa and silver tinsel and run toward the field at the end of the street, into the dark wilderness beyond it, where no one would follow or find me.

"Jade, are you coming?" Loren held the door open for me.

"Oh, yeah. Sorry."

The four of us walked around the hodgepodge of a store, picking up knick-knacks and placing them back. The store reminded me of the old Woolworth on Main Street in the city where I grew up. Shoes, clothes, makeup, ice cream, toiletries, gift wrapping, cards, and souvenirs. I picked up a postcard that featured a brighter version of the wilderness I imagined escaping to. As I turned the card over to the mostly blank side, I was reminded that I had loved sending handwritten letters when I was a young girl. A writing love affair ignited when I began sending letters to a pen pal in second grade. Ann-Marie was her name. That exchange continued for five years, then abruptly stopped when my mom, stepdad, brother, and I moved out of our house after my parents' divorce. I put the card back. My time in Alaska was not a life moment or a vacation destination that I wanted to share with anyone, and although it was only a dime, I made a promise to myself that I would only spend money on food and any other necessities that came up. A postcard was not that, and what would I write anyway?

Dear roomies, I am having a grand time taking my clothes off in Fairbanks, Alaska. How are you both doing? How are your cats?

I wasted more time looking at hats and gloves while Loren bought herself a small twinkling Christmas tree. She and I clearly had different priorities. I was not looking to decorate my temporary space. I let her have her holiday moment, but to me, the decorated, mostly vacant streets felt like a creepy holiday scene that hid a dark undercurrent.

"It's on sale," she squealed. "It just doesn't feel like Christmas without a tree."

"Maybe it's not supposed to," I chided under my breath.

"What?"

"Nothing. It is a cute tree," I added, and everyone chimed in with their own tree adorations.

I was just glad that Loren bunked in the room across the hall. I did not want to look at the twinkling lights or her lit up face every time she looked at it.

We left the hoarder's paradise (my nightmare) and made our way to the grocery store, around the corner and two blocks over. A shared shiver and a collective *burrrrr* was said when a gust of penetrating wind found the four of us on the street corner while waiting for the light to change. One car, with one bundled driver inside, was also waiting. If the streets hadn't been covered in slippery ice and snow, we could have easily outpaced the car. I learned about the unforgiving nature of frozen asphalt when running into the club before the start of my second shift. A slip and smack on my ass left a black and blue reminder of life without sunshine. A reminder easily covered with makeup, but I preferred to cover my smiling cheeks versus those that covered my seat.

"Yes," I said quietly and excitedly to the wind that blew from the direction of the rugged wilderness. I let it wrap around me, then I had these thoughts while the four of us walked: You found me, wild wind! I knew we were meant to be together. You, my partner, and me, your lady, willing to be covered in white. Till death do us part. Make it a short matrimony, please. Freeze me solid, my love. Squeeze me tight, my freedom-robbing and life-stealing partner, right here under this holiday banner covered in glittery white. A swaying illusion of heaven's cascading light. A sparkle borrowed from the changing and swaying streetlight, not by the sun's rays or by a full moon, lit bright. The locals will speak of our passion for years to come. Their eyes and voice will lower when speaking about the tragedy of our brief love, but time will turn our story into a lovers' legend, surpassing the romantic tale of two other star-crossed lovers who also died in each other's arms.

The fluorescent lights of the grocery store snapped me out of my ill-fated matrimonial daze. I was once again reminded that I was in a strange foreign land. The store design devoted more space to alcohol than to fresh produce or anything else edible or nutritious. Like the four of us, everyone was padded and bundled. Like stuffed sleeping bags, characters slumbered their way down the aisles. I had found ground zero for a zombie apocalypse. These people actually live like this, I thought. Not just for eight weeks, but they *choose* to stay here. *God, please let me make it back to the valley of the sun*, I prayed fervently while standing between the shampoo and tampons.

Please God, don't let my face show up on a fucking milk carton that someone recognizes five years from now as the lady who waddles in every Saturday for her cart full of hard liquor and bag of potatoes that she makes soft and fluffy in her single-wide. Of course, they will only recognize me if the milk-carton photo is just the center of my face, aged by the hand of a milk-carton artist. If not for the hard liquor that I will need to drink every night to drown my misery, my face will not age a minute beyond its current condition. It may get a bit freezer burnt though.

Four became two. Loren and I stood in front of the milk section, commenting on the price of milk, like two moms on a routine grocery visit. We were anything but that. The milk was the first item we noticed as being twice the price of items back home. I was not a seasoned shopper, but I did eat, and I did buy my own groceries. We passed on that section and quickly learned everything was more expensive here.

"Everything costs more," Loren complained.

She was right about that. Fairbanks is a long distance from everything. Alaska is part of the

Union, but a distant cousin it seems.

I bought a few apples, and some bread and peanut butter. That would sustain me until the next trip to the store. I might have to sustain myself on bar liquor and olives if I stuck with my low-budget plan. We found the other two girls and once again became the four bundled-up dancers who did not look very glamorous at that moment. Our lips were blue and cracking from the cold outside, and our cheeks were rosy, but not from life's pleasures like sex or joy. So much for the dream that the inebriated patrons created each night when they saw us under the lights, skin exposed, with alluring smiles. That was an illusion. Everyone knew it. *Or did they?* We were just young ladies trying to survive. Right now, we needed to survive the cold again and make our way back to our storefront abode.

The chilling wind that met us on the street corner had turned angry. We clutched our grocery bags and held our heads low as we retraced our steps down the quiet and slippery sidewalks. The locals were somewhere, tucked warmly away. The four of us, who were temporarily retained by a club owner in Fairbanks, Alaska, owned the city, but not the night. From the look of the empty street and the one streetlight that was precariously swinging from a loose cord, we did not have anything to write home about, but we did have a warm place to escape to and we had each other, and each of us had our health and, although we had not yet talked about them, I am sure they each had dreams, too. I was too occupied with not freezing to death on the sidewalk to ask the three of them what brought them here. In time.

We pushed through the glass doors and were welcomed by warmth…and smoke, flowing toward the open door from the strange gambling room that never closed. The owner of the club was a proper entrepreneur, investing in more than one seedy business. I suppose he was doing what he needed to do to survive. Survival seemed to be the first objective in this frozen dark mysterious land. The four of us separated to our respective bunks, our only personal space in this makeshift dormitory. I peeled off my layers, to my bare skin. Shivering, I quickly covered my chilled body with my warm pajamas and crawled under my cold covers. I turned my back to the next bed. I did not feel like socializing. With my eyes closed and my mind racing, I worried about the next shift, but mostly I ruminated about what I might return to in seven weeks and how much money I would have in my wallet. Unaware of time, sleep finally found me.

As the first dancer to rise the next day, I indulged in a long, hot shower. A luxury that the last waking sleeper would not experience. Like being part of a large family, we each needed to fight for our place and our slice of the pie. We did not have a supercharged matriarch watching over everything and directing our every move. Just a feisty, tiny woman to make us dinner before work and to drive us to the club each night and return us safely home, but she was not a House Mom. *Thank goodness.* I already felt like a child away at camp. Not church camp or band camp, maybe more like a camp for delinquents.

Chapter 7

well-spent government checks

I was halfway through my seventh shift when a group of GI Joes walked in. Their pulsating energy and unapologetic voices bounced off the walls and reverberated through our restless minds and tired bones. They came to shake off the cold and in doing so, they shook us, the dancing mannequins, out of our stupor. I was on stage two when a wall of buzz-cut men formed around me. Dancing topless was uncomfortable but looking directly into their lustful eyes was nauseating. The Fairbanks stages were closer to the ground than the Phoenix stages I had danced on. An unfortunate design decision. Even though my first dancing experience during "amateur" night was dreadful, the elevated stage somehow made the experience more of a show, compared to how I felt in that moment: under siege and surrounded by a wall of testosterone. The entire awkward situation was made worse by knowing that all the men were close to my age. I tried to smile while I danced but what I really wanted to do was spray green vomit across their camouflage pants, waking them out of their hypnotic trance. I was just skin to them—a gyrating woman to get their blood flowing. They smelled of manliness and fresh spruce from the great outdoors. Cheap cologne floated from their sweaty pores. They should have left their skin naturally exposed. A rugged scent, under different circumstances would have been heaven-sent. The embarrassment I felt dancing close to men my age was bordering on the edge of ridiculous. *Why did I step into this mess?*

I needed to stop this mind torture. I spun away from their baby faces and bulging biceps. I kept spinning, searching for the center of me—my sacred place. I would much rather dance in front of a scruffy fifty-year-old logger than a young man whose eyes penetrated me with his hunger. There was less demand and judgment from the old guys, or they were better at hiding it. Though surging with testosterone, the younger men did seem to understand the rules of the game. They did not just stand there gawking at my bouncing body parts; they were paying customers, eager to spend their government checks on a dancing girl and her perky breasts. They left tips and tipped their heads at the end of the song, then the hungry pack moved along. *Good.*

No longer suffocating from their collective breath, I was the one being entertained by their mingling and moving through the room. Their egos were a gift to no one else but them. I should have been more concerned with how entertaining I was, but I did not expect pipeline tips from government subsidized soldiers, though every dollar was appreciated, and their energy was needed.

I stepped down from the stage after dancing to "Welcome to the Jungle" by Guns and Roses. *Again.* The Axel Rose DJ could not go more than one hour without playing his favorite song. No one complained, but I was about to lose my fucking mind in his fucking jungle. Holding my top and trying to cover my breasts as I walked to the dressing room, I was stopped by one of the army guys.

"You are very pretty," he spoke shyly.

"Thank you," was my response while trying to get away from his syrupy stare.

"Are you available to talk for a while?" he inquired with a smile that seemed genuine.

"Yes. Let me put myself together. I'll be back in a few minutes. Order a few drinks and I'll find you," I suggested to the shy soldier.

As if I could put myself together at this point. I don't know why I bothered getting dressed. I don't know why any of us bothered getting dressed. I suppose part of the allure was watching the dancers undress. A fantasy brought to life before the patrons' eyes. Real flesh. Not a slick magazine page worn over time, but real flesh and real smiles. Well, fake smiles that were real enough to make their three-minute fantasies come true. Real flesh and real smiles that the men would remember later, when they were lying in bed alone. Maybe they weren't entirely alone. Maybe they had a slick magazine lying next to them on their bed. Memories and magazines that would bring them to a climax, if not the height of ecstasy—*that* would require two people exchanging bodily rhythms, flesh, and heartbeats and anything else two people can share during passion. This heightened sense of pleasure takes two, but a biological release in its basic form, that *can* happen alone. An orgasm they would remember when watching the same dancer two nights later. A secret behind that smile.

They weren't hiding anything. Except maybe their cash from time to time. We all knew the rules, or at least we should have. Even the least experienced flesh among us, which included me, understood this charade. We were all doing what we needed to do to survive. Day by day. Surviving daily, complicated by the desires that were assigned to us when we took on this human form.

I came out of the dressing room wearing my hot pink bikini top and fresh pink lip gloss. More fantasies. Only in the confines of these walls, could one find lip gloss or a bikini top in this freezing land. The gloss on my lips would probably turn to tiny glass shards if exposed for more than ten minutes outside. I found the young man seated at a two-top table close to the dressing room. He was tapping his foot and watching stage two when I approached him. I was a few steps from him when he quickly stood up and extended his hand to me.

"Hi, you look so pretty put together. My name is Sean," he offered.

How sweet, I thought. A proper date.

"Hi, my name is Jade, but you already know that," I replied.

"What's your real name?" he asked.

"That's as real as it needs to get," I countered while holding his gaze.

We spent the next two hours talking, when I wasn't being called to the stage. Each time my name was called, he made his way casually over to the lights and placed a few dollar bills near my feet. Not a proper first date, or any typical date, for that matter. The slow saunter in his feet did not match the expression on his face, which looked flushed and excited. After my stage performance, I walked around the club as we were expected to do, and then I found my way back to the young man who had short, sandy-blond hair and was taller than me but shorter than everyone else in his crew. Physically, he was not my type, not that I was looking for any type beyond the type that could help me put a deposit in my bank account, but he was kind, and he seemed genuine.

During our conversation, I learned he was from a small town in Nebraska, and he learned I was from the suburbs of Phoenix. We talked briefly about school, friends, and hobbies and even less about our families. With that subject, he did most of the talking. I did most of the avoiding. To talk about my family meant I had to think about my family, my parents, and to think about my family meant that I was reminded of the fact that they had no idea I was in Fairbanks, Alaska dancing at a topless club. He told me a little bit about what it was like in the field. Training in the field required that they put Vaseline on their eyelashes to prevent the tiny fragile hairs from freezing and cracking off, which could happen when temperatures were seventy degrees below zero. I could not imagine surviving those extreme temperatures, nor did I want to. The thirty below zero that had blasted me when I stepped off the plane was extreme enough. My first night in Fairbanks was a chilling night for many reasons.

I kept sipping and listening and adding to the conversation, when needed. Our extended time together was beginning to feel like a date, and based on the looks I was getting from the bartender; I was not the only one who thought this. A serious glance from the man behind the bar motivated me to tell Sean that I needed to mingle, and he needed to order another drink. As an army man, Sean seemed to understand the importance of following rules. We both let out a sigh, then stood up. I was the first to speak after doing so. I told Sean it was a pleasure to talk to him and asked him if he would be coming back to the club. He told me he had fun talking to me too and that he and his friends would come back the following weekend. Sean shook my hand again and we went our separate ways. More mingling rounds for me and one more round at the bar for Sean.

I sensed that Sean was ready to leave the club after our conversation ended because he no longer seemed interested in his surroundings, including the other dancers. His friends did not seem to share his attitude. I think Sean felt obligated to buy one more drink, having extended his time talking to me. A nice boy, he appeared. Not surprising that two young people accustomed to being told what to do would feel the need to make amends after breaking some arbitrary rule that was meaningless in the grand scheme of things.

In the warm SUV during the twilight hours, packed in with the other dancers, I thought about Sean and wondered if I would see him again. I did not have romantic feelings for him, but he felt like a friend. I needed a friend.

Chapter 8
eyes don't lie

The next four shifts passed just like the first eight. My dancing legs were getting stronger, and I was becoming familiar with not only who the regulars were but their voices and preferences. Most of the patrons were older men. The same men ordered the same drinks, and I sipped slowly while talking, when I wasn't walking or dancing in circles. I heard the same songs, played by the same Guns N' Roses DJ, and I rotated my two dance outfits. I don't know if the men were tired of looking at my hot pink or black bikini and G-string duo, but I was. They probably paid more attention to what I was *not* wearing. I watched the same local dancer, Jo-Jo, dance her unique theatrical style of dance, and each time she dramatically kicked her leg or held an invisible patron's stare, I said a quiet prayer to myself: "Please God, let me leave this place and not end up as a sideshow here." She did add some entertainment to the slow-paced place, so I suppose my destiny could land a worse fate. If only her style of entertainment was performance art and not the result of a mind that had lost touch with reality.

During my Friday night shift, Sean walked in with his friends. I was on the stage closest to the entrance, stage three, when he stepped through the door. Wearing only a G-string and pasties, my body shivered from the chilly wind that the men allowed in. An offering of tiny snowflakes and nature's chill delivered to my dancing feet. Seeing Sean's kind crystal eyes distracted me from the goosebumps covering my bare skin. Next to the doorway that led to the great outdoors, I finished my set and stepped down from the stage. Standing next to the steps, Sean offered me a hand. What a gentleman, I thought. I wondered if he'd learned that in the army or if he'd arrived with those manners. Thoughts that led to my brother; two years older than me, he was also an enlisted army man. I had not seen him since attending his boot camp graduation almost two years prior. My brother had found his escape and I was living mine. Sean held my hand longer than he needed to. We smiled at each other, and I told him I would be back soon. He knew the routine. Every patron did, unless it was their first time in *any* club, but there were none of those men around this place, as far as I could tell.

Fairbanks, in the middle of winter, was not exactly a tourist destination nor was this a club that catered to men in fancy business suits, having their business "lunch" stage-side. Sean nodded at me while I held my top in my right hand, attempting to cover my chest. He did what few men did. He gazed at my eyes, not my exposed boobs.

I found Loren in the dressing room, putting on more cherry-red lipstick. Her lips were so naturally large and red, I wondered if more lipstick and fussing with her appearance was her attempt at avoiding the "crowd." I noticed that about Loren. Once in the dressing room, she did not want to leave. I was not the only one to notice this. She had already been talked to, but it did not seem to bother or motivate her. It seemed like the little topless club was more of an escape from a life back home than it was a paycheck to return home with.

I wanted to hide in the dressing room too. In fact, I wanted to put on my sneakers and run the fuck out of there, just like I had wanted to do after completing my first amateur contest; but I had college graduation goals, and this seemed the fastest cash path to get me there. Maybe a full purse was a far-fetched dream that would freeze and die on the crystallized leaves. These moments of doubt I had to shut out. I had to keep dancing and believing that each spin and drop of sweat would get me one step closer to walking across a university graduation stage. So, on these three stages, I danced. Scooping up dollars, swishing down drinks, and holding onto hope and belief. I was no longer an amateur on these stages, or in this thing called life. I was no professional, either.

I told Loren about Sean. She looked at me with her large dark eyes and asked me if he had a friend. Her eyes did not sparkle at the thought of a wintery romance. She had sad eyes, like a puppy looking for a home.

"He has a few friends. They travel in packs. You would know this if you ventured out of this dressing room," I nitpicked at her.

And with that comment, her eyes, clinging to my words, looked away and back toward the mirror in front of her. A reflective world that seemed to have swallowed her. I wondered what she saw, what she thought. I saw vacancy when I looked at her.

"Aren't you here to make money?" I asked. "Yes, but I hate this," she whined.

"Yeah, well, I don't love it either, but I did not come here to sit on my ass all night and then freeze my ass off when I am not sitting on it," I retorted, before departing from the smudged mirror that held her frozen face in its warped structure. Her desperate eyes begged me for pity, for understanding. I had none of that to give her.

I was here to save myself, not to fall into the pity well of a lost and lazy girl. I had not come here to hide, or to find a burly mountain man and become his mountain bride. I arrived with one suitcase and one goal in mind: to earn as much money as legally possible, to pay for next semester's tuition and books, then make it back home, alive. I did not have the time nor patience for sad eyes, pleading me to fix everything, from another dancer or a lovestruck drunk man. I would not fall prey to her drag-me-down attempts or the mirror's trap.

I turned my back on her and walked toward Sean. I met his cheerful eyes and noticed they held a hint of longing. Not desperate like the eyes I had just abandoned, but hopeful with hints of innocence. Looking deeper and longer into his crystal pools left me feeling content. A feeling that appeared without warning and one I seemed powerless to stop. His look of longing had either not been there when I had first met him, or I had failed to notice. I knew that look. More needs I could not feed. I could sit and talk to him, though, and do my best to ignore everything not said.

Less than one hour later, my needed stage presence interrupted our conversation. Before rushing to stage one, Sean surprised me with a request. "Would you like to go out some time, before you fly home?" he asked. I felt my body, getting ready to dance, become tense. I looked at him, but I could not speak. The nineteen-year-old in me wanted to say "yes" without hesitation, but my internal stage mom, who needed to manage what no one else was—my future—wanted to blurt out "no." I could do neither. I sat in silence while my brain split in two. Battle lines drawn. "Yes" versus "No"— each word fully equipped to stand its ground and die for their beliefs, if needed. Although my future depended on it, a winning side, I could not predict. Sean must have recognized the internal struggle going on behind my teary green eyes and not wanting to feel the sting of rejection, spoke first.

"I know you're here for only a few weeks, and it would be a shame if you flew home without seeing the Northern Lights. They really are spectacular. A fireworks show in the middle of winter." His words were a rush. He was like a young boy trying to convince his mom to take him to the county fair. His lips did not form the word "please." They did not need to. His eyes did the pleading. His request was not a hard sell; it was pleasant with just enough persuasion to twist my heart and my arm. I felt my breath slow, and my face relax out of its dilemma.

He did have a point. I was focused solely on the dirty green bills, but bright lights in the sky did sound incredible. "That sounds nice," I conceded.

"OK, great," he said. His attempt to hide his excitement left his body unnaturally stiff but his ocean eyes reflected golden rays. His slight smile revealed a dimple just below his left cheek that I had not yet seen. Maybe this was his effort to hide the excitement he felt inside.

Maybe that moment revealed genuine happiness bubbling up from his muscular core. A sweet charm that did not flitter from petal to petal, nor did it flourish in a place that froze everything solid. A cold so cold it burned.

Buried under the pristine snow and sheltered by twenty hours of darkness, our lack of advantages was exposed. We were part of the disadvantaged crowd forced to trade freedom for survival and then mocked for our choices by those who are free to choose. All depressingly true; but in that exchange that happened above a flickering tea candle on a sticky tabletop, we could smile and have something to look forward to. What would become of this flirtation, inspired by loneliness, and created in a false world, under neon lights and with skin that was shared too readily, I could not pretend to know. But in that moment, I was content to pretend that we were just two young people free to love and free to choose.

Chapter 9

a black backless dress

On my Monday off, I found myself strangely and unexpectedly getting ready to look at the Northern Lights with a young man who did not light me up but did warm my heart. *What does one wear to view the Northern Lights?* Fashion was the last clothing concern in this frozen land. Practicality and survival were what mattered most. Dressing in layers took precedence over dressing to impress, and it occurred to me that Sean had not seen me in street clothes. Since he had already seen my tush, I was more concerned about not freezing my tush. I layered in a tank top, thermals, warm socks, jeans, long shirt, sweater, scarf, heavy coat, gloves, boots, and a hat. I was ready to go, except for one small issue. I could barely move. *Oh, how I missed the sunshine.*

I was not the only girl dressing to meet a boy and then venturing into a frozen field where the lights could best be seen. Loren was joining me. If anyone needed light, it was her. Except the thing about bright lights, you can't count on them, nor can you expect them. If it is meant to be, you will find them, and they will shine for you. My inviting her to join us was not completely altruistic. Safety in numbers, I suppose, even though I was less concerned about my safety than I was my future.

I was a contrast in emotions. In life choices. Opposites that pulled at my brain, that sometimes pulled me apart. One half of my brain, fighting fiercely to live. To achieve. To win. The other half of my brain, pulling me into the dark frozen forest. Pulling me under. Into an eternal sleep. I could hear one thousand dark shadows calling me at night when everyone and everything was quiet.

Come join us. Lie down. Let us cover you with snow. Let us absorb your soul. Let us take you home. The whispers were a slow and steady hum. They kept singing the song—a chant of finality and doom. The persistent whispers hitchhiked with snowflakes and found their way to me. The one wrapped in warm layers. The one with a slow and steady heartbeat. The one longing for peace, longing for sleep.

Voices drifted from snowflakes; they invited me to join their ride. Dressed in a gorgeous black, backless dress and sexy black heels, I longed to follow those voices up the steps covered in snow—toward one last dinner party. One last opportunity to dazzle and be known. With snowflakes on my breath, my words would spill and intoxicate all who had the pleasure of falling under my spell. Partygoers would laugh and delight in my charm and magnetism, bringing some to the edge of orgasm. They would drink in rapture and intoxication, yet something would want to pull them away— survival instincts, telling them if they stay, they may not see the light of a new day. Walk away, they must, while mumbling and glancing down at their slow-moving polished shoes. "I have never met anyone like her," they would say. Sweet and sensational, she is seduction and mystery. Onto the damp grass, they would step, looking confused and scratching their heads.

This is how I would like to spend my last evening living—mingling with others, who are easily amused, and with my presence, easily confused. I would like to arrive without a purse, not needed where I am going. A purse implies attachments—keys, an ID, a credit card, or cash. I would not need any of these things, except lipstick, perhaps. Wearing lipstick, the color of blood on my parted lips, I would breathe in one more scent of preserved jasmine mingled with enchantment, before slipping out the back door and walking toward nothingness. I would lie down on the angelic white, let it wrap me in its seduction and on this worldly plane I would forever close my eyes. There will be nothing sensational about the night, except it will be a night no one will ever forget. Why this is so, no one will be able to say, for sure. They will quickly forget the young woman robed in the darkest night, with lips the color of fresh kill from the wild, and yet, the memory of her will haunt them for the rest of their lives.

These were my fantastical suicidal thoughts while Loren fussed over shoes.

Sean and his friend, Trevor, arrived just in time. I was one minute away from tying a shoelace around Loren's neck. Bundled up with sensible shoes on, we followed Sean to his truck, where his friend was standing next to the passenger door. Trevor greeted Loren, then he opened the door for her. They had only met briefly at the club prior to our date. Sean opened my door and offered me help into the backseat. I took his hand, even though I did not need the extra lift. I thought it was sweet. I looked at him before he closed the door. We smiled at each other, and both our lips and our eyes spoke without saying a word.

I am not sure if Trevor smiled at Loren behind my back, and if he did, I am not sure if she smiled back. I am not sure if he saw her full red lips that smiled a slanted smile. A slant that hid more insecurities and shyness than it did deception. Her smile was beautiful when she let herself enjoy the moment. A moment that rarely happened, I had noticed. It appeared her lips had been trained to resist all hints of joy, and her body knew how to follow. I wondered if she had twenty years' worth of half-smiles stored in her body, and if she did, what does that do to a person? Feeling joy should be a necessity, like drinking, eating, or sleeping. Can one feel joy inside while masking it from the world?

I sat behind Sean and Loren sat behind Trevor. Trevor was taller than

Sean and his hair was dark, a contrast to Sean's sandy blond. Neither of them had long hair. The army made sure of that. They wore the standard issue haircut. Trevor's eyes were brown with a hint of sadness. Another contrast to Sean, but a complement to Loren's large deer eyes. I doubt they would ever see each other again after Loren's dancing card was full, but they would make an attractive couple. I did not notice any sparks flying between the two of them, but it was nice to see Loren away from the harsh lights of the dressing room and making her way to the Northern Lights in a magical sky.

The lights of the city grew dim as Sean drove down a snow-covered road, pointed in the direction of the forest I had seen from a distance. A sudden chill came over me, and the source of it did not come from the outside. The windows and the heat were up, and I was covered in layers. The chill came from my inner being and extended to every inch of my body, making my spine and fingers tingle. So powerful it was, I shuddered. Sean, being the observant soldier he was, asked me if I was OK. I caught his eyes in the rearview mirror and told him, "Yes, I am fine."

I was not fine, but what else could I say? "No, I am not fine. That forest we are driving toward has been calling me since I arrived in Fairbanks. Calling me to walk into the deep woods, lie down, and never leave. Thank you for asking."

I was excited to see the lights in the sky, and hoped that we would, but this outing, like most everything I did, felt like nothing more than a distraction. An experience that I could not fully immerse myself in. Always guarded, I could not allow joy to overtake me. A taste of that feeling would ruin me. From the look on Loren's face, she felt the same. Maybe. Or was her look one of sadness? She was preoccupied with something. Maybe it was homesickness. I had a longing, but it wasn't for home. What was "home" anyway? A dwelling? A city? We had left my childhood home seven years ago, and I wasn't sure I could even call it that, given I only spent five years of my life there. Not a long time, but longer than I had lived anywhere, so maybe I was justified in calling it my childhood home. A title earned, not by being the longest compared to the experience of some people, but the longest for me and the one where so many of my younger friendships were formed and cultivated, several that had remained to this day, although those were now distant in thought and location.

Except for the radio turned low, the truck cab was quiet. An awkward quiet multiplied by the double-date scenario. I wondered if the four of us would be together if we were back in Phoenix. I doubted it. In-search-of-a-better-life-fueled-by-desperation brought us to this moment, together, in this 49th faraway land. I suppose most life scenarios are the product of a single choice followed by random encounters. This felt incredibly random. The forest voices in my mind were growing louder than the low staticky radio. The tension was escalating too. Being one to please, I sensed that Sean was just as uneasy, or more so, than me. His constant glancing in the rearview mirror and his stiff body told me I was not alone in wanting to open the door and run out of there. Facing the freezing outside would be easier than continuing with the chilly atmosphere inside.

"What should we expect to see?" I asked, not so much out of real interest, but as an attempt at slicing through the silence.

To my surprise, Trevor responded before Sean. "It varies," he commented. "Sometimes it's faint and quick and other times the display lasts for a while."

As I pondered Trevor's lack of clarity in explaining what we might see, Sean blurted out "Look!" We tried to do as he advised, but we weren't sure where to look or what we were looking for. He pointed to the left of the front window. "There!" "Do you see the green lights?" Loren and I crouched down and attempted to see what he was pointing at.

"Yes!" I said, surprised by my reaction and sudden interest. "Yes! I see the lights!"

Sean's reaction to my excitement was to speed up. An exhilarating moment was unfolding in the skies. I felt a surge of adrenaline when he stepped on the gas, driving faster into a scene of white. Loren's stressed frame turned rigid, and both hands grabbed hold of a false sense of security.

Her right hand clutched the door handle, and her left hand grabbed the side of the seat.

Her date noticed her hand and said, without turning around, "Don't worry, Sean is an excellent driver. He knows the fields like the back of his hand."

Loren's missing smile must have found a new home in me because I was beaming. I felt alive in that moment. This was more than a distraction. Sean's capable and take-charge driving made me look at him in a new light. Surprisingly and unexpectedly, I found myself into him and suddenly excited to be on a date with him. It was more than the rush of flying into the unknown, it was knowing that he cared enough to show us, okay me, a sky show knowing it might light me up.

Sean must have read my mind because, in that moment he looked at me in his rearview mirror and smiled. "I have to hurry," Sean said, "because the lights can disappear as quickly as they appear, and I want to make sure you see them."

I smiled back. It happened in an instant. It was almost as magical as the lights hovering above us in the distance.

"This looks like a good spot to park and take a look," Sean pulled the truck off the road.

We had entered the forest and were pulling into a clearing. I prayed that Sean had parked on solid earth and not on ice that might crack sending us plunging into the freezing depths. We were in capable hands, but they were Army soldiers, not Navy SEALS.

"Are we parking on dirt?" I asked.

"Well, we're parking on snow that is covering dirt, yes," Sean replied.

"OK, smartass, you know what I mean." I was presently not a huge fan of living, and had not been for some time, but I wasn't quite ready to die just yet. This was a hopeful sign.

Sean opened my door and took my hand. His hand felt different this time. This time his hand warmed my entire body. Another hopeful sign. He kept holding my hand as we walked away from the truck and onto higher ground. We both looked up and saw the undulating green and purple lights. I gasped. He smiled. I could feel tears pooling in my eyes; I summoned all my strength to not let them form and fall. I was not going to cry. I would not let Sean see me cry at the sight of flickering lights in the sky. Mostly, I did not want the tears to form because I was afraid they would not stop. They might gush out of me, freezing my eyes shut and freezing my body to the ground when a fountain of water sprang forth. Sean would either need to use his powerful GI Joe arms to pry me loose or I would become a misplaced statue for locals and random tourists to point at. Their pointing would lead to a story about my history, about how I came to be a statue. The story would change with each passing onlooker. No, I was not going to cry.

Sean pulled me close, as we both looked at the sky. To keep me warm, he said. Except for a few "Wows" and drawn out "Ohs," we said nothing else. We just kept looking toward the changing colors in the dark sky.

"Hey, the dancers are being entertained with a sky dance," Trevor mused.

Sean and I looked back at Trevor, who was standing close to Loren, but not too close. We both chuckled at his joke.

We kept watching. Each of us dreaming our own private dreams. I thought about how I would never forget this moment and how it might be the highlight of my time here. I was happy to be here, not falling into an eternal sleep under the trees, but looking up at that amazing sky. A gateway that cracked open hope—well, gave it a nudge, anyway. As thoughts of gratitude flooded my eyes and brain, I noticed my head was resting on Sean's arm. I wonder what he was thinking as he looked toward the dancing green lights. I looked up at him, even though everything inside me told me not to. He looked away from the green lights and into my green eyes. There he stayed for a few seconds.

In that moment, I felt the snow melt into a sea of warm water, rising from our feet and reaching our hearts. We were floating. My head was spinning. This was not happening. The dark whispering trees morphed into a thousand-people chorus singing a song I had never heard with my ears, but my soul recognized. My sigh released steam into the air that seemed to hiss when it collided with my dreams. The sound of my bitter pain rising from the surface of the melted virgin snow. Not all my breath was dispersed to the wind or the water. Sean leaned toward me, breathed in my released breath, making it his own, then we kissed. Cold lips instantly warmed by a rising and surprising passion. I let myself sink deeper into the warm water. *I don't know if this is love, but I know in his arms I feel safe, even if I fall too far.*

Chapter 10
bored with bearded men

It had been four days and four nights since I'd last seen Sean. With the Northern Lights in his rearview mirror, our night together ended with a kiss on the sidewalk under a peek-a-boo moon. I was standing on the sidewalk and he in the gutter, which put me a few inches closer to his lips. I became so overheated while kissing him, I wanted to rip off my jacket and layers and let him hold me with nothing on but my G-string and bra. Nothing he had not seen before. I felt an urge to bare myself to him in other ways, too.

I wanted to tell him how alone I felt and how terrified I was about going home. I told him none of these things. I just lost myself to his lips and his blue eyes and the swelling between his thighs. I imagined him carrying me to a nearby alley, both of us ripping our clothes off and making love on a discarded emerald-green couch with a hungry gray tomcat lurking near our feet. I told him none of these things, either. My suppressed thoughts bubbled up on my brow. I felt like I might pass out under all these layers. I was buried under more than just layers of clothes. I gently pushed him away to avoid embarrassing myself with a fainting spell. He would catch me, but a damsel in distress I would not be.

"It's getting hot." I admitted.

Sean chuckled. "Yes, yes, it is." His eyes revealed his own alley-cat thoughts.

Our stare lasted a few more minutes because neither of us wanted to say goodbye. Neither of us wanted the night to end. We both had our stories of loneliness, beyond the boundaries of Fairbanks, but in this moment, we were not alone. I felt connected. I felt love. I felt loved. *Is this what hope feels like?*

Still holding hands, covered in gloves, while our bodies were separating, he whispered goodnight and told me he would see me at the club soon.

Soon? What did that mean and why did that word alert sirens in a girl's brain? "I will be there. Where else would I go?"

We said one more goodbye with our lingering eyes as he walked toward the driver's door. Trevor, who had been sitting on a short wall and talking to Loren who stood in front of him, jumped up when he saw his comrade walk toward the truck. A little too fast, I thought. I already surmised that Loren was not an engaging conversationalist. Trevor took his cue, told Loren goodnight, and lifted himself into the truck. I watched the taillights bounce off the shiny black road as Sean's truck traveled down the deserted street before pausing at the swinging stoplight next to the grocery/liquor store. I saw Sean look in his rearview mirror. This was a good sign. The light turned green, and they drove on. I stood there until I could no longer see Sean's head. I did not need to shake off the cold, but I did need to shake off my feelings for Sean.

Loren, who had remained on the short wall, walked toward me. Slowly. She was in no rush, either, to walk past the strange smoky gambling scene and into our labyrinth of lounging dancers and questionable dreams.

I suddenly became very sad. Then angry at myself for being sad. *About a boy.* I came here to make money. Period. Men! I could not be angry at Sean though. He was sweet and I already missed his company. Damn green lights and blue eyes!

Four nights passed. Four nights of gyrating, stripping, smiling, drinking, smiling, talking, smiling, collecting, gyrating, stripping, smiling, drinking, and trying not to notice every time the door opened, bringing in the cold air and another man who was *not* Sean. *No, not Sean. No, not Sean. No, not Sean.* Each time I felt my shoulders and smile drop, pretending to not care while I carried on listening to some old, bearded geezer dressed in a flannel shirt talk about a car he was working on.

"You know, as soon as I find myself a used carburetor, I will come pick you up and take you for a spin in my convertible Cadillac," he said. I heard dozens of conversations that sounded strikingly familiar. Each time, a different car, but it wasn't always a car. Sometimes it was a house or trailer or boat. But there was no shortage of to-be-finished projects in this place.

"Wait till you see it, little lady," they would boast. "You won't want to go back home after I take you out in my boat and show you a part of the wilderness you can't see from the stage."

I felt nauseous and I wasn't even bouncing on the waves yet.

Never poetic or romantic or seductive, just to-the-point with their attempt to show off what they did not yet have. Have *finished*, anyway. These men were not refined nor were they under any false pretenses that a young dancer from Phoenix would stay and fall in love with them and their fucking fishing boat. They were straightforward because they understood the rules. It was refreshing, I suppose. Just good ol' boys doing what they needed to do to survive. Trying to make it through another day, with a little girly as their company, pleasant to look at, which helped and made their drink that much more enjoyable. Banter from the bartender, bouncer, and other regulars, lifted their spirits more before closing their tabs and swaggering back into the cold, past their undone projects and into their tomorrow.

I did not see too many wedding rings. With so many downed drinks, their fingers were probably too fat, or the matrimonial symbol might be put safely away in a small box for special occasions only, because their day jobs were not conducive to wearing jewelry. This place was certainly special, but it was not a special occasion. There was a difference.

It was 2 a.m. One more hour to go. One, maybe two more stage sets, and a few more conversations, then I could sleep and forget about not seeing Sean again. Fourteen hours, or more, without looking toward the door or *trying to not look* toward the door. Strangely, my sadness and disappointment spun away from me while dancing on the stage. The club speakers pulsed with "Sweet Emotion." I remembered hearing Aerosmith's song on the radio while the four of us were headed toward the Northern Lights. I kept remembering…the song, Sean's kiss, the lights, another kiss, Sean's eyes. Joy sprung from my core and expressed itself on my singing lips, forming a genuine smile. The man who slipped a five-spot in my G-string seemed to appreciate my mouth's response to a mind's remembering.

I did not come here to be happy! I did not come here to meet a boy! I left the sunshine with two goals: to make money and make it safely back home. I kept repeating this mantra to myself. If I said it enough, maybe I would convince myself. We were nothing serious—Sean and me. Just two young people, keeping each other company during the long dark days.

The bartender's bell snapped me out of my thoughts and told us it was time to go home. I felt relief, knowing I could put something warm on and go to sleep.

Chapter 11

dance for me

Another week passed before I saw Sean again. I was on Stage One when he rushed through the door. I felt him before I saw him. A wall separated the stage and the door, but I had a feeling it was him when I heard the only door open, a creaking sound I tried to ignore, because each man *not him* brought too much disappointment. Sometimes their lack of tips brought more disappointment. I was on my second song when Sean walked up to my stage; his eyes caught mine while I was spinning. For a moment, I wished that he could have spun me out of there. Maybe we were just spinning sticky webs.

"Hi! I'm so happy to see you. You look beautiful. I'm sorry I've been gone so long. We were training at a base a few hours north of here. It was so cold out in the field. I wasn't able to make it down here until tonight." His rushed words almost knocked me over. Easy to do to an almost naked girl in stilettos.

"Slow down, cowboy," I teased. "It's OK. I hardly noticed."

His excitement turned to concern then quickly dissolved into disappointment.

"I'm kidding! I missed you." *Did I just fucking say that?* "Let me finish this set, then I'll find you."

"OK. I'll sit at our table." He walked away with a smile on his face.

Our table? Hmmmm. Maybe not a web, but a fairy tale that is not going to have a happy ending. This I knew, but this I also tried to ignore. For now.

I found Sean after talking to the DJ, Lex. A talk I had put off for a few weeks, but during that shift I was suddenly motivated to approach his spinning throne. Maybe Sean's presence gave me a jolt of courage, or maybe it was more a feeling of suddenly caring. Maybe having someone care about us makes us care more about ourselves.

"Hey, Lex, how's it going?" *I couldn't care less; I was just being polite.*

"Hey, Jade It's great. What's up?" he asked while cuing up the next record.

"I love Guns and Roses too, but I can't dance to "Welcome to the Jungle" one more time. When I'm on Stage One, will you *please* play from the list of songs I gave you?"

"You gave me a list?"

I am going to tie that stupid rock-n-roll sash tighter around your fucking neck.

"Yes, I gave it to you last week."

"Oh, I don't know what I did with it," he said, pretending to scan his DJ space. Spinning bullshit is what he was doing. "Can you write it again?" he asked. His sarcastic smile revealed a gorgeous full set of pearly whites, brighter than the snow outside, which I guess wasn't very white, especially near the edges of the parking lot. A gross thought. I don't know why I was surprised by Lex's perfect smile. Maybe I had stereotyped him as a drug-addicted DJ hiding out in an Alaskan topless club. Maybe I was wrong. Maybe he had music dreams. Maybe he was just doing what he needed to do to survive.

"Sure, I'll write *another* list."

He smiled.

"You have a nice smile. You should smile more often. This place could use it."

He immediately closed his mouth.

Making my way to "our" table, I thought about the randomness of this place and how and why each of us ended up here. I saw Sean's drink, or at least I think it was *his* drink. He must have been in the bathroom. In his absence, my mind wondered, *What would I be doing if I was back in Arizona right now? Of course, I would be working at the video store, then crying myself to sleep.*

My days at the video store, surrounded by families checking out movies for the night, were some of my loneliest days, and I have had a few. Standing for hours in the same spot in front of a cash register, ding ding ding, watching happy, bouncy Scottsdale people come and go, on a late Friday afternoon to pick out their movies for the weekend. Often, customers would already be dressed in their comfiest clothes, sometimes even pajamas. "Not a care in the world" is what that look said. In they would skip toward the New Release wall. Like little moths, they were drawn to the bright "New" neon lights. Everyone wants the latest in life and movies were no exception.

Together, in twos, threes, or fours, they would look at the shiny boxes, talk about who was starring in the movie, other shows those actors had been in, what others were saying about the movie, or get disappointed because the movie they really wanted was no longer available.

"You can put a movie on hold," I would tell them when they would moan about how they were excited to see Crocodile Dundee II but couldn't because it was gone. They were nice enough; no one ever yelled at me about an absent movie box, but their tone was void of all understanding that there *were* problems in life beyond not being able to see a movie. Problems, like not knowing if you were going to have electricity when you arrived at your apartment after working eight hours at your shitty video job, smiling, and helping privileged teenagers who drove away in their parents' Mercedes. The video store was their fun, their there's-nothing-else-to-do-tonight escape, or their I-am-too-young-or-too-lame-to-have-plans plan.

If I wasn't renting movies to shiny, happy people, I was selling albums or recently added CDs, at the front of the store. People who came in just for music were a bit more serious, more focused, and more often than the video people, they came in alone.

"Do you know the song…" they would ask. Desperately trying to recall a few words or hum a tune. It was usually a disaster and a crime to discerning ears, like two people not speaking the same language trying to understand each other. Sometimes we could figure it out, but usually they left humming the song, not out of happiness, but frustration. If they kept humming, the song would come to them; then they could buy the album and memorize every damn word.

With video store memories tumbling through my mind, I became profoundly happy to be sitting at a table in a topless club in Fairbanks, Alaska. Even if I never saw Sean again.

I would not need to test that theory, because I did see Sean again. With light blue lips just below his rosy cheeks, he told me that he had left his wallet in the car.

"Yeah, I've heard that before," I joked with smiling lips that had just pursed a straw. "At least you took the time to find it. Some guys say that and don't bother to go get it. You'll need it when it's time to pay for your lap dance," I said, teasing him, not expecting, or wanting, that to happen.

"Yeah, about that. Can I have a lap dance?" he suggested in a shy tone. I imagined he had practiced that question a few dozen times based on the way his voice rose at the end of his question.

"Sure, you can have a dance." *Fuck.*

Now what? We just sat there looking at each other.

"How about the next song that comes on, that you like, you dance?" The lack of urgency in his words did not match his tense body. A body that might explode and light this place up like an Alaskan bonfire. That might attract more patrons. Come, have some s'mores, stay warm while you watch a little lady freeze her ass off in the slushy snow!

"That sounds like a plan," I hesitantly agreed, noticing his rosy cheeks turn three shades redder. *I think I'm going to throw up.*

Four songs passed before I found one danceable *enough.* The song was "Patience" by Guns N' Roses, of course. My legs began to shake as I walked toward Sean. *Interesting.* They turned to concrete legs when I began to dance or *tried to dance.* Sean's buddy saw what was happening and whistled from across the club. *Kill me now.*

Calm down. You've done this dozens of times. Keep breathing. Don't pass out! My thoughts were racing as I began moving my hips and my body closer to Sean. I looked at his eyes and kept looking until it became too intense. The only thing saving me from collapsing onto his muscular thighs was looking away every few seconds. I would have preferred to have worn a blindfold. That could be alluring. Customers might like that. Since I did not have that to save me, I did the next best thing. I stared at a stain on the worn carpet while my hips swayed. Staring at the stain took the edge off. It reminded me how unromantic this moment was, and it jerked me out of the tunnel I was falling into while looking at his eyes. His playful blue eyes became intense, like deep ocean waters. A look I had not previously seen from him. Maybe my gyrating hips activated his focused solider training. Maybe my swaying hips became the enemy…don't take your eyes off the target.

Hips still swaying, I began to turn my body so that he now had a view of my back. I could not see his eyes, but I could feel the heat radiating from his body. *I wonder if he noticed my shaking legs. Of course, he did, he's trained to be observant. He must have been loving every minute of it. I, on the other hand, was a swirling mess inside.* It was not my first lap dance, but it was the first time I felt like that. Dancing for and close to men is not sexual or arousing; it is just the means to an end. There was some sensuality involved when falling into the rhythm of a song, when my body moved in sync with the music, but those sensual feelings were never motivated or enhanced by a man. Until that dance.

I waited as long as I could to make this an official topless dance. During the last bar of the song, I untied my top and placed it across Sean's left thigh, in the way that dancers do…gingerly, like the top is made out of gold shards that might fall apart if not held with the utmost care. The slow and sensual approach lets the receiver of the tiny triangles know just how fortunate they are to be in possession of such a splendid gift, if only for a few minutes. These things are not taught. There is no dancer "school." It is partly watching and emulating, but mostly it is having an awareness of slow and steady movements that help build the intensity rising in the men. Sean did not stop looking at my eyes. *Interesting*. Relief washed over me. This was awkward enough without Sean staring at my breasts like a hungry baby. Not until the end of the song, when I needed to put my top back on, did he look at my breasts. *Oh, he's good,* I thought.

"You are beautiful," he said as he slid a crisp twenty-dollar bill under my G-string. *He must have visited the bank on his way here. Or maybe it was two days ago… who knows how many hours or days he has been preparing for this dance.*

"Thank you." I acknowledged his compliment while glancing at the carpet stain that seemed to be growing larger. Maybe I was falling face first toward the disgusting carpet. I was at the end of my capacity for staring directly into someone's eyes, especially at such a close distance. "Excuse me, I'll be back in a few minutes," I told him.

"Take your time. I'll freshen up my drink."

"Perfect, because I'm going to freshen up my face."

"No need to, you are glowing."

"Oh," *ha ha,* "thank you." *Fuck!* I thought as I walked away.

I walked calmly to the dressing room; then I collapsed on a chair at the end of the dressing table. I needed to sit alone and breathe. Fortunately, Loren was on Stage Two; I could not deal with her right now. I looked at myself in the mirror. Focusing on my eyes, I tried to see what Sean was looking at. What held his attention. What captivated him for five minutes. I tried to make sense out of the feelings that had turned my legs into jelly, then concrete, then jelly again. There was no making sense of any of this. There was also no time for any of this. I was on a mission, and it was not to play Barbie with GI Joe.

I slowly pushed open the dressing room door and noticed one of Sean's buddies patting him on the back near the bar. I imagined what they were talking about—if they were talking at all. The secret man code. Just a look at his friend's eyes and a knowing smile was the only exchange needed after the close encounter had taken place between him and me. Already feeling like I was the focus of that exchange, if not through words, then through gestures, I stopped at "our" table which was now the source of my most embarrassing moment. One of them, anyway. I drank a sip of my watered-down gin and tonic with a lime wedge that looked like a little floating corpse.

I could relate. I wasn't thirsty and I did not want any more alcohol—I was just keeping myself busy, unsure of what to do next. Too nervous to sit, I began to feel the pain of the evening's shift radiate through my feet, calves, and brain. Seeing me, Sean patted his buddy on the back, mouthed what looked like, "See you later," then made his way back over to me.

After ten long seconds of awkward silence and shifting eyes, we both started laughing.

Comic relief. It's all just part of the show.

"I'm going to leave soon. I have an early morning. I'm wondering if you would like to go out on your next day off? Just us. Dinner, maybe a movie?"

"There's a movie theater in this town?" I asked. I already knew the answer to my question. I was stalling.

"Yes, it's been around forever. I am not sure what's playing, but I can find out."

Say no, say no, say no… "Sure." *What the fuck is wrong with me?* This is going to be a bitter goodbye in a few weeks. Maybe it doesn't have to be goodbye…maybe we can see each other again. *Stop this nonsense!*

"OK, great! I'll pick you up at your place at, say, five? Will that work?" "Sure!" Behind my genuine smile, my internal mom was lecturing me.

We hugged. Being wrapped by his arms felt so warm and comforting. I wanted to stay there and pretend nothing or no one else existed.

"Good night." "Good night."

He stepped into the cold night, and I stepped under the bright lights of Stage One.

Chapter 12

buttery lips and simmering sauce

Figuring Sean would be on time, I stepped outside a few minutes early. The breeze, although bitter, was refreshing on my face. I was smiling and looking forward to going on a date, but those romantic feelings were temporary. Four hours with Sean were not going to change my status in life or erase all my problems.

Like trying to ignore a cute boy at a middle school dance, I was avoiding looking down the street toward the forest. I did not feel the same pull as when I had first arrived, but the dark and deep continued to tempt me with its whispers. The dark enticer of souls is strategic; this I had realized when I was a teenager, spiraling toward suicide. It is also cunning and wise, sending energy where it can be most effective. The dark pull had lost *some* interest in me, but it was still there. Watching and waiting. Should I send out a distress signal, it would be the first on the scene, offering permanent relief from the pain.

Just one look wouldn't hurt while I waited for Sean's truck to arrive. I turned my head and gazed toward the forest. I noticed a fantastical scene of dancing shadows that were spinning in circles, first two, then four, then a dozen of them. Shivers shot through me. Armlike shapes rose from the singular silhouettes that were dancing independently. Reaching out, the strange shadow dancers clasped each other. Sometimes floating and other times touching the ground. With hair flying, and the tops of their heads tilted back and up toward the sky, they seemed to laugh, exhaling cold vapor the color of ash. Their heads snapped in my direction. I gasped. The black centers of their eyes changed to bright red. Red eyes that stared intently at me. I almost choked on the bitter cold before looking away. I closed my eyes. My body struggled to regain balance. My body was losing. I sat on the short wall to avoid letting my head smack against the snow-covered sidewalk. Heaving heavy breaths, I was a mixture of freezing and overheating. I closed my eyes again. When I opened them, the penetrating red pupils had transformed into brake lights.

Sean engaged the emergency brake then, jumped out of the truck, and with a quick pace he came around to the passenger side. I was relieved and happy to see his friendly face. I had never dated anyone in the military, but my own brother's army buddy did ask me to marry him when they were visiting while on leave. Not a playful request, but a heartfelt, I-have-fallen- madly-in-love-with-you-and-might-die-if-you-say-no type of proposal. More of a plea than a proposal. It was well after midnight when he proposed. We had been up late, talking in my mom and stepdad's back yard in the suburbs of Denver. I laughed at his offer, then I said no. He was very cute, but I was seventeen. I carried on with life and graduated from high school. He found someone else and became a father. Maybe dating a military man could have its advantages. No, I decided. I am not matrimonial military material—Sean is a fluke; this place alters reality.

"I hope I didn't keep you waiting long."

"Oh no, it's okay. I came outside a while ago to breathe some fresh air." My body quivered as I thought about what I had just witnessed.

"Are you OK? Do you want me to turn the heat up?"

"No, I'm fine. It's just a chill. I'll warm up soon enough."

"How was your day? What did you do?" he asked with a genuine interest.

"I slept until noon, ate breakfast, read a book, then got ready to meet you. What about you? What did you do?" I responded with less enthusiasm than he offered me.

"About the same, except for the reading part," he laughed. We both laughed. "Are you ok with going to the movies first, then dinner?" he asked.

"Of course. What's playing?" I inquired, with genuine interest this time. "*Working Girl*."

"That sounds appropriate," I said laughing at my response. "Who's in it?" "Melanie Griffith."

"Oh good, I like her."

I did not care if the movie was good or bad, if it was a silent movie or one with nonstop explosives, or if it was an adult movie or two hours of cartoons. I was just thrilled to be going out. It gave my existence some normalcy. With only four weeks to go, and my dance purse not as full as I had hoped, I was anxious. I tried to put my cash flow out of my mind. *I am just a young woman going out on a proper first date with a proper boy.* That's the story I told myself. He wasn't fooling me, though; I saw more intensity in his eyes. There was a caged wild animal pacing behind those angelic blue pupils.

We found seats toward the top row, to this we were both in agreement. Perfect. I liked to have a full view of everything. I am not sure how interested Sean was in the movie or if he wanted to be out of view of everyone else. Two cold sodas to wash down our buttery popcorn and comfy seats to slip into. More perfection. For the first time in a long time, I felt content to just be. As soon as the lights went down and without looking at me, Sean put his left hand over my right one. If seeing my breasts during his lap dance counted as first base, he had already been there. In vision only.

He would have been bounced out of that club in two seconds if he'd tried to touch my breasts, whether he was friendly with me or not. The bouncer did seem to care about the dancers, but his first responsibility was with the club; they could be in trouble with their license if any "funny business" took place. I tried to put the club out of my mind and just focus on Sean and the movie coming up.

During the previews, which I enjoyed watching, Sean put the popcorn bucket in the empty chair next to him, then he leaned over and kissed me. His lips were buttery and salty, and he confirmed what I already knew—he was a very good kisser. I might not watch two minutes of the movie, but I had a feeling it was going to be very good.

We watched. We laughed. He smiled at me and offered me a napkin. *This guy.* We kissed each other's buttery lips. We held each other's buttery hands. We kissed some more, cozying up to each other as much as we could. I was lost in the movie. I was lost in the moment.

When the movie was over, we walked to dinner. I was so heated up from all that butter that I did not notice the freezing temperatures. Seeing my breath reminded me that I was *not* in Phoenix. Walking along the sidewalk with Sean holding my gloved hand, I was glad for my change in location. At the only stoplight between us and dinner, Sean spun me around and kissed me again. Any trace of butter still on our lips was devoured during that passionate kiss. We kissed so long, we missed our chance to walk, at least once. If not for a car horn beeping at us, we might still be kissing. We both chuckled, grabbed hands, then walked across the street. It was more like a skip than a walk. Just two kids, playing and having the time of our lives.

There weren't too many dining options in Fairbanks. We chose Italian. I am glad we did because I could smell the simmering garlic and tomatoes a block away. The freezing temperatures had a way of muting and dulling life, including smells, but their sauce woke the senses. Sean noticed it too. We looked at each other, said *mmmmmm,* then picked up our pace to the restaurant's doors. We had worked up an appetite.

We were seated at a table for two by a young woman who did not look like anyone else I had seen in this town. She had long, silky black hair pulled back in a ponytail, and large dark graphite eyes. Stunning, she looked quintessentially Italian. It felt like we had been transported to Italy after our romantic kiss. If only.

Sean's eyes sparkled above the flickering candle, and his rosy cheeks matched the red tablecloth. We sipped dark, red wine that I was not legally old enough to drink, but no one seemed to care. We slurped rich, red sauce, and we talked about our life back home and what we would be going home to after leaving Alaska. Neither of us had solid plans. I would be leaving sooner than him—a truth that I did not want to talk about. I did not want to ruin the perfect moment.

He brought up the subject first. "When are you flying back to Phoenix?" he asked.

"Never!" was my quick response, "I have fallen in love with this Italian food; I can't possibly leave this!"

"No, really. When are you going home?" his smile disappeared, and his tone turned serious.

Damnit. Can't we just enjoy ourselves and pretend like there is no tomorrow? "I leave in four weeks," I said while wiping the corners of my mouth with a red cloth napkin.

"That's so soon. I may have to kidnap you and hide away in the forest." Shivers. "Ha ha," *If he only knew.*

"Well, I am going to steal every free moment you have until you leave. Of course, I can't leave without another lap dance." His baby blues had turned playful again.

Oh, he is getting bold. Must be the red wine giving him courage. "Ha ha. Good, because I need to make more money before I leave. Tell your friends," I said, laughing at myself.

"No, I'm not sharing you with anyone else. Definitely not my friends," he replied with a look that had grown serious.

In that moment, I saw a glimpse of Sean's possessive side. *Fortunately, this was just make-believe. At midnight, I would turn into a pumpkin and roll myself back to the makeshift dormitory, or I would turn into a pumpkin pie with extra whip cream and Sean would feast on me until sunrise. The wine must have gotten to me, too.*

The waiter put the bill on the table. Just in time. Our conversation had become too real, and my mind was getting lost in a sticky sex scene. I would have liked to change the conversation into a real sex scene. From the look in his eyes, I don't think Sean would have minded.

"I'm not ready to say goodnight yet, do you want to go for a drive? I know a spot, you'll love," Sean said in a manner that did not sound spontaneous, and I was sure he had plenty of gas to get us there.

What I wanted to tell him was that I knew a spot I thought he'd love, too, but I could not be that bold, not even with red wine as my courage. "Sure, where do you want to go?"

"There's a park just outside of town with a lake surrounded by trees. The lake is frozen right now, but there are benches. We can sit and look at the stars. I have blankets and a thermos of hot cocoa in my truck," he said, wanting to say more, but he had already said too much.

"Well, aren't you prepared, Mr. Army man?" My comment made him blush. *The wine was talking for me.* "Did you bring the stuff to make s'mores too? That can be our dessert," I teased with a sugary sparkle in my eye.

Without taking his eyes off me, Sean replied quietly, "I thought you would be the dessert."

His words danced in front of me before they penetrated and heated my skin, already made warm by the fermented grapes and his growing intensity. This was not the Sean I had met in the club a few weeks before, I thought. I like this guy. *Too much.*

I said nothing in response. I just looked into his eyes. Everything faded away, except his eyes. I was getting dizzy. I wanted to excuse myself and go to the restroom, but I thought I might faint if I stood up. He stood up for me.

"Excuse me, I'll be right back," he said, placing his napkin on the table.

I had not thought about having sex with Sean, well, maybe once. It was a terrible idea. Not because I was a virgin. I was not. I had lost my virginity when I was seventeen to a boy I barely knew. It was a terrible idea because our flirting had already gone too far; giving him my body would expose my guarded heart.

Sean returned, interrupting my thoughts. *Good.*

"So, are you ready for some star gazing?" he asked.

"Yes, I am, as long as you keep me warm," I whispered from across the table.

"Oh, I will keep you warm," his voice lowering when he said "warm."

I felt all the blood rush from my dancer legs. His words left me flushed and disoriented. I think he knew and was secretly loving every minute of it. *This must be foreplay. How am I going to walk to the truck without proper blood flow to my legs?*

Ever the gentleman, Sean must have sensed my hesitation. He reached out his hand to help me up out of the chair.

"Take my hand. You've had two glasses of wine," he offered.

"Thank you." I smiled at him and placed my hand in his. His smile told me he understood the effect his words were having on me. His sudden smoothness left me wondering how many other dancer girls he had played innocent and charming with before serving them wine and the stars? I didn't care. At least I would have a view of the stars and not a flickering fluorescent basement light like I did when I lost my virginity. And I would be wrapped in Sean's arms. A place that was going to be hard to leave.

Chapter 13

bare bodies below

We stared at the stars. We stared into each other's eyes. Then we stared some more. For two young people raging with wine-infused hormones, we were in no rush. Sean's pace matched what I was feeling. With limited time, we were going to take all we could. We were going to enjoy every breath, every heartbeat, and every wish made upon a star.

My timid smile morphed into beaming radiance when Sean lit three large white candles, before placing them near a blanket. He was prepared. The unused wicks caused me to sigh. Either this wasn't a regular date for him, or he had bought new candles just for me. Either way, those unused candles made me feel special. *So, this is what romance feels like.* Maybe I did care. His warmth and passion were going to be my new memory of how making love should be. My mind's photo of this scene would be glued over other memories. If only Sean could be my first. He couldn't be, but if he were, I would give him the satisfaction of knowing. We could have frozen to death under those stars, and I wouldn't have cared. My frozen smile would let our would-be rescuers know that I had died happy, in Sean's arms.

An hour of drinking hot cocoa, laughing, kissing, and clasping glove-covered hands lifted toward the starry sky, led to a slow and sensual removal of layer after layer of clothing until we were two bare bodies under the glowing moon. Our skin glowed and our eyes glistened. That van Gogh moment lasted about ten seconds, before we needed to cover with blankets or freeze our asses off, and in my case, freeze my ass and tits off. I could not afford either of those losses—they were my bread and butter. They became Sean's bread and butter, and he handled them with care. He slowly kissed my nipples, something he must have imagined when they were six inches from his face. His charm paid off.

So charming he was, he stopped kissing me and looked into my eyes and asked, "Are you sure about this? We can stop now if you want to."

"I'm sure," I said. I wanted to tell him that I had never been so sure of anything in my life, but I could not say the words. I felt them, but I could not say them. "I don't want to stop."

"Neither do I," he whispered, before leaning in to kiss me.

The truth is, my heart would have been content kissing and holding Sean, but my body wanted to feel his against mine. All of him pressing against me. I wanted to feel his breath in my ear. I wanted to feel him inside me, thrusting. I wanted to hear him escalating and moaning to climax. Before any of that took place, Sean stopped and put a condom on. Smart.

We made love under the moon, breathing out heated crystal breath. We quietly held each other and watched a shooting star stream across the sky. We were the only people left in a freezing world. We kept each other warm.

Chapter 14
Sonny's lap

I was back at work the next night. It was a Tuesday night, the start of my fifth week in Fairbanks. I could not stop smiling. I was floating six feet above the ground. Not once did I ask myself during my shift if I had fallen in love with Sean. I didn't have to; my heart knew the answer. I had had sex before, but for the first time, with Sean, I had made love.

My mind kept playing highlights from the night before. I remembered watching the tempting dark forest shrink in the side mirror as we drove away from the frozen park. The sight of the forest did not make me shudder like it had earlier in the evening. I saw the square spot where the blanket had lain, where we had lain—where I got laid. The frozen park had thawed my heart. At least for the evening. That is all we had. Our drive back to my temporary home was quiet, but not awkward quiet. It was a peaceful, content quiet. I felt safe. I felt warm. I felt love.

During the drive, my legs were drawn in and my body was facing Sean. I kept looking in his direction until the truck came to a stop in front of the commercial building. He glanced and smiled at me several times while he was driving, reaching over to kiss me at each stop sign. His kisses were sweet, and his smile left me with no regrets over having made love to him. I wondered if I would see him again after my contract was over. I wondered if he thought the same thing. I wondered if it would be more awkward when he came into the club. I wondered if he had dated other dancers. I wanted to talk about these things, but I didn't want to disturb the perfect moment or the perfect image of two carefree young people enjoying life and each other. My questions would shatter that image and reveal tears that lay on the other side of this frozen façade. Sean asked me to wait in the truck. After riding with him a few times, I understood why. He put the truck in park, then came around to open my door before taking my hand to help me out. I did not need help, but I loved every minute of his chivalry. Before taking one step, Sean wrapped his arms around me, looked into my eyes, then told me how much fun he'd and that he would love to see me again before I flew home. Fly home. My purring heart stopped. Words that had kept me motivated at the beginning of my time there now made me sad. I didn't know what I was flying home to. I knew it would not include star gazing on a blanket with Sean.

"You know where to find me," I said playfully.

"Yes, I do."

With that, we kissed. If he had not been holding me, I might have collapsed on the slick sidewalk. My legs became weak. I lied to myself and said it was because I was tired. Wrapped by his right arm, we kissed and hugged one more time before I said goodnight, then I disappeared behind the glass doors and into the strange world of gamblers, smoke, and dancers.

My mind kept wandering to the past night's moments while I was dancing on the stage and next to and in between laps. Laps that became legs when they stood up—not necessarily manly legs, but legs that belonged to men. None of them reminded me of Sean's strong muscular thighs. They did not have to—Sean's physique and smile were carved into my memory. Sean's greatest hits were spinning in my mind. His gentle hands brushing my stomach, his whispers in my ear, his body melting into mine under the starry sky. He was nowhere to be seen during my shift, but my mind was lost to him. To his eyes. To his lips. To his smile. To his hands on my body. To his...

"Jade, you're up!" Sabrina shouted. "Lex called your name three times."

"Oh, thanks," was my response to her pinched face.

I put my drink down and hustled to Stage One. Lex played, "Hot, Hot, Hot" by The Cure.

Finally, he played a song from my list.

"The first time I saw lightning strike I saw it underground

Six deep feet below the street the sky came crashing down..."

My twirling body calmed my spinning mind. I lost my memories and myself to the music. Inward I dove—away from the stares that probed my skin. Faces that looked at me like one might in a gallery, or with this crowd, a car show. Eyes that connected and memorized my freckles and talked about the dimples on the back of my thighs like they were imperfections that could be smoothed out and painted over. Imperfect manly faces, sizing me up and putting me on a pedestal where I did not want to be.

I wanted my feet firmly on the ground so that I could run wild, away from their mouths with missing teeth. "Smile pretty," those imperfect mouths said: we did not brave the cold or trudge through the snow to see sadness on the stage, their eyes did say. This is not a theater where all ranges of emotions are encouraged. This is "flesh" performance art. We came to see you smile and spin, like a little doll that keeps spinning when we wind you up. A few dollars tossed into the musical box, and she will keep doing what is expected. We were like the small, spinning ballerina in the jewelry box that I had as a little girl. The tiny ballerina on my bedroom shelf, at eye level, had mesmerized me as she spun to *Swan Lake*. Resting my head in my hands, supported by my elbows, I watched and fell into an enchanted land.

Dancing on a small club stage gave me insight into how the spinning ballerina from my childhood felt, if she had feelings. We weren't expected to feel either and like her, we were trapped. Spinning in one spot. Dancing only when summoned to do so. I remember when her music permanently stopped. Maybe I wound her too tight. She became forever stuck. Frustration came over me, then panic, then sadness, then tears. I wondered what had happened to my broken ballerina.

I began to wonder about me. I had become her, and she was forever stuck in my memory. Maybe she freed herself and found a grand stage to dance upon. That spinning ballerina was the one patrons wished to see, the pretty one who never stops smiling. No sad faces here, "pretty please." The patrons saw enough of that at home. If not from their significant other, then from their own mug staring back from their mirror.

Not human, just a symbol of womanly consumption. Never perfect, but under the right lights and with enough alcohol consumption, one could pretend to be. The closer to perfection, the more tips and the more affection. Lost in my thoughts while the music played on. While my heart pretended to not care.

"There's your smile," George, one of the regulars said. *Fuck off.* Words thought, not expressed.

My smile turned to an eat-shit grin. George could not distinguish that look, nor did he care. He saw teeth glisten and a mouth slightly open. Just enough of a small crack to open his imagination. Imagining himself slipping into that crack, with tongue, finger, or dick. None of these things would ever happen—at least not with me. But he could dream. He could tease with his five- dollar tip while his own tip lay shriveled and hidden away. Holding an Abe Lincoln in his hand—pretending, wanting to believe he had a ticket to the promised land. Another promise broken. A vast tundra scattered with broken promises. Mostly to himself.

"Jade, that guy over there wants a lap dance," Krystal ordered, pointing in a direction I was not looking. "Jade, did you hear me?"

"What?" I asked her. I heard every word she said, but I did not feel like smiling pretty. I was stalling and if I ignored her maybe she would go away. "Did you just give him one?" I asked, while looking blankly in her direction.

"I asked if he wanted one, but he asked for you," she said, before turning to walk away.

I let out a deep sigh, then made my way over to the old man bent forward in his chair, leaning toward a glass of amber-colored liquid that sloshed like a turbulent sea between his short fat fingers. Walking toward the old man who asked for me transported me back in time, ten years prior, when another old man asked for me. No reward came with that visit, only uncomfortable torture. It was our yearly school field trip to the nursing home. In single file, we walked there. I remember music playing. Someone must have been carrying a boombox. I distinctly remember hearing the song, "Only the Good Die Young," playing on the battery-operated radio. Singing and walking toward the old people. How ironic. The man who asked for me, the man who asked for a few young girls by pointing at them, was creepy and gross and when I complained to my teacher, I was told, "Be nice to him. He's old." From discomfort, I twisted in my plaid skirt. I wanted to scream and stomp my feet. I did none of those things. I followed our teacher's command. I despised her for that.

The old man in the club would at least give me a money tip, but that was not the reason my reaction to this man was different. I pitied him. Seeing him slouched in his chair, with his eyes straining to look up at me and his alcohol spilling on his legs because his hand shook uncontrollably made me sad. A different sadness from watching my broken ballerina, but a sadness all the same. The dance I danced for him was uniquely his. I barely moved, just a slight shimmy while resting my right hand on his left shoulder. His strained eyes did not reveal a sexual longing or an unfulfilled fantasy. They revealed deep loneliness. Hard to imagine him to be anything other than his rumpled and crumpled frame, but he had been a young man once. He had kissed women, made love to women, dreamed of women, chased women, maybe he buried a woman or maybe she was at home, watching reruns of *The Rockford Files* and having her own fantasies. Unlikely, but maybe.

"What's your name?" I asked him, leaning into his ear. "What?" he said, pointing at his ear and shaking his head.

I repeated the question, louder this time, "What's your name?"

"Oh, my friends call me Sonny. Call me Sonny."

"Will do, Sonny." I smiled empathetically.

He reached for his wallet when the song ended. From the looks of his shaking hand this was going to take some time. I sat down. I was going to anyway. I did not want to run away from Sonny, like I wanted to as a young girl in the putrid-smelling nursing home. I felt a genuine warmth from and for this old man. A kindness covered by the effects of time and a lifetime of experiences carved into his face.

"Do you have a Mrs. at home, Sonny?"

He looked at me, started to speak, then stopped. He took a few seconds to respond. His eyes looked beyond the paneled wall. I don't know what he was looking at, but it wasn't the black velvet picture of the bare-breasted woman, crookedly hanging on the wall—another stuck ballerina.

"My Mrs. is at home," he said while a smile formed on his face, "she is in her final home." Another long pause followed. "She is in the most glorious home. She's at home with Jesus. God rest her soul," he said while holding his shaky glass up, toasting the air in front of him, before taking another drink. A frustrating sight to watch. I wanted to help him, but he had come here to be reminded that he was still a man.

"I'm sorry," I told him.

"Thank you, dear child. She died five years ago of cancer…" he began to form his lips, but words did not come. I was relieved. I started to ask him if he wanted another drink, but I stopped myself. I couldn't handle more of that either. I sat for a few more minutes, listening to him talk about when he, his wife, and their two children moved to Fairbanks. He brought his family to the area in 1953 when he began working for the Haines-Fairbanks Pipeline. He told me about his job as a systems engineer. He told me his wife taught Sunday school. He told me they had another child after moving here and that he was the only one who stayed in the area. He told me they stayed after his work with the pipeline ended because they fell in love with the land. "It has a way of getting under your skin," Sonny said. I was in and out of focusing on his words, but with my own thoughts of a dark, dancing forest, I understood. My eyes and attention bounced between him, the dancer in front of us on Stage Two, and my obsession with the door. I could not stop myself from looking at every man who walked in the place. Not too hard of a task in a slow-moving casual joint. Disappointment followed every time the happy-to-see-bouncing-boobs-and-butts smile was not Sean's.

Chapter 15
caged chicken

White was swirling through the air and blurring past me on the way to the airport. I was numb. Eight weeks ago, I had come to a faraway frozen land to make money. That's it. Dance, show some skin, and go home with a few thousand dollars. Easy plan. Easy money. *Easy mistake to make.* I had deviated from my plan, and it may have cost me my heart. I desperately wanted to curl up into a fetal position on the vinyl station wagon seat and moan like a sick baby. Or jump out of the piece of shit paneled wagon I was riding in and finally give in to the dark forest that had been trying to lure me in for weeks. Hundreds of distinct voices, shaking loose from their frozen limbs, inviting me to join them. Casting their seductive voices toward the dirty white and brown vehicle, carrying the lost girl—the one they were determined to not let get away.

"Get her…she's ours…she belongs here…" High and low tones calling me, calling me, calling me.

"Shut the fuck up!" I blurted toward the forest.

With one eyebrow raised, my driver, the same lady who had picked me up eight weeks before, gazed at me in the rearview mirror.

"What? I said nothing." She was confused.

"Not you. I know. Sorry." My response was hollow.

Nothing else was said. I was just another strange dancer chick that she would laugh about later with her friends around a card table. Short of reaching into the wired cage in the back seat, yanking a chicken out and biting its head off, drinking its blood and spitting feathers at my driver, both arriving and departing, I don't think anything would have surprised her. And why the fuck did she have a chicken in the goddamn car? I was glad to be going home, even without my heart. I didn't need it, anyway. It was better that it was ripped out of me and tossed onto the frozen sidewalk, then stepped on by a dozen drunk men on their way in and out of the frozen fairytale factory. My blood began to simmer. I looked toward the enchanting forest and flipped it off. This place got my heart. It was not taking my soul too!

I leaned my head against the cold glass, then closed my eyes. I was tired. Too tired for a nineteen-year-old. I already carried a lifetime of hurt, pain, and disappointment. I couldn't carry any more. The weight of it all brought me to my knees. I desperately wanted to surrender, but I had to keep going. The only other option was to take matters into my own hands and end this life with them, or my own feet by walking into the dark forest, without a blanket and without food. I could sense the snow-heavy tree limbs vibrate with glee in response to my distressing obsession. I stared at the old door handle, just below where my head was resting. I considered how easy it would be to pull it and hurl myself out of the spinning coop, letting the voices bury me.

No! was my soul's silent scream. Don't give in! Don't let the darkness win! I needed to keep fighting for my life. I almost gave up the fight when I was a despondent sixteen-year-old. My guardian angels intervened. They saved my life. I had been fighting ever since.

I tried to push thoughts of Sean aside. I wanted to not care. I wanted the heartache to end. *It will,* a calming voice told me. *It will not happen soon enough,* was my response. I wanted to believe Sean did not intend for me to depart this way—a broken bird sitting next to a caged bird, being driven to the airport by someone who might not even say goodbye to me. Sean should have been driving me. He should have been hugging and kissing me on the sidewalk in front of the Fairbanks Airport. We should have been two young lovers, kissing, crying, laughing, and inhaling each other's visible breath. Clinging to each other until the airplane was dangerously close to leaving and telling each other how we would meet again, as our tears fell, freezing before they reached the ground. Salty drops that I would take home after they shattered into a thousand tiny diamonds on the frozen sidewalk.

I would wear the sorrowful souvenirs around my neck, next to my heart when the longing became too much. Others would notice and comment on their exquisite sparkle. Behind my "thank you," would be a knowing that the glisten was not the makings of earth's compressed time, but of the jagged sediment that poured from my broken heart. In that moment, on the sidewalk, we would convince ourselves that our love was true and the belief in that truth would soften the pain of two kindred hearts, forever separating.

None of that had happened, except the tears streaming down my face. Tears that turned into stains, not diamonds, to be stepped on by muddy boots. *I knew better than to fall in love.* I should have listened to my own voice, telling me to stay focused on the prize, not on a boy with sparkling blue eyes. *You knew this was not going to end well, you, dumbass. You fool!* It was no one's fault but my own. Unless the story about Sean getting unexpectedly called out to the field was bullshit. He wouldn't do that to me. *Would he?* His friend sounded believable. Even Sean's deep sadness and regret, conveyed by his friend, seemed convincing.

Two young lovers deeply in love, forever separated by life circumstances. Two lives not in control of their own destiny. Just pawns in the flesh trades: a soldier and a dancer.

I wrestled with two stories, trying to decide which would be easier to tell myself for the next several days, maybe even months. Story one: Sean's friend was telling the truth and now Sean is a twisted heartbroken mess in the middle of God only knows where, anguishing over not saying goodbye to me with each snow-crunching step. A broken child in a man's body. Or story two: Sean is a liar who had his friend lie for him, just so he would not have to say goodbye to me. Then he could rest up and stock up on candles for the next dancer chick dumb enough to fall for his romantic bullshit.

The scenarios bounced around in my head, scrambling with each bump in the road. The stories mingled together, and I imagined Sean both crying in the cold field and laughing over cold beer with his friends. The laughing Sean was easier to process, and I could easily turn my heartbreak into anger with that scenario. It would be much easier to curse at him and turn him into a prick than to imagine the tragedy of two young lovers who lassoed a most powerful love under the dancing green lights, now ripped apart by fate. *I can't bear it! I can't spend the rest of my life pining for this perfect love that escaped me in the middle of a land faraway—a land and a young man I would likely never see again. No, I just can't carry this deep sadness.* My arms and legs were tired. Much better to imagine him laughing over all of it. Dumb dancer, he was saying. He was right. He was also a prick. End of story.

We bumped along for another twenty minutes or so, until we came to a stop in front of the large Fahrenheit sign in front of the airport's only terminal. Five below zero. Warmer than when I had arrived, eight weeks before. *A lifetime ago.* I arrived as a hungry young naïve desert native. I was leaving as a jaded, broken-hearted, experienced dancer with a stash of cash. At least I chose my name correctly. I did something right. The cold had enveloped me, from the inside out. Just as well. I would need some protection from the bright sunshine.

Chapter 16

falling through the soft white

My flight back to sunny Arizona was a teary, cloudy blur. If I wasn't sleeping, I was crying. I no longer had the buoyancy of adrenaline to keep me moving. I crashed hard 35,000 feet up in the sky. I was flying home with just over five thousand dollars stashed in my purse, resting near my hip. It was more money than I would have made at the video store over a two-month period, though less than I had imagined. My purse was lighter than I had hoped for, and my heart was heavier than I had bargained for. Flying high, strapped under a seatbelt, I was a stuck ballerina without a tune. "Be Kind—Rewind" were the words that kept coming to me. A friendly message I had said a thousand times, to remind video customers to rewind their VHS tapes. The plane was rewinding the route from which I had come, offering a different view of the Space Needle, Mount Rainier, and the skies I had soared through eight weeks before. The clouds seemed darker this time. Sights rewinding before my eyes, but there is no way to rewind time. If only I could rewind time and say, "No thanks," to the boy with sky-colored eyes and muscular thighs.

I must have fallen asleep somewhere over Northern California, because I don't remember seeing any of the Golden State. Too bad. Too bad I didn't have a parachute to jump out of this plane and fall into the ocean and let the waves swallow me. The blue liquid squeezing me tighter and tighter, pressing on my broken heart, creating the illusion that it was mended before collapsing on itself then rupturing into a thousand pieces with a final squeeze. Tighter, tighter, tighter until the person I was, became a nothingness. My entire being reduced to a bubble floating to the surface. Like my life up to that point, barely a ripple, I would make.

Dreaming, dreading, crying, wishing. Not wanting to be going home to warm sunshine and cold whispers. Not wanting to return to the vast tundra where I let myself trust a solution to a problem that was now looming larger than ever and where I opened my heart to romance and love. Just an inch, I let it crack, but enough for its broken promises to reach in and grab. I did let its tight grip cling, then it tossed me around and slammed me against the cold concrete. A cold, hard smack reserved for the less privileged. I should have known good things, like long goodbyes, long-distance whispers, and love letters sealed with sweet kisses were not for people like us, Sean and me. We were too busy selling our flesh to pay for our existence.

Irish writer Jonathan Swift was on to something. Sean and I were too old for that Swift exchange, though. No easy way out for the likes of us. Destined to toil and eke out an existence in the flesh trade until our flesh was too leathery and old for dancing and soldiering. Who was I to think I could be swept away by love? I was no princess. Just a lonely video clerk trying to earn my way to a college degree. *Fuck this.* I had a good time with a nice boy, I earned a few dollars, I saw the Northern Lights and Alaska—at least one quiet street and a frozen field anyway. I was not going to fall apart. I would get off this hurling pile of metal and carry myself with pride back to my life, even if I was dying inside. I was not giving up on my life, or on my dreams. I just needed to stop being so damn dramatic and carry on.

With my eyes open, I may have made the decision to carry on without Sean, but my sleeping brain had another plan. I was dreaming about Sean chasing me in the frozen park when the pilot interrupted a perfect, playful moment—one that was miles away from reality.

"Passengers, fasten your seatbelts and prepare for landing. We will be landing in fifteen minutes. It is a warm winter day in Phoenix—eighty-two degrees."

The jostling of the plane shook the rest of the sleep out of me. Another hit from reality.

Groggy, grumpy, and depressed, I wondered if I would ever dream about Sean again. I imagined us carrying on a love affair over phone lines. Laughing and flirting for hours, like a schoolgirl, I would sneak calls under the covers. Believing this was possible softened the pain surging through my heart and body.

"Miss, please put your seat up," the stewardess requested, as she made her final cabin check before securing herself into her seat. I watched her lean down and make her final requests to other passengers. She never stopped smiling. She was very pretty. She had long, jet-black, curly hair pulled into a high ponytail. She wore a navy-blue, knee-length skirt with a sweater and tights the same color. The red scarf around her neck added color to her monotone outfit. She must have sensed me staring at her, because she slowly turned her head and looked toward me. I noticed her long eyelashes in her profile. She smiled a knowing smile. I could not help myself; I smiled too. For a moment, I considered if I could do her job. Of course, I could *do* her job, but I wondered if I could do what she did, day after day after day. Serving drinks, smiling at people, smiling at men who stared too long and said too much. Another stuck ballerina. I did not want to do her job. I needed more. My body could go through the motions, but my brain needed so much more. I was sure hers did, too. I was sure she was doing what she needed to do to survive.

"Flight crew, prepare for landing," the captain said. I heard his deep voice, and I wanted to follow his instructions, but it would take so much more than putting my seat upright and buckling in to prepare for stepping into my apartment and facing my two roommates. As we descended over the Valley of the Sun, I considered one more time hurling myself out of this plane. What a grand return that would be. I was sure I would make the news.

"A young woman jumped out of a plane and fell ten thousand feet to her death, landing on the ASU football field," the news woman would say. "They will need to work fast to clean up the bloody mess she left behind before tomorrow's game. They just put down new turf, what a shame."

Shock, horror, and sadness would permeate the campus and city, followed by pity. They would learn I had applied and had been accepted, and they would speculate why I was not a student there. They would read that I was returning from Fairbanks, Alaska, where I had danced topless for eight weeks. "Maybe she was on something," they would say. "Oh, yes, yes, I am sure she was," would be the collective response. A false assumption that would help to make sense of the tragedy and put the blame back on me. Much easier than looking at the many reasons why a young intelligent woman, who had "everything going for her" could end her life in such a dramatic fashion. No one to blame, really, just a series of steps, or in my case missteps, that young, lost people take. Steps that are more manageable when someone is there to hold their hand, or at the very least, to say, "This is how you do this, follow my lead." I did not have that person.

Eventually, sooner than later, the chatter about my tragic demise would cease, and everyone would be left with confusion over what to do about this horrible and tragic episode of a young woman falling to her death and the scar it left on the airline and the university, and on the football field. They would unanimously decide that a park bench, with my name on it, would be a generous and thoughtful tribute to my memory and a place to put their temporary feelings.

Then they would carry on with their business of molding young minds and cutting grass. Everyone would carry on. I would be just another lost and desperate falling teenager.

I was becoming quite enamored by this storyline when I saw the approaching runway.

Smack, bounce, *smack, screech.* I did not have the courage or the strength to go through with my 11th-hour plot. I could never hurt anyone else, either. I was looking for a solo jump and I was not about to suck the two children, sitting two rows up, closer to the emergency door, into my farewell. Coloring and holding dolls, the two little girls were shining with hope. I would not be the one to extinguish that light.

Chapter 17

solo traveler

I dragged my tired body and scuffed suitcase through the terminal and glass doors. The sun had set about an hour before, and it was still warm outside. The thought of returning to my apartment and facing my two roommates made my heart race and my palms sweaty. My thoughts were distracted. Stepping into the warm winter evening made me sweat more than I ever did on the Alaskan stage. My head began to spin. I found the nearest bench and plopped down. I tore off my sweater and contemplated throwing it in the trashcan next to me.

I was in no rush to leave. No one was waiting for me, and I didn't have a job to prepare for. No boyfriend would be arriving to lift me into his arms. I was balancing on a thin rope, teetering between flying—feeling freer than I ever had, and falling—like my body was plunging toward a crashing finale. I wasn't waiting for a taxi. There were plenty of those to choose from when I was ready to face my fears. I could sit here for eight hours, and no one would say a word, not the strangers here or the women in my apartment. I contemplated what life is like for people who move from bench to bench, who try not to take up space but become a nuisance to those who would rather not have to see or deal with their troubles. I wondered how long I could sit on the bench before the man in uniform, patrolling the sidewalk would tell me to move along. A few days is my guess, with different schedules and my ability to blend. Until then, I could sit and watch people. Some looked happy to be returning and others sad to be leaving. Happy or sad, most curbside moments began or ended with a hug.

I closed my eyes and imagined Sean pulling up in his black truck, with its piercing red lights, arriving to pick me up, from the curb and off my feet. I began to cry. *Fuck.* I did not want to open my eyes. Doing so could compel me to look into the eyes of another who might be noticing the sad girl crying. A pathetic scene or a painted masterpiece, I couldn't decide. Neither vision properly described me. A passing older mom might be the first to notice these details. She might see her daughter in me. Or a passing child might notice me, the grown-up crying. A sensitive and curious child might even approach me for a closer look. I imagined she would lean in, like children do, wondering what's wrong.

"Why are you crying?" the precious child might ask while placing her tiny hand on mine.

Just long enough for her hurried mom to notice what was happening before grabbing her daughter's hand and hurrying her along. The mom would look at my eyes and see that I was upset. Her decency and maternal instincts would make her want to stop and comfort me, but she would quickly decide that she did not have time for a stranger's despair. She and the child would rush off to catch their flight. Oh, to have a hand to hold. To feel the embrace of arms around me. Neither would solve my problems, but they would give me a little strength to lean on—to take one more step into my fucked-up life, feeling like I didn't belong.

I opened my eyes and saw no one looking into mine. Just the usual curbside busyness.

Stressed drivers. Stressed travelers. Quick goodbyes followed by a punch of the gas and a quick merge left, or brief hellos that continued inside the vehicles. Happy faces, sharing details about their travels, and laughing drivers talking about how they had to circle the airport six times.

I walked to the farthest yellow cab. My driver tossed my suitcase into the trunk. Except for telling him my address, we said nothing else. I watched the bustling airport disappear from my view as we drove toward my shared Tempe apartment.

When we turned down the street that led to my place, I saw the same homeless man I had seen countless times, digging through the trash. He looked old with his long, dirty beard, but I wondered how old he really was. I could always join him if life got too hard, I considered. He was surviving. The street was lined with tall and crowded apartment buildings, and a drive down the road reminded me of the many parties I had attended since moving in. Fun memories that were overshadowed by the persistent feeling of being an outsider who should not be there intruding on *their* college experience.

The thought of going to another lame college party no longer appealed to me. I just wanted to go to college classes, graduate, and get out of there. I wanted to get far away from there. I was done with the parties. I was done with the lame drunk people who did not appreciate how good they had it. All the while judging those of us who did not have what they had, including support with all of it. I suppose it is easier to hurl stones when you are standing upright.

The driver put his cab in park then hustled to his trunk to retrieve my suitcase. He would have been amused if he had seen the contents of my bag. Sweaters and wooly socks and tiny G-strings and triangle tops. A curious combination of items. I counted thirty-seven ones from my purse. He watched and counted along with me, every dollar going from my right hand to his open right palm. He was not amused, but he was paid in full, and he did not have to take his top off or shake his ass for any of it. Good for him. His job, I could not do. I would be accused of padding my mileage. It would not be intentional but getting lost was my talent. I would smile though, unlike this serious man, who sped out of the parking lot headed toward his next paying customer.

After a deep breath and loud sigh, I made my ascent up the stairs to the second floor. Plop, plop, plop, went my suitcase with each step. *Please don't be here, please don't be here*, I prayed with each stomp. I would have loved to take a long hot shower and slept for twenty hours before facing either of my roommates or any of their friends or boyfriends. I turned the key slowly and pushed open the door. The smell of the litter box almost knocked me over. *Really? You really must put the shit next to the front door?* I didn't even want to move into this apartment. I'd already put a deposit on a studio apartment. I was excited to be moving into *my own* place when my friend Alena called to ask if I needed a place to live. I didn't regret taking her call. I regretted saying *yes*.

"No, I don't. I am moving into a studio down on Main Street," I had told her.

"Oh," she replied, followed by a long pause that was more of a hanging question. "Have you signed your lease yet?" she asked.

"No, not officially, I just put down a holding deposit."

"Awesome! What do you think about moving in with us? Me and Christina."

"I don't know. I'm really excited about living alone." I did know and the answer was no, but I didn't have the courage to say it.

"We really need a roommate, and you and I would have so much fun living together."

Her gentle arm-twisting went on for a few more minutes. I was torn between doing what I really wanted to do and feeling like I owed her something. She had been a very close friend in middle and high school. She and her parents were there for me at the start of my senior year in high school when I needed a place to live. They had opened their home for me and tried to make me feel welcome. Something my own father did not do after I returned to Arizona to graduate in my hometown, after living with my mom and stepdad in Denver for a year and a half.

I lived with Alena for about a month before the uncomfortableness of being a long-term guest in her home became too much for me. After saving enough from my video store job, I was able to buy a piece of shit car, then I moved into an apartment with a friend of a friend. During the first semester of my senior year in high school is when my foray into barely surviving began. I was broke, but I no longer felt like I was imposing on anyone.

So, I hadn't been able to say no to a friend who had been there for me.

"Hello, is anyone here?" I directed my question down the hallway. I was intentionally quiet: I did not want to be heard.

Alena and Christina, another high school friend, shared the larger room with a bathroom and I had my own room. At least I could retreat to my own room. With no sign of my roomies, I could breathe a bit easier. I unzipped my suitcase, unpacked a few things, noticed the inch of dust on my dresser, and then exhaustion overtook me. I fell asleep in my clothes and slept for thirteen hours.

I woke to the sounds of laughter and the smell of bacon. What a charming scene, I thought. Unlike any I had risen to in Alaska. Mostly, we were offered cereal options, even though a warm breakfast would have been more generous and fitting. I was nervous about facing my roommates, but I could not spend the rest of my life in this bedroom. I slowly sat up, then plopped back down on the pillow. I spent another twenty minutes mulling over my misery and wrestling with a body that felt like it had aged five years in the last eight weeks—most of it in the previous twenty-four hours. I peeled myself from my futon bed and lifted my body into an upright position. It was time to leave the safety of my room.

Chapter 18

grab a bagel instead

Facing the two laughing girls in the kitchen was much harder than facing strangers from a stage. I wondered if they had heard me come in. It smelled so good, and I was so hungry. I doubted they would offer me any and I thought, if they did, it would be done in a way that left me feeling like a pauper. "Please sir, I want some more," would be my reply. They would probably look at me with their heads tilted, not knowing my reference. They might love the groveling me. The me that I should be ashamed of. The me they could look down on. If only I did not care. If only I had stayed in the freezing tundra where the greetings were warmer. I considered greeting them wearing only my G-string. At least it would shock and silence them, giving me time to grab some bacon and run back to my room.

Alena, pausing in the middle of flipping bacon said in an upbeat tone, "Well, long time no see!"

"Hi," was my one-word, one-syllable ice-breaker.

"How was your flight?" Christina asked, "What time did you get in?"

"Long. Fine. Thanks. Sometime around 8 p.m., I guess. I'm not sure," I said.

An awkward and familiar silence followed our brief hellos. A familiar feeling that always precedes a break-up and move-out. I was too tired and too outnumbered to be the bigger woman and turn this into a heartwarming reunion. One where I would run to my room in excitement, grab the gifts I bought my two besties, while thinking how much I hoped they would like what I bought for them. I did none of these things. I had nothing to give them except a blank hungry stare. They smiled back. Not a friendly, "we are so happy to see you smile," but a "you look like shit" smile.

Alena grabbed some bacon and plopped the pieces onto their cute little matching plates, then slid the spatula under the shiny white eggs and let them cozy up to the bacon. It was a delicious greasy-looking feast. The popping toaster interrupted the thick silence. *Use that butter knife to cut through this bullshit,* I thought. Alena handed Christina her plate then took one step toward *her* barstool, before stopping to ask if I wanted anything.

"Thanks, but I am going to shower and run some errands," I told them, while they crunched on bacon. I closed my mouth tightly, so the bacon-searching saliva would not drivel down my chin. "I left my rent money on the coffee table," I said before closing the bathroom door behind me. Not a slam. I did not have the energy for anger.

The bathroom, *my bathroom,* was dirtier than I had left it. I *guess their bathroom is theirs and my bathroom is ours.* The warm, flowing water drowned the growling in my stomach, but not the ache. That pain was growing beyond my stomach and quickly working its way into my limbs, leaving me weak. Maybe I should have asked for some breakfast, but that felt awkward and uncomfortable. I decided if I could survive the last eight weeks, I could survive another hour of hunger. I dressed in dirty clothes that smelled like the gambling dormitory, slipped on my black boots, grabbed my purse and keys, and left our apartment with my wet hair dripping onto a fresh pile of cat shit.

My car was covered in leaves and bird droppings. I had seen and smelled enough shit for one day, and I did not want to stare at the crusty white splatter while hunger gnawed at my being, but without something to clean up the mess, I was stuck staring. *Please start,* I said silently with my eyes closed before turning the key to my VW Rabbit. Not immediately, but my car did turn over. *Thank God.* My big break for the day…maybe the week. I looked behind me, reversed out of the parking spot, then left our apartment complex without glancing back.

I did not "have errands to run," except the big one that involved finding a job, but I wasn't up for that task today, I just needed to get out of that greasy bacon and cat shit-smelling apartment. I remembered a bagel joint a few blocks from our apartment. I let my stomach guide me to the nearest food location, a task my brain was not up for.

Nothing had changed in the food joint, including the people who worked there. I had only been gone eight weeks, but since I had changed so much, it made sense that everything and everyone else should too. I suppose the comforts of college life ages young adults at a slower pace than the biting cold of the Last Frontier and the bright lights of the stage. The secondhand smoke and first-hand alcohol didn't help, either.

"Hey, how's it going?" the cute boy behind the counter said while quickly looking away when I made eye contact with him. His left eye was covered by his wavy, chestnut-colored hair, and after spending the last eight weeks surrounded by bold and mostly older men, some bald, it was nice to interact with a young man who blushed when I looked into his eyes. He was probably my age in biological years, but I felt so much older than him, even if I didn't look it.

"Jade, your order is ready," the tiny girl behind the counter said. I hadn't meant to say my stage name to the cute boy, but after answering to that name for the last eight weeks, it just rolled off my parched tongue. I ate my bagel alone and contemplated using my stage name going forward when meeting new people. After fueling my brain with a few bagel bites, I decided that was a terrible idea that would require too much energy to keep track of. Or would it? Maybe it wouldn't be that hard. No one was too concerned about me or pried too much. Certainly not my parents. I believed that if I just kept paying my bills, I wouldn't need to explain myself to anyone or ask for anything from anyone.

I slowly ate my bagel and watched the busy intersection from my window seat. Only two blocks from the university, the bagel shop window gave me a front row seat to college students weighed down with heavy backpacks, who seemed to be lifted by big dreams. I had dreams too, but I was weighed down with burdens and insecurities and the constant feeling of not fitting in. It would take more than a backpack of textbooks to feel like I belonged in "their" world. I contemplated what it might feel like to be hurrying to class, going over notes in my brain with each quick step on the sidewalk, instead of hurrying to grab a bagel or look for a job so that I did not end up on the streets with the other hungry people who had discarded their dreams long ago. Carrying broken dreams seemed like a heavy burden, a monkey on their backs. A painful reminder of what could have been, whenever they saw themselves in a store reflection. Maybe it was easier to tear the monkey free and toss its ripped limbs in the overflowing trash bin.

I stayed in the bagel shop until my butt and legs were numb and the boy with chestnut hair and dreamy eyes had ended his shift. I should have left when he left. Maybe we would have struck up a conversation, both of us laughing and admiring each other's eyes, just long enough to be flirty but not too long to be uncomfortable.

"Hey, do you want to come to my place?" he might have asked me. "It's nothing special, but my roommate is out of town, and I have some movies we can watch."

I would look at the ground, pretending to be unsure about his request. "I don't know, I have a lot to do today," would be my coy response. A bullshit response. I did have a lot to do, but it was bullshit to think I was going to do any of it. "OK, just one movie and then I need to get going. What movies do you have?" I would ask him, as if it mattered. We would never watch a movie because we would spend three hours on his balcony just talking and sipping sodas. No table dances, no alcohol, no dirty dollars tucked in my G-string, just talking. My mind was lost in my imaginary scene, and my heart began to ache for the simplicity of it, when one of the bagel shop workers knocked into my table with her broom. *I get the hint. It's time to get going.* One more stop in a restroom that did not smell like cat shit, and I would be on my way. Where that was, I had no fucking clue.

Chapter 19

a dress to impress

Eyes still closed, my mind woke to the sound of a cat scratching in the litter box, just outside my door and a few steps to the left. *Scratch, scratch, scratch, spin, turn, spin, scratch, scratch, scratch.* Stillness. Here comes the squat and shit, I thought. Sleeping with my back toward the door and my face toward the rising sun, I watched a determined ray of light dance through the curtain's crack, then disappear back. So beautiful, the dancing light inviting me outside to play, to be free. Oh, to travel on a ray of sunshine from the nearest star to the center of me, I dreamed. To know what amber gold feels like, oozing slowly down my skin. *Scratch, scratch, scratch. Shit. That's it! I can't take any more of this!* I turned my body away from the flirting ray to face my closed bedroom door. I scanned my floor, skipping over dropped clothes and shoes, looking for the litter box that sounded, and smelled, like it had been moved next to my bed. I would not have been surprised to find the box placed at the foot of my bed, as loud as the scratching was.

I pulled my heavy body and heavier head to an upright position, catching a glimpse of myself in the full-length mirror across from my bed. Falling asleep with wet hair after taking a late-night plunge into the apartment swimming pool had caused my hair to dry in a mountain of layers, each going in a different direction. *Perfect*, I thought. *I don't know what direction I am supposed to go with my life right now, and neither does my hair.* Maybe if I could wake to smooth flowing hair, my life would follow. Doubtful. I could not help but laugh at myself. Not just a little half-hearted chuckle, but a big belly laugh that continued for a few minutes. Needed comic relief and less harmful than jumping out the window. Jumping from our second floor would not be worth my trouble. I didn't need a life-altering injury, I needed an end to this shit. The shit. The smell. The shitty smell of my life. I could not stop laughing at the irony of the turdbox alarm clock.

How I ended up in this predicament was the question I could not seem to answer or escape. This was not the vision I saw for myself when I was a young girl and yet I couldn't seem to get myself on the right path. My vision included living in a dormitory and reading books on a manicured lawn. Maybe a cute boyfriend would be part of the scenario, but mostly I dreamed of learning and graduating. All the striving and studying and sacrificing as a younger person…for what? I should have tossed those dreams into a litter box and let a fat, gray cat bury my dreams under a pile of steamy crap.

My nerves were beginning to exhibit the anxiety my mind was trying to conceal. I was not very good at keeping secrets from my body. Going through life alone had created the perfect scenario for my mind and body to become the closest of friends. I needed those close friends to unite and help me find a new dancing gig, in Phoenix, or visit my old boss and ask for my job back. The preferred choice was to stay in bed and figure out how to climb on the sparkling steps of a dancing ray and tap my way out of this shitty existence. Like in an old black and white movie, I would dance confidently up the steps of the ray. The golden staircase would be lined with swaying cats, who turned their furry little faces toward me when I sauntered past them. I would get to the top of the steps, where a big litter box sparkled, then I would kick it, sending shit flying everywhere, before I was carried forever away on the golden ray. Musical fantasies that I needed to turn off so that I could deal with my jobless reality.

I slumber-walked through the maze of unpacked and dropped clothes and opened my bedroom door, making sure I inhaled a deep breath before I headed into the hallway of floating feline feces and urine traces. My plan to rush into my bathroom was thwarted by a closed bathroom door. I was not about to stand next to the litter box and wait for whoever was in my bathroom. I knocked on the bathroom door to let whoever was behind the door know that there was a line forming. Needing to breathe, I went back to my room and plopped myself on my bed. I was just waiting for the door to open so that I could take a shower and leave. I was hoping the shower would wash the shit smell out of my nose.

I thought about where I would go and what I would wear while the barely warm water washed over me. *Bitches took all the hot water*! Just as well since I didn't have all day to luxuriate under a steamy shower. I dried off then sprinted to my bedroom, across the hall, praying I would not run into a roommate's boyfriend. I am sure my roommates' boyfriends knew about my vocation and the last thing I wanted was one of them to see me wet and naked, barely covered by my small towel. I made it to my room without incident and shut the door. Now the task of getting dressed to visit a strip club with the goal of leaving with my name on the shift board. It felt pathetic and embarrassing, but I was not sure what else to do at that point. *No one's going to rescue me, and I do need to eat occasionally*. What does one wear to a strip club interview? As little as possible, was my first thought.

I looked at my sparse closet and then at the piles on the floor. I wasn't going to the library—I was going to a strip club where my number one job qualification would be to look sexy. I contemplated asking my roommates if they had an outfit I could borrow. "What for?" they would ask. I would rather show up in my birthday suit than ask either of them for a sexy dress. It would be a pointless request, regardless of the occasion, since I was a few sizes and inches smaller than both. I did the only thing I could do—I searched through my unwashed clothes pile and found my only black dress.

It would do the trick, well not a literal trick, I only danced. It was stinky though. I should have spent my time doing laundry the day before, instead of daydreaming about a boy with chestnut-colored hair and watching college kids skip across the intersection toward *their* dreams. Wanting to get moving before I changed my mind, I ironed my dress with my roommate's iron, fixed my hair and makeup and left the apartment, not without a full body check look from Christina.

More looks followed; this time from a pack of overgrown boys in the parking lot as I walked toward my car. The boys stopped talking and watched me walk. Left, right, left…with each step and stare from them, I grew more uncomfortable. I wished I could walk with pride and confidence—after all, my eight weeks of dancing the night shift in the land of darkness had transformed my body into a toned dancing dream, but I did not own any of that outward facade. Under my firm muscles, I was an awkward girl, caught between wanting to hide and trying to fit in. My pace did quicken, but what I really wanted to do was sprint to my car and get the hell out of there. I felt less exposed in a topless bar than I did on that parking lot blacktop.

"Damnit!" I shouted. I had forgotten to clean the bird shit from my window. I was a mess. I needed to take care of my shit.

Safely protected by metal and locked doors, I could breathe. I let out another sigh before I attempted to start my car. Oh God, please let this car start. *Please. Please. Please.* It wasn't a pretty start, but the engine did turn over. "Thank you, God!" I whispered sincerely. "Now, will you help me find a place where I can take my clothes off and dance for dollars?"

Chapter 20

a personal escort

I did not have any confidence walking past a group of gawking overgrown adolescents.

I sure as hell did not feel confident when I turned into the parking lot of the Phoenix gentlemen's club, Desert Rose Cabaret. The "me" determined to pay for a college degree would need to take the lead. That ambitious woman would need to convince my legs that I could walk into this place, alone, dance if asked, and leave with a reason to come back ready to work a full shift. I parked in the back row of the parking lot, facing the entrance, and watching customers come and go. The standard blue-collar crowd, with a few ties, much looser around the collar on those who were leaving compared to those who were arriving. I was not sure what else I would learn staying in my car. I was stalling. I must have stalled too long because the tall bouncer who had been guarding the door was walking toward me.

I rolled down my window when he approached. I had no reason to fear him—he *was* security. "Are you a dancer? Are you here for a job? Do you want to come inside?" he asked me, while crouching down and leaning toward my open window.

A personal escort. How nice, I thought. He gave me and my legs courage. "Yes," was my response. I did not have to tell him that going inside was more of a need than a want. Although there were a few perks, I am sure it wasn't his life's ambition to work as the bouncer in a strip club in an industrial corridor of Phoenix. I am sure he was doing what he needed to do to survive. I am sure I was not the first girl he had rescued from the parking lot, and I doubt I was the last. I grabbed my purse (getting lighter every day), locked, and shut my door, then followed him in. I asked him how long he had worked there. "Two years," was his response. He had wavy, light-brown hair, with a cowlick on top, just above his large forehead. He had strong, solid thighs and an upper body in equal and impressive proportion. I was relieved to be walking in with him. I felt safe with him. This could be a positive sign—*or* a trap.

With the ushering of his hand, I stepped into the club ahead of him. It took a moment for my eyes to adjust to the hazy interior. My body did what my nervous energy was preventing me from doing: breathe. I inhaled a deep breath through my nose and released through my mouth. Doing so prevented me from passing out, but the secondhand smoke I inhaled made me nauseous. Slow sips of alcohol and secondhand smoke. I might become an alcoholic and get lung cancer before I earned enough money for college.

Too mesmerized by the activity happening on every stage and in every corner of the large open room, I did not hear the bouncer ask me my name the first time. It took a nudge against my right arm from his left hand for him to get my attention. Leaning down again and speaking directly into my right ear, he asked, "What's your name?"

"Jade. My name is Jade," I replied, trying to convince myself this was true.

"Pretty name. Matches your eyes," he said matter-of-factly.

"What's your name?" I asked while leaning toward him, but without looking away from the show—the lights, the sparkles, the smiles—I was terrified *and* enchanted.

"My name is Doug."

"Oh, nice, solid name," I told him and then, after peeling my eyes away from the circus-style attractions, I looked into his brown eyes that were a good foot above mine. "Thanks for helping me."

"Don't mention it; that's why I'm here." His smile revealed a silver tooth in the left corner of his mouth. His eyes looked tired, but they also looked kind. I wasn't sure what would happen with this place, but if I did come back, I hoped he'd be working.

"What nights do you work?" I asked him. His response was interrupted by his need to check the I.D.s of two young men. The young men waited at the door while Doug scanned their IDs with a flashlight and their faces with his intimidating stare. The taller of the two, a tanned blond who looked like he rolled in from a San Diego beach, was trying to keep it together, but he could not stand still, moving from one foot to the other and tapping his fingers against his thighs before shoving his shaky hands into his pockets. The other young man was a redhead with a frozen pearly grin that perfectly advertised his frozen body. He might have needed to be carried in or out by his nervous friend. Imagining that comical scene made me laugh. I needed that. Relief that quickly disappeared when my thoughts turned to Sean. As much as I didn't want to and as hard as I tried not to, I often saw Sean in other young men. Nothing else about the odd pair reminded me of Sean. Sean didn't have to *try* to be calm and cool, he just was. Sean had an energy that calmed others. I had noticed it with his friends, and I had felt it. *Oh, how I felt it.*

The Sean train was taking over my brain and there wasn't a damn thing I could do to stop it. *Not here! Not now!* I pleaded with myself. My blood which pulsed for Sean was beginning to bubble in my core, pushing its way toward my throat, which it would choke just after making my heart flip and flop. Not little taps, but a heart that was throwing itself against my interior, trying to end its tormented existence and prison, either through escape or suicide. A fiery blood that I could not control. It was rising, like a volcano, pushing against the back of my eyes, threatening to rupture and flood the entire room with fiery red lava, burning everyone and everything in its path. The aftermath would be a tragic scene caused by the most powerful force in the universe: love. A tragic scene that would pull other casualties into its smoky embers when women from the outside world, outside of this place, would have to come and identify the bodies of their husbands or boyfriends. "I thought he was working late," they would cry. "I can't believe he died in a strip club!"

I tried to turn off those thoughts. I tried to turn off thoughts of Sean, the boy I never meant to fall in love with. I tried to extinguish the slow-moving lava consuming my heart. I tried to prevent the tears from falling, but I was powerless to stop *every* drop. I had no more control over monsoon storms than I did over the storms raging in my love-lost soul. Nature was going to take its course. I just had to wait out the storm and, like a claims adjuster, I would assess the damage after the lava cooled.

I needed to appear strong—not like some desperate dancer chick crying at the entrance of a strip club. Crying about her fucked-up life and why she ended up in a place like this on a Tuesday, late afternoon. Crying about how desperate she was for money. I closed my eyes and took another deep breath, longer than the first. Too long. Fire-charged blood mixed with stale cigarette smoke expanded my lava-scorched lungs and made my head spin before sending me into a coughing fit. The four customers seated at a four-top closest to the entrance, who had not glanced my way prior to my spitting and sputtering, took notice.

"Do you need a drink of water?" one of them asked. I am not sure if he was being kind or sarcastic, but I said, "Yes" between coughs.

"Here, you can have mine," he offered, "I haven't drunk any yet." I took it and nodded a thank you before taking a big gulp, then another.

While I was fighting for my breath—*and soul*—Doug finished checking and intimidating the men at the door. In between coughs, I heard him going over the rules of the club, "The girls need to stay twelve inches away from you and absolutely no touching or lewd language…" before ushering them in with a wave of his arm. They let out a sigh when they walked past me. I understood the anxiety caused by this place. Doug wasn't the only one to scan their faces. I did the same as they scurried past me. Searching for any familiarity. *Did I know them? Did I go to high school with them?* Unlikely, but I couldn't help but wonder. The club was several cities and worlds away from my old neighborhood. But…there was a possibility. I stared and searched my memory bank of faces, looking for a match. I needed to put an end to this staring routine before it became an obsession. If I was going to survive this experience and stuff my college purse with dirty dollars, I could not worry about the identity of every man who walked through the doors into this seedy world.

Anyway, what about their identity? Shouldn't they be concerned about being recognized too? *No. Life doesn't work that way,* I was beginning to realize. *Guilt and shame are not equally distributed, especially between the genders.* The girls who walk into these places with their costumes and stilettos shoved in a bag, or left behind in a musty locked trunk, are sluts who take their clothes off for money. The guys are just being guys, having a good time.

Done with his bouncer duties, Doug walked over to me.

"Are you OK?" he inquired while placing his left hand on my right shoulder. I did not mind. I needed the support. "I saw you coughing. Do you need more water?"

"No, I'm fine now, thank you." Either he really was a nice person, or he was trained to show a little extra tender loving care to the desperate girls at the entrance. TLC with an ulterior motive.

"OK, good. Well, if it were up to me, I would hire you on the spot, but it's up to the house manager and the club manager, so have a seat here and wait a few minutes"—he gestured to a small table close to the door—"and I will see who I can find first."

I was relieved by his instructions. I needed to sit. With a mind spinning and a heart breaking, I could not think or act for myself. I finished drinking my warm water while I let the smoky haze cover and swallow me. Like every other person in the place, I was transformed into a gray shadow, watching women do dog-and-pony tricks. It was still light outside, but it was obvious from the empty beer bottles, loud voices, and staggered steps walking toward stages to drop dollars, that some of these men had kicked off their happy hour hours before. At least *they* were happy to be there.

"Hi, I'm Tracy, the House Mom," a woman approaching said while thrusting her hand toward mine. Her radiant smile matched the afternoon sun—a different energy from the first House Mom I had met during my ill-fated amateur night.

"Hi, I am Jade." I stood up and shook her hand. She had a firm grip.

"Yes, I heard. That's a beautiful name, and you're very pretty. Have you danced before?"

"Yes, I just got back from Fairbanks, Alaska, where I danced for eight weeks at a topless club. Before that I danced one night at a club on Van Buren, for their amateur night. I never went back there." The nervousness welling up in me was about to highjack my thoughts and send my mouth into a flurry of words that did not need to be said.

"It helps that you have some experience, but all the girls must dance one set before we can add them to the roster. Did you bring something to dance in?"

My stomach reacted to her request with a violent thrust.

"Yes, I have a few outfits in my car. I can run out and get them."

"Great. Do that, then Doug will show you where the dressing room is." She started to walk away, then turned. "Oh, ask Doug to walk you out. We like our girls to be looked after in the parking lot. Some of these guys can be obnoxious."

"Some?" I asked.

She laughed, then darted away from me.

"Hey, Doug, Tracy said that you would walk me to my car. I need to get a costume for my audition." I wanted to bust out in laughter at the sound of that. I had been in band auditions and dance and cheer auditions, but this was an entirely new experience, and from the looks of the other dancers on stages and sauntering around the smoky room, I wasn't too worried about my "audition." That truth did not stop me from needing to throw up.

"Sure," Doug said. "Johnny, watch the door, I'll be right back," he said to the young man cleaning glasses behind the bar.

Doug and I walked to my car without saying anything. I grabbed my bag of costumes, shoes, pasties, and pasty glue from the trunk, then we walked back in. He told me to not be nervous and that I would do great, then he walked me to the dressing room door. That was as far as his support would go. I was now on my own to either sink, float, or swim with the girls in the dressing room and the customers on the floor. I wasn't sure which group would be more intimidating, but I was about to find out.

Chapter 21

dance audition

I stepped into the lion's den, or rather the lionesses' den, when I walked into the dressing room. Not a single dancer hissed at me—not exactly anyway. I did see a few backs curve when I walked past the colorful row of tiny-top-wearing women. Backs curved just before giving me The Look. The look that catches your eye just long enough to make sure you see theirs, before the giver of the look deliberately scans your body from your eyes to your toes, before casting their eyes away from you with a smirk that matches their bitchy disposition. We all know The Look, though not all women use it. A look that stirred some fire in me. I wanted to scream, "I did not drive myself to the middle of industrial Phoenix to be intimidated dancer chicks, with stretch marks and smoker lines. It's going to take more than your downward glances and bitchy turned-up lips to send me and my purse packing." I said nothing and kept walking, searching for an open seat.

No two women, down the dressing table, looked the same: long, dark, straight hair; bleached-blond, wavy hair; light skin; dark skin; small frames; voluptuous frames; intense stares; empty stares; welcoming faces; intimidating glares—an overwhelming portrait of skin, makeup, and sparkle blurred past my eyes, as I scanned the long, narrow dressing room for a chair to call my own. The chairs belonged in a 1970s sitcom, an ugly orange-and-yellow vinyl floral print seat cushion, with a tall slender back. I suppose the club owners would not want the chairs to be too cushy or the girls would spend too much time sitting on their tushies, like Loren in Fairbanks. Relieved, I found an open seat near the end of the row. I laid my bag on the counter and looked again at the long mirror that doubled the number of women in the room. Some of them were still looking at me. No doubt, they were trying to figure me out, making up stories about me, as I was about them.

I turned my attention away from the women and toward my own reflection. I looked even younger than my age, even though I felt much older. My hair was a tousled mess, as usual, and my plump cheeks were flushed by extra heartbeats that were rapidly escalating. With shaky hands, I began to undress. I wasn't concerned about messing up my hair or my makeup, which had mostly disappeared, as I pulled my black dress up and over my face. Standing in front of the mirror wearing only my bra and thong panties, I noticed a few women look back at me. *Gym class all over again.* If I can't get undressed in front of a room full of women, I sure as hell can't get undressed in front of a room full of drunk men.

I thought I might vomit. My eyes searched the ground for the nearest trashcan, just in case. I found it among the long string of shoes, clothes, and locked trunks. *If I make it official here, I will need to get my own trunk. Something to strive for,* I chuckled at the thought. I had been wise enough to leave my wallet in my locked car. I didn't trust a locker room full of chatty, naked girls in high school and I wasn't about to trust a dressing room full of dancer chicks, either. Seeing the floor littered with sparkly costumes and shoes gave me a flashback to dance recitals. *Yeah, that's what this is,* I told myself. *Just a dance recital and a room full of adoring parents, grandparents, and annoyed siblings.*

I unclasped my bra and exchanged it for a fancier one from my bag, then did the same with my G-string. Why the hell didn't I just wear this getup under my clothes, like wearing a bathing suit under my clothes on lake day? I gave myself a body check, complete with a turn and look back. I looked more like a gymnast than a sexy long-limbed dancer. Muscular thin arms, small waist, and strong thighs. I had breasts though; unlike most gymnasts whose disciplined regimen gave them zero body fat. A hard-to-find bra size—a 32C. A full C cup. A quick brush of my hair and a swipe of lip gloss and, except for my too-tall heels, I was ready to hit the stage. While looking down at my shoes, I did not notice Tracy walk in. She was looking for me.

"Are you ready?" she asked looking into my eyes. She looked at my body, too, but not in a bitchy way. Her eyes were welcoming. They matched her playful smile. "Cute bikini," she complimented.

"Thanks. Yes, I am ready." *To throw up.*

"O.K., super. You'll be up after Cat. Listen for her name," she said as she pointed toward Cat. "Cat! Wave." Cat did as she was told. She even smiled in our direction. How nice. She reminded me of the curvy cartoon lady in the Roger Rabbit movie. She had the curves and the long hair, more auburn than red and more straight than wavy, but she had the same sex appeal. I felt like a girl child next to her womanly presence. I will get there one day, I told myself and when that day arrives, I hope I am a million miles away from this place.

"You won't be able to choose your song today," Tracy told me. "But if we invite you back, you can give your records to the DJ. Do you have any questions?"

"No, I'm ready. I'll watch for Cat to leave, then follow her. Thank you." Tracy turned and left the dressing room. Not without a smile and not without telling a few loitering ladies to get out on the dance floor. She was nice *and* stern. I was too nervous to sit, so I remained standing and stretched my legs and arms. More looks. Then I waited. If I had learned anything from years of dance recitals, it was how to wait patiently in the wings. That was a dance skill I had mastered.

What felt like an eternity later, I heard the DJ say Cat's name and a silly comment about how tips make her purr. Oh, brother! At least the DJ was trying to help. I wondered if he would say anything corny about me. Maybe he would comment on how my vomit matched my name and neon green bikini. My nervousness had taken up permanent residence in my body, like an alien pushing its spikes into my skin and splintering my brain, and I couldn't even pace my way through it. If I attempted walking nervously behind the row of women, they might stuff me in a trunk. *I can do this,* I assured myself. *Just breathe. Breathe. Breathe.*

Cat's song, "The Chain" by Fleetwood Mac, was ending and the crowd began clapping. That was my cue. My stomach was doing somersaults, and the dressing room began to spin. The alien in my core had turned into a washing machine stuck on the spin cycle. I should have asked the bartender or Tracy for a glass of water.

I heard the DJ's voice through the dressing room speaker as I pushed open the door and stepped into the smoky scene, "And now, for the first time to the Desert Rose stage, it is my pleasure to introduce, Jade. Please welcome the sexy dancer who will sparkle in your dreams."

Oh, brother. I did not want any part of their dreams.

I was too busy holding the brass rail and looking at the thinly carpeted red steps that led to the stage to notice the bloodshot eyes beginning to look in my direction. Focusing on not falling, I heard the song selected for me. Maybe not *for me,* but the one that would introduce me to this crowd. Boston's "More than a Feeling" began playing. Based on the applause, the crowd seemed to like this classic rock tune. Maybe they would like me too. This song would not have been my first choice, but it was one I could dance to. I began moving, not too gracefully. My nerves had turned my legs into concrete pillars. The song's slow intro helped. I could ease into this neon nightmare. I wondered if this was a request or if this was their standard audition song. A song that was easy to sway to, like I remembered doing at a house party in Denver that I attended a few years ago. *Just a few years ago. Look at me now! Don't look at me now. Step sway sway, step sway sway. I am ready for Broadway!* Okay, maybe the alley behind the theater. More like an alley cat scrounging for scraps. The music and my movement began to find each other, and I began to find eyes in the crowd. Presentation 101: make eye contact. Remember to smile. I remembered that we put Vaseline on our teeth in cheer to remind us to smile. I should have remembered that trick before my first audition.

My heart rate was increasing but my nerves were settling. I knew how to dance, I reminded myself. Keep moving. Keep smiling. Keep your eyes on the prize. A college degree. *Hopefully that would be more than a feeling,* I wished.

I began spinning with the song's escalating pace. Like my childhood stuck ballerina, I captivated the crowd with my spinning—a neon blur spinning faster and faster. The stuck men were becoming hypnotized. My spirit was fleeing my body with each rotation. Like the line in the lyrics, I was getting lost in the music.

A few dollars were tossed on the stage; one was held in the air by stubby fingers, with a prominent pointer finger gesturing me to join him. I knew from my time in Alaska how to playfully shimmy my way to a dollar bill. Dollars that were too good to be tossed on the stage, apparently. These dollars were special, they needed to be tucked directly in the string of the G following the dollar strut, which was a sultry walk toward the patron, a slight bend at the knee, with the dancer's side accessible for grabby and grubby paws, before the patron launched into their teasing game: *Do you want this dollar? I know you do. I will give it to you slowly, or if I'm a real prick, I will pretend like I'm going to tuck it in, then I will draw it back, before tucking it into your G string and brushing against your skin with my stubby dirty fingers while you smile a smile just for me.* "You are welcome," their smile says. Fuck off is what I wanted to say. There wasn't anything special about that dollar game. I had learned to smile and say thank you.

"Take it off!"

"Yeah, take it off!" The crowd was getting restless.

Eat shit, I said behind my smile and sparkles. They could wait a few more minutes. I wasn't a trained pet. Not yet anyway. More than halfway into the song, I did untie my top and let my pasty-covered breasts flop. Perky and bouncy, my teenage breasts should have given them something to smile about. Just like other half-exposed young breasts they might see at a lake, if they ever went to the lake. Probably not. Being here gave them more control over young bikini babes than they would ever have had beyond these smoky walls. After all, the customer is always right.

Up on the stage, I felt the sinking feeling of the difficult road ahead of me. One dollar at a time, it was going to be a long and sweaty road to a college degree. The end of the song brought hands together and a few thumbs and fingers to lips, whistling in appreciation. With my triangle top in my hands, I scooped up my dollars and left the stage.

Tracy was waiting at the bottom of the steps, beaming. "You did great!" she exclaimed with sparkling eyes. "Can you come back tomorrow?"

"Yes. What time?"

"The night shift starts at 5 p.m, ends at 1 a.m.," she said, still smiling. "Okay, I'll see you then. Can I bring my own music?"

"Yes, bring your records and the DJ, Tommy, will take care of you."

"Okay, thank you." With that, she and her glowing face darted away. She seemed to enjoy her job. Maybe I would learn to as well. The restless alien that had taken over my body was now resting. I, however, felt like a twirling mixture of elated relief and escalating fear.

Chapter 22
the daily grind

Spring was still one month away, but that did not stop my apartment complex from getting a start on adding fresh flowers to the grounds. I watched a gardener add new color and life to the area below my window. Lifting, bending, planting, and repeating. His hard work left dozens of light pink flowers lined in perfect rows. *Spring. Renewal. New life begins.* I guess that applied to me, too, as a newly hired topless dancer with a regular shift. I told myself it's what I did, not who I was. My dance shift didn't start for another two hours, but I could not sit in my bedroom for one more minute, regardless of how cute and entertaining the gardener was. I threw on a pair of jeans, my Vans, and my light blue Izod polo, the only one I owned, grabbed my dancer bag, and left the busy gardener behind. I drove myself to my one meal of the day. Using three of the twenty-two dollars I earned during the previous night's audition, I bought a bagel from my favorite bagel boy. The rest of the money would go in my thirsty gas tank. That would be plenty of gas to get me to work and back home tonight. *Thank God for small favors.*

I should have celebrated my accomplishments. I should have thrown myself a party and invited the entire apartment complex. A ridiculous thought while I waited for my bagel. My thoughts turned to reality and the money I made while auditioning. Twenty-two dollars was nineteen more dollars than I walked away with after my first night of dancing. At that rate of increase, I could be a millionaire by the end of the year. Then I could just buy a degree. My icy-cold experience was leading to great things or at least some fuel in my tank.

If only I could guzzle a few gulps of gasoline to energize my tired body, to keep my own wheels turning. I was a tired soul trapped in a fit body. My limbs were active, but it was hard to override a mind that wanted to collapse. I needed to keep pushing and keep showing up, for myself. Unlike my roommates, my financial savior wasn't a phone call away. Only a busy signal or a click. I was the caller and the receiver. A one-sided conversation, for sure. My father had already turned me away—or his wife had, but it was all the same to me—and my mom was dealing with her own drama, leaving a man who was not what she had hoped for. Both my parents were on their second marriages and neither of them seemed to be headed for a *happily ever after* storybook ending, *if* there is such a thing. I was angry at them. I was also sad about their marriage predicaments, but I did not have the luxury of dwelling on their troubles. I had to feed myself and keep a roof over my head. More than anything, I was detached.

From the same bagel store window, I watched more students walk across the crosswalk that led them to their future. I held back the tears that were forming, a compromised dam ready to burst open. I couldn't fall apart over a bagel, just before my first official shift. I couldn't show up at the club with black streaks running down my flushed cheeks. Why couldn't I just be one of those kids wearing a backpack loaded with books instead of a bag of tiny tops and stilettos? How could I get myself off this hamster wheel and become more than I was? With my appetite now flooded with suppressed tears, I forced the last few bites of my cold bagel past the growing lump in my throat. I needed to pull myself together. I did not want the cute bagel boy to see me crying, so I kept staring out the window while I finished my last meal until the next day. A concern only if I survived the night.

I stayed too long. The last image I saw before rainy salty sadness splashed on my tabletop was a young man who reminded me of Sean. That did it. *I was stuck.* In more ways than one. I did the only thing I could do: I let nature take its course and let the tears flow. I still had plenty of time to make it to my first shift, so I let it rain. My rainstorm drew a few looks from two girls sitting not far from my pity party. Guest of honor: me. *Yeah, go ahead, look at me! Rain is a rare sight in the desert.* When the gushing dam dwindled to a trickling stream, I gathered my trash and purse and made my way to the bathroom, doing my best to avoid eye contact with bagel boy.

If I could, I would have locked myself in the bathroom, sleeping away the afternoon—or better, flushed myself down the toilet. At the end of the long shit tunnel, I might find myself swimming in a crystal blue ocean. It would be a fight for my life, but the prize at the end would be worth it. *Freedom.* Like all the other traveling turds, my head would pop up to greet the glowing sun, except that I would not float and fry and decay away; I would suck every molecule of oxygen around me into my compressed lungs. They would not expand quietly. My reaching for life would be a fierce two-handed clutch and a loud disturbing inhale that would cause beach-goers to glance in my direction. They would scan the shoreline, squinting and searching, but they would never locate the source of the loud wailing. A distressed whale? A stranded porpoise? A spinning seagull? A mischievous mermaid?

"Did you hear that?" and "What was that?" they would say to their sunbathing neighbors. "I did hear that," would be the response. "I don't know what that was."

The strange noise would hold their attention until their goosebumps disappeared, then they would carry on doing nothing, only to think about the strange scream later that evening. An aggressive knocking on the bathroom door told me it was time to end my pathetic daydreaming and wipe away my salty tears. I splashed cold water on my face, then rushed out of the bagel joint as quick as my dancer legs could take me.

Alone in my car. Always alone it seemed. Trying to survive is a lonely business. A hungry lone lioness looking for her next meal. Rest would find me later, sometime after 1 a.m.. Until then, it was time to put on my happy face and my superhero cape and drive my sad self to the glowing and vibrating room of adult entertainment. A room of spinning ballerinas stuck under spinning car tires. The noisy dance club drowned out the freeway above.

With only one wrong turn, I made it to the club with fifteen minutes to spare. If I was one thing, it was punctual. One more face check in the mirror, then it was time to face the music, or at least dance to it. This time, I would be dancing to a few of my own songs. That would help. I grabbed my bag and purse from the passenger seat, took one more deep breath, then headed to the door. Thank God Doug was there. He would help, too.

"Hey, Doug." I nodded with a tilt of my head.

"Hey, Jade, what's up?" he responded with both word and gesture.

"I guess I'm about to be," I smiled.

"Your first shift. Are you nervous?" the kind bouncer asked.

"Yes, I am, but mostly I just want to get started so I can calm down," I admitted.

"I understand. I could never do what you girls do," he said.

"You're right about that! You would not look good in pasties and a G-string," I laughed at him. A real laugh. I needed that.

"You are right!" he laughed. From the change in his demeanor, he needed that, too. "Break a leg, Jade. Go get 'em," he said as he stepped out of the way, and I stepped into my new life. *Just another turd floating in a shit show*.

My legs wanted to turn and run, and my lungs instantly revolted against the thick gray smoke. My hungry-for-cash brain took control and told my legs and lungs to buck up and be quiet. I needed both my legs and lungs to dance for dollars, but they would need to stop complaining and adapt. Immediately. My brother had to endure inhaling tear gas and running long distances during Army basic training. He survived. I could, too.

"Smile, Pretty," a wobbly, old, short man, holding onto a barstool for support, commented as I passed him.

I responded with an "eat shit" grin.

"That's better," the little man said to my disappearing frame.

Fuck off, were my trailing thoughts as I approached the DJ booth.

"Hi, I'm Jade. I'll be starting tonight. Can you play these songs for me?" I asked while handing the DJ my small, blue-and-white checkered record box secured with a gold clasp.

"Hey, Jade. Welcome to the Rose, I'm Tommy. What kind of music are you into?" he asked.

"There's a sampling of what I like in there. The Cure, Dead or Alive, Violent Femmes, The Call…"

He stopped listening and started flipping through my albums. "Cool, this will be a nice change from the classic rock that mostly gets played in here. It's what the crowd prefers."

"Yeah, I see that. Well, let's keep the crowd happy and tipping." I smiled at him. "I can dance to anything, but if you could rotate in a few songs I actually like that would make this entire experience bearable," I told him.

"For both of us. Will do."

"Great. Thank you,"

"Hey, is your name on everything?" he asked as I was walking toward the dressing room door.

"Yes, my name is on everything, including the box. Thanks."

I turned again and braced myself for the curvy crowd primping and posing behind the swinging dressing room door. I took a deep breath and puffed out my chin and chest. They would not eat me alive. *There is enough for everyone*. My new mantra. My new lie.

Chapter 23

Jade to the stage

I pushed open the swinging door and the chatter quickly turned to a hush. All eyes were on me as I walked past the heavily made-up and scantily-dressed row of cash-hungry women. Cash hungry, too, I fit in. I did not have the strength to meet the piercing pupils that singed my skin. So intense their vibes were, I could hear the collective hiss and smell my burning flesh. I was fighting enough battles; I did not need to fight these women, too. *I am nobody, no one to concern yourself with*, I wanted to shout at them. *I am just here to get my share of the topless pie to pay for classes and books.* Crumbs will suffice, I thought, and if I can scrape them together into an ugly misshapen cash pie, I will be fine.

With shaky legs and a calm smile, I found an empty seat at the end of the dressing room bus. Again. I was fine with that chair location. Seeing myself in the mirror stole my breath. Faint streaks of mascara remained from my bagel shop tabletop rainstorm and my hair was wild and windblown. I did not look like the same person who left the cat turd apartment a few hours ago. Something about my appearance looked haunting. A ghost of myself. I was shocked by my appearance. I looked hauntingly beautiful.

I recognized that my pain had exposed an inner beauty I was not aware of prior to that moment. I did not look like a lost girl; I looked like a fierce woman. I understood why the other women fell silent when I walked past them. Stepping out of a dream or a nightmare, I wasn't sure. It appeared that my cracked-open heart had unleashed a lioness into the world.

I stripped out of my dress and bra, then I painted my nipples with the white sticky substance that secured the sequined pasties to my circles—a delicate job that required a steady hand, focused eyes, and precise judgement. Missing the mark meant having to wash off the white mess and start over. That was not an option. Slow and steady. Two times. Done. Covering the nipples is not a costume enhancement. It is state law. Legalities addressed, I slipped into my dance costume: a white G-string with a matching faux-jeweled triangle top, all covered with a tiny tight dress that I could easily slip in and out of. I completed the look with my pair of white stilettos from Payless ShoeSource. High heels, not high dollar. Costume complete, I reapplied my makeup, heavier this time. I didn't touch my hair. I didn't know who this wild woman was staring back at me, but I decided to let her control tonight. Maybe her wild ways would get me closer to the prize. I did not want someone to get closer to my cash, so I brought a small purse that I could carry on the dance floor. That would suffice until I was able to buy a trunk and lock up my belongings. More items to invest in. Business expenses, I told myself. Skin was the business, and I was the merchandise. *Flesh for sale. You can look, but don't touch. State law.*

Time to sit and wait, except I could not sit. I put my clothes in my backpack, zipped up the pockets, placed it on my borrowed seat, and pushed the chair under the counter. I prayed the backpack would be there when I returned. I made my way back down the long hissing catwalk, holding my head a little higher this time, I gave up my attempts to smile. I decided to adopt the "fuck it" attitude, realizing I didn't need to impress or befriend the other women. I just didn't want any trouble. I had no problems being a loner. In that role, I was an expert. I pushed open the swinging door and made my way to the raised DJ platform.

"How long before I'm up?" I asked Tommy.

Looking over his list, "There are four girls ahead of you. You're up after Star," he said, pointing toward a long-legged girl with long golden hair.

"Ok, thanks. I'll listen for her name."

"Cool."

I decided to walk around and walk off some nerves. This club felt very different than the one in Fairbanks, but the routine was the same. Mostly. The girls did not drink here. Good. Not that they couldn't sneak a drink, but it was not looked at favorably by the Iranian club owner, I had learned during my quick check-in with Tracy before heading to the dressing room. Like the Alaska club owner, the owner of the club rarely visited, but when he did, everyone needed to be on their "best behavior." The day-to-day operations were handled by the club owner's cousin, Omar, who worked behind the bar. He seemed to watch every move. His jovial disposition hid nothing. I did not want to get on the bad side of the club owner, even if it was through the eyes of his joke-telling cousin. I could disappear from this place and not a single person close to me would have any idea that I had spent my evenings in a seedy joint on the other side of town. I would not be drinking or breaking any other rules that I was yet to learn about.

I made my way around the club, moving around and in between tables. My movements through the club were met with looks, smiles, and a few whispers. No requests for table dances or friendly welcomes. Another difference between Alaska and here. The men were just watching, making their assumptions about my story. As I was them. City folks are less trusting and more guarded. I was still missing Sean. I was starting to miss Fairbanks.

"Hey, little lady," I heard from an old man in the corner, near Stage Three. "Are you new here?"

"Yes, this is my first night here."

"What's your name?"

"Jade."

"Where ya from?"

"Arizona, and you, where are you from and what's your name?"

"I'm from Arkansas, but I've been here for over twenty years, so this is home now. My name is Wilbur."

He may have left Arkansas, but I don't think Arkansas had left him, based on his overalls and cowboy boots. "Nice overalls," I complimented.

"Thanks," he said with a chuckle. "I'm a farmer. They get the job done. How 'bout you get the job done and give me a table dance. I'll be your first," he said with a glimmer in his eye and a flirty smile. He was trying. I was trying not to throw up.

"Super. Next song," I said, which fortunately would be soon. "Until then, tell me about the club." I sat down in the empty seat across from him.

"What do ya wanna know?" he asked.

"How long have you been coming here? What do you like about it? What do you think of the girls? What can you tell me about the club owners?" I had not intended turning into my old high school newspaper reporter self, but the questions just rolled out of me. I was nervous.

"That's a lotta questions. Not sure I can remember them all. I started coming here after my wife left me five years ago. Hadn't planned on making it a habit. I was just lonely one night and found myself here. My farm's just a few miles outside of Phoenix. Sometimes I bring in produce, when I feel up to it," looking like he wanted to say more, he stopped there. "What was your next question?"

This is going to take all night. Hurry up and end, song. "What do you like about this place?" I repeated.

"Oh, yeah. The girls," he said, laughing.

"I see that," I laughed with him. "That leads us to my next question, what about the girls? Are they nice?" I asked and then I immediately regretted asking him. I wanted to not care.

"Some are. Some aren't. Ya know how women can be," he said, this time not laughing.

"Yes, I do know." We both rested on that thought for a moment before I reminded him of my last question. "What can you tell me about the club owners?"

"Not much. I see a man with slick black hair and fancy suits come in here every now and then and once I saw him turn into the parking lot when I was leaving. I don't stay late on account of my eyes not being too good. He drives a black Lincoln Town Car. Real nice. Wish I could afford one of those," he said. "He bought this place a few years ago. Changed a few things, including the girls, and this place stays busy all the time now. That's 'bout all I know."

"Thanks." I had more questions, but I did not have more patience. Another time. Maybe. The next song began. I immediately recognized the drum beats as belonging to "Life's Been Good" by Joe Walsh. I laughed at the irony of that song selection. That was my cue to dance cute for the old man in overalls. I remembered that my great-grandpa from Iowa wore overalls when he came to visit us. *Great.* That was a visual I could have lived without. It was the perfect time to turn away from the old man, from a memory. I watched the room while the old man watched my bare back and mostly naked ass. I caught a reflection of my profile and the old man's downward stare in the mirrors across from where we were sitting. Those mirrors had seen a few things, and many others had seen themselves looking back in a stare. Whether it was blank or not, I can't say, I wasn't there. Whether they liked what they saw, or not, I can't say that either. As for me, I wanted to cover the mirrors with a funeral cloth, just like my great-grandpa was covered after his passing. Two images I did not care to be reminded of.

So strange, this world I found myself in. Loud music. Flashing lights. Liquid courage, until the last drop, when the customers' courage and desires fell flat. Spinning ballerinas, spinning stories for the men, the ones who showed up with money to throw away. Money to throw our way—toward hungry hands and mouths, and toward those picking their scabs in the dressing room with a need to feed their hungry veins. Anywhere else, these scenes would be disturbing. But in here, life took on a different normalcy. Each of us was breathing life into this skin circus and looking away when the mirrors revealed more than we wanted to see.

Look away, look away, but remember to sway, sway, sway, then shimmy, dip, tease, and turn. Start from the top, then do it again. Oh, and remember to "smile little lady." They aren't paying to see you cry. They come here to get away from their troubles, not to listen to troubled dolls wound too tight. Dolls don't have emotions or tears, just bodies that satisfy, but never completely. Not until later when the men relived the moment, meeting their own flesh, when they became the best man for the job. Tension released. For the moment. Tomorrow is a new day to squeeze, shimmy, and sway. Start from the top, then do it again. Bury that visual. Bury it. Bury it with your dead grandpa. Thoughts flooded my mind while the old farmer watched my behind.

What I really wanted to do was give the old grandpa a hug and take him out for ice cream, but no touching was allowed, and I wasn't going anywhere with any man from this place. Ever. Not after Sean. The song came to an end and Wilbur handed me a twenty-dollar bill with his earthy left hand. "Thank you," I said while putting the money in my empty purse and putting my tiny top back on. A perfectly normal conversation—talking to an old man I just met while my pasty-covered, perky breasts pointed in his direction—just a few inches from his face—twelve to be exact, and not an inch closer.

"Next up, on Stage One, put your hands together for Jade, our newest dancer here at Desert Rose Cabaret!"

That was my cue to say goodbye to gramps and make my way to the stage, as an official dancer. No pretending. *Who am I kidding?* We're all pretending in this glittery meat market where the hungry can come watch and smell but order up a sandwich with all the trimmings—well, that ain't for sale. At least I was warmed up for my stage performance and I would not be dancing alone. Wilbur's soil-stained Andrew Jackson would be joining me.

Chapter 24

first shift, first short stack

It was fifty-five past midnight, and I had not turned into a shriveled pumpkin in the corner of the dressing room, nor did I have a sunken pumpkin smile. Last check, an hour ago, I looked energized and alive. The smoke might kill my lungs, and the stares were more than I could bear, but dancing was good for every other part of my body and soul. Other than farmer Wilbur, my night began with a slow start, then something happened just after ten, that I couldn't explain, but I hoped it would happen again. I went from stage to table dance to stage to table dance, barely resting except for using the restroom a few times. *Beginner's luck?* I hoped not. *The way and sway of this place?* I hoped so. How many dollar bills filled my purse, I could not say, but my purse was much fuller than when I arrived, just before five.

"This will be our final song. Last chance to tip your favorite dancer. Last chance to ask for a dance before these ladies head out the door and into dream land. If you are lucky, maybe they will meet you there."

Like hell, I thought.

I immediately recognized the first few notes of what I would learn was the closing song, "Rock and Roll All Night" by KISS. I also learned that this is when every girl not dancing table-side for a paying customer, joined a stage. No exceptions. All three stages full of color, glitter, smiles, and sweat. Circus tigers brushing bare skin and strutting their stuff in hopes of being tossed another dollar. The perfect scenario for a catfight. Not on this night, though. The song ended, and we exited stage left, some of us, me included, with a few more dollar bills than when we joined the finale.

The dressing room vibes were much lighter than when I arrived. Quitting time has that effect on people, no matter the job. My legs were tired, and my feet were rebelling, but I was elated to have made it through my first shift. A shift that delivered actual dollars. How many, I had no idea. Yet. A proper job. That might be a stretch. Maybe not proper, but legal. That's what I told myself.

"How was your first night?" Cat asked.

I heard her repeat the question, this time looking directly at me.

"Oh, sorry, I didn't know you were talking to me. It was good. How good, I don't know yet," I told her.

"Every time I saw you, you were doing a table dance. The regulars are usually nice to new girls, if they like you and want you to come back. I hope you come back," she said.

"Oh, I will. As long as I keep making money."

"Do you want to join us for breakfast at Village Inn? A few of us go after work."

Is that what this is? I thought. I didn't have a lot of work experience, but this did not feel like work. It felt like a night of club dancing, except that I was mostly naked, and the men tipped with cash, not drinks. I preferred the form of payment in this joint; I didn't need alcohol. Another rejected, hope-filled man in a club scene, I did not need to disappoint by saying, "No, I don't want to dance or drink your hopeful drink."

"Sure, why not. Except for my legs, I'm not tired," I told her.

"Okay, great. We'll walk out to the parking lot together and then you can follow us there."

I wasn't sure who "us" was, but I smiled at these instructions and at her offer. I suddenly felt less alone in this concrete jungle.

My purse was full, I made a new friend, and my backpack survived the night. A backpack that did not contain textbooks, but it was still there, which meant I did not have to go to Village Inn wearing a dancing costume. If the restaurant was anywhere nearby, I was sure I would not be the first one to arrive in next-to-nothing, but I did not want to be a wandering weirdo leaving people wondering. I noticed that the haunting look I began the night with had been transformed into a glowing radiance. Dancing had painted my cheeks red. My eyes sparkled, my skin was covered in a sexy sweat, and my thighs and calves looked tight. *This place is good for me*, I thought before laughing at the thought of it. I changed back into my street clothes and Vans, then sat down to count my cash. I was careful to count with my back toward the remaining girls. The vibes might be lighter, but I was no dummy. I counted. Only two more dollars and it would have been an even two hundred. Damn! I then made three stacks of lesser cash. One for the DJ, one for the bartender, and one for the bouncer. Ten dollars for the bartender and DJ and five for the bouncer. My piles felt generous. I hoped so, because much more and I would not be able to maintain this.

I made sure each man looked me in the eye when they took my cash. All three did, and all three said thank you. The bartender added in a joke, calling me, "Jade the dancing gem." *Could be worse*, I thought.

I saw Cat and another dancer standing by a black Buick.

"Thanks for waiting. I'm over there," I said pointing to my white VW Rabbit. A decent-looking car that hid its unreliable side. For a moment, I thought that might be me, too, then I corrected my thoughts about that subject. Especially, the voice of my evil stepmother, my dad's second wife, who considered me unreliable. Did she call me that before or after her stint in a mental ward? I couldn't remember. My dad took his pots from the front lawn, then he jumped from the frying pan into the fire with that lady. I was not unreliable; I just didn't have time for the whims and schemes of others. I was a survivor, fighting for my life. There is a difference.

"OK, pull around, then you can follow us. Village Inn is a few miles down the road," Cat instructed.

"Thanks." I would have driven even farther away from my apartment. I wanted to drive far away and never return. Someday. For now, I was just happy to have somewhere else to go and someone pleasant to go with.

I drove my car around to where Cat's car was idling and waiting for me. A small gesture that made me feel grand. She waved her left arm out the window and away we went, into the cool city night. I kept my window down and let the cool city air dry my sweat and whip my hair. I was the energized, electric blond, traveling on a quiet Tuesday night toward 2 a.m. short stacks. I was an adrenaline angel with crusty nipples. I was elated.

The 24/7 café was about two miles north of the club—farther away from Tempe, but I didn't care. I could have driven all night. If only my car ran on my sweat.

Before going in, I met the two other girls, Krissy and Angel, who I had seen in the club but had not met. They looked to be around Cat's age, twenty-five to twenty-eight-ish, I guessed. I was the young kitten in the group. Good. I felt safe with them. I felt protected by them.

We made our way into the neon diner and found a booth. Not hard to do. Only two other booths were occupied. A young couple, pale as milk, dressed in all black including their nails and lips, took up space in one booth: two skinny sleepless souls slipping through the cracks and stopping for a late-night meal. The third café customer was an older, thick man, wearing jeans, black boots, and a red-and-black flannel shirt, who looked to be in desperate need of a shower. He was drinking coffee, smoking, and staring into the dark night. I saw his scruffy, gray, weathered face in the window reflection. I saw our reflections, too, which he didn't seem to notice. So close he was, yet a million miles away from this place. He looked in our direction when Cat started talking. He did so without smiling or looking amused or impressed. Just a stare.

I turned my attention away from the late-night flannel man and toward Cat. "How long have you worked at the club?" I asked her.

"I've been there two years. I started working there, just after starting a graduate program at ASU. I needed fast cash. That didn't last, but topless dancing did," she said with a sly laugh.

I felt a chill race across my skin; then I swallowed the growing lump in my throat before asking her more about her program. "What were you studying?"

"Psychology. I was studying to be a child psychologist. I'll pick it up again. I just needed a break after my mom was diagnosed with cancer. She passed three months ago. Now, I drive her Buick and use my education on the customers," Cat said with a wink and smile.

"Yeah, a year break," Angel said, laughing at her. Cat laughed, too, but her eyes told a different story.

"I hope you do go back," I told Cat, looking into her eyes. Her slight nod told me she felt understood.

The waitress asked Cat if we wanted the usual. "Yes, make it four."

"What about you, Jade? What's your story? Everyone has a story, especially in a topless bar," Krissy contributed. "Is this the first club you've worked in?"

"No, I worked at a club in Fairbanks, Alaska before trying out at Desert Rose. I just got home a few days ago, and now, here I am."

"Here you are, in the big city under the bright lights of the Rose," Angel said in a sarcastic tone.

"What was Alaska like?" Cat inquired.

"Cold."

We all laughed. Our combined laughter drew another look from the loner man, and maybe a slight smile, too. It was hard to tell. I was hopeful, anyway. He seemed so lonely. I wanted to invite him to our table, but as an invited guest with people I barely knew, it didn't feel like my place to do so. I wished that two years ago, when I was the new kid at a high school in Denver, someone would have invited me over. I pushed those painful memories aside and refocused on the conversation.

"Other than cold, what was the club like? Did you make good money?" Cat asked. She seemed genuinely interested.

"Well, I didn't make 'pipeline' money, but it was decent. I left with over five thousand dollars in my purse. The start of my university tuition and living expenses, of course."

"A student taking a break, like me," Cat laughed again.

"Yes, unfortunately. No offense, but I would rather be up late studying than eating pancakes at an all-night diner in Phoenix," I shared with a smile to soften the sting of my truth.

"I have a year's worth of credits from the community college, but even those classes are expensive when you're only making five dollars an hour. Plus, I can't get a four-year degree from a community college."

"What are you studying?" Krissy asked.

"I would like to get a degree in journalism."

"You wanna be a news girl?" Angel asked.

"Sure, but my real goal is to be a traveling journalist. I would like to write, research, and interview people around the world. I would like to see the world." I beamed. I must have felt safe with them. I had only shared those goals with a few people. Maybe dancing for dollars until 1 a.m. was a truth serum for me. Or maybe I was sitting with people who understood that dreams and goals were the only things that would keep us from being swallowed by a soul-sucking business that did not support or care about futures. Cash, now, was the concern.

"I know you can do it," Cat told me. "You seem smart, and you're very pretty. Just don't get sucked into the dancer lifestyle. You know what they say. 'Once a dancer, always a dancer.'"

"Thank you," I told her. I knew I would like her. She offered me more encouragement in ten minutes than any friend ever had on the other side of town. The electric euphoria that had been racing through my body for the last several hours was calming down and contentment was beginning to take its place.

Our talk was interrupted by four orders of pancakes. I didn't think I was hungry until I looked at the stack placed in front of me. My mouth began to water as I watched the ball of whipped butter melt and ooze down the round sides. It was quite possibly the most beautiful picture I had seen in a long time. I was breathing in the fluffy buttery goodness when Cat asked me, "Are you going to eat or just stare at it?"

We all laughed. I sliced through the fluffy vision with my fork, then placed a bite, too big, into my mouth. Heaven. Home. I had not expected to feel a sense of home with three dancer chicks in the middle of a Phoenix industrial area at 2 a.m.. A feeling I had not felt in many years. Stuffed, I had to stop at half a stack. Breakfast or lunch tomorrow. With a full stomach, I felt the last of my dancing adrenaline fight to stay in control, but it was losing.

I was not alone in this feeling. We stared at each other with sleepy eyes. Our relaxed bodies now occupied the booth. A late-night short stack must be a natural downer for the dancer high.

We paid our bill with our singles, then dragged our tired bodies to the parking lot where we said goodbye. Cat and I hugged. I did not want to let go of her. Letting go of her meant turning and driving myself home to a place that felt less like home than the dirty diner. I caught the loner man's eyes in the window. No smile, just his sad eyes. I held his gaze for a moment and smiled. Maybe that was enough to let him know he wasn't alone.

Chapter 25

one thousand bombs

I was dreading the drive home, and more than anything, I was dreading the being home, but the distance gave me time to think about my first shift, my future at this new club, and my late-night short stack, forming friendship. I enjoyed being one of the few drivers on the road. Peaceful. Magical. Bad things *can* happen after midnight if you aren't careful, but there is also a mystery to the bewitching hours. It feels like moving forward in a waking dream, surrounded by floating dreamers.

I turned into apartment row and felt a knot growing in my stomach that was not caused by the pancakes. So late it was that even the college partiers were nowhere to be seen. They were passed out in their beds—or someone else's—where futures could be forever changed. My future was changing, too, working in a new club. A future yet to be revealed. For now, I was content to have survived my first full dancing shift in Phoenix and to be passing out in my own bed with an extra hundred sixty-seven dollars in my purse. Every single Washington earned by the blood pumping through my veins, my sweat dripping from every pore, and my tears that were never far from bursting forth.

The wave of cat urine that poured out of the apartment destroyed my remaining ability to breath after inhaling secondhand smoke for eight hours. A few customers smoked in Fairbanks, but there were more guys blowing smoke in the Phoenix club. I knew topless dancing was going to be a challenge, but I did not expect cigarette smoke to be my biggest hurdle. So far. I was sure there would be others. I really needed a shower, but all I wanted to do was collapse on my unmade bed. A note taped to my bedroom door would delay sleep by a few minutes. No hellos, how are you doing, or how was your night, just a list of utility bills and the monthly rent amount. The utility bills split three ways. *Bullshit*. The stinky cats used more utilities than I did. I should pay one fifth, not one third. The smelly pussies should get a job and pay their share. Maybe I could include them in my stage act. Three pussies strutting their stuff. It would never happen but the thought of me as a cat trainer and their cats jumping through hoops while I wiggled my tush made me laugh out loud.

My catlike grin gave me just enough lift to move me into the bathroom to wash my face and brush my teeth after tossing my bag and their lame note on my dresser. "Damnit! Who left me an empty toilet paper roll?" *I hope they heard me! I hope they woke from their privileged beauty sleep.* I had toilet paper on this roll before I left to dance my ass off, now I don't have anything to wipe my ass! Maybe the cats had learned how to use the fucking toilet! Wouldn't that be nice! *I have had enough. I am moving out of here! I will work seven days a week if I must. Better than being here anyway.* I really wanted to barge through their princess quarters and get a roll of toilet paper, but I also wanted to keep the peace for my remaining days here. *Not* tiptoeing to the kitchen, I grabbed a handful of their dinner napkins to replace my missing toilet paper. I would need to remove my paper roll before going to work. Maybe I needed to keep it in my dancer bag. Maybe I could turn myself into a toilet paper mummy on stage.

Done with this day, I fell into a nine-hour sleep. A deep sleep that turned my body to stone and my brain to a disoriented daze. Not fully present, I was sure I was still in Fairbanks, sleeping away the scents of sexy sweat and seductive snow. Over 3,500 miles away from my Tempe apartment and yet I could hear Gabriela playing Paula Abdul, *again*. I could hear her and Loren talking to each other about their favorite lip color and their boyfriends back home. I must still be dreaming. A better state of mind, I decided, than waking up to my current one: rooming with two smelly pussies and two inconsiderate princesses.

With my eyes still closed, I imagined myself in that tiny, hard, twin bed in those weird, dorm-style barracks in Fairbanks, getting ready to wake to my only day off. The luxury of a day of freedom fell on me like a soft sheet smelling of fresh linen. A reminiscent scent that could only be created under a golden sun with freshly washed clothes dried by a gentle breeze. I did not have to jump and rush; I could enjoy five, ten, fifteen more minutes of sleep. A few extra drops of beauty, landing softly on my face, adding to the flushed glow left by Sean. Lying there, resisting reality, I let my mind go where I had resisted. I could resist no more. I thought about Sean. I longed for his touch. I imagined our wrapped and warm bodies, surrounded and protected by the virgin snow. A heavenly purity folding us into each other, then blanketing our sensual sins.

A few inches above my resting head, I imagined seeing the white candle flames, flickering and dancing, sending sporadic spurts of smoke into the air when a snowflake landed just so. My eyes followed the smoky dancers rising toward the heavens, as if being pulled by an invisible string, held by an invisible hand. A hand that guided the wavy gray line toward a sky full of Northern Light ballerinas, swirling, spinning, and swooping down then back up again. The thin gray line carried the memory of our love, then offered it to the sky dancers, making them sparkle. *Those* dancers were not stuck. They were free. The most glorious freedom I have ever witnessed. I watched this dance, felt Sean's warm breath on my face and his strong thighs wrapped around mine for several more minutes before the dream began to stretch and disintegrate. Smoke, snow, flames, the blanket, our naked bodies, stretched until they were unrecognizable, loose threads loosely held in the space between the white field and the sky dancers. Then all was sucked into the atmosphere, and I was left with nothing but a black void.

An emptiness that would swallow me up if I did not get out of my bed.

My head was spinning, thinking of the possibilities of my day. My life. It was just after noon and I had nowhere to be until 5 p.m., the start of my second dance shift. Shaking off my deep sleep and dreamy Sean scene, I decided I would head to the pool and read for a while. It was winter, but not too cold to sit poolside for an hour or so. First, I needed to eat. *Shit!* I forgot to ask the waitress for a to-go box for my pancakes. I hadn't bought groceries for myself, and I dared not eat a crumb of the princesses' food, properly labeled with their names. A direct message to me, their pauper roommate. *I didn't care. I didn't need their crumbs.* I tossed on a pair of jeans, a t-shirt, and my flip-flops, grabbed my purse, and headed to the corner convenience store to buy some food. That would sustain me until tomorrow; then I would do some proper shopping.

I returned with some vanilla zingers, two bananas (the third I ate in the car), a small frozen pizza, a day-old tuna sandwich and two sodas. The breakfast of champions. I wrote my name on the pizza—I can play that game, too—and tossed it into the freezer before changing into some shorts. Then me, my beach towel, book, sandwich, and one of my sodas made the way to the apartment pool. I hadn't been to the pool since the past fall when I had a day off from the video store. Felt like a lifetime ago.

A young man seated at the table under the poolside gazebo caught my attention. He had thick, black, wavy hair with a sexy swoop that covered his forehead, and it moved with the gentle breeze. He was wearing shorts and a tank top that revealed his smooth, toned and tan arms. His flip-flops were kicked away from the table. With my eyes on him, I almost tripped over a chair. *Get it together!* How embarrassing would it be to splash into the pool in front of this gorgeous boy. Maybe that is a brilliant idea. Maybe he is a lifeguard. Maybe he could give me mouth-to- mouth resuscitation. *I really need a boyfriend. No, I really do not need a boyfriend!* I found a lawn chair with a view of him, but not obviously so. I spread out my freebie KUPD beach towel and planted myself behind a book and pretended to read. I could not focus on a single word with this guy nearby. *Focus!* How was I to make it through four years of college if I couldn't concentrate in the presence of one cute guy with his head buried in a book, let alone thousands of cute guys!

It took me thirty minutes to read two pages. In that time, I looked at poolside cutie at least a dozen times. I watched him stare into space while he tapped his pencil on the table, making me melt on that winter day. I watched him get up and stretch. I died on that winter day. I was enjoying the view, but I wasn't making any progress with Tony Robbins' book, *Unlimited Power*. The scenery was sexy, but the studious tan man was not helping me find my own power. I turned my body toward an overflowing trashcan, spending the next thirty minutes actually reading.

So immersed I was in Robbins' advice, I almost missed tan man walking toward the pool gate. Almost. I caught the cute boy looking at me when he was throwing his trash away. With his eyes focused on mine he failed to see that his wrapper fell from the top of the trash heap.

I laughed, then I told him, "Your trash fell on the ground." Walking toward me, he asked, "What?"

Smiling at him, I repeated myself, "Your trash is on the ground."

"Oh," he said, turning to pick up his trash. "Thanks."

"You're welcome. Looks like someone needs to empty it."

"Yeah, you're right. I'll just throw this away at home."

"Good idea." With my book still raised, I kept smiling at him.

He smiled back, hesitated for a moment, then thanked me again before turning toward the gate.

The departing view of my poolside lifeguard was equally captivating. He had a well- defined back and by the look of his glutes and calves, he was a runner or athlete. I kept watching him until he was out of view. He may not have guarded me, but he added some life to my afternoon. I might be spending more time at the pool. *Reading, of course.*

It was time to head back to the apartment and get ready for my second shift. I was a tingling mixture of feelings. I was excited to dance and earn more cash, but I was also annoyed and sick to my stomach over all of it. I would much rather be spending my evening writing and studying than wiggling and strutting, but I had to rise above those feelings that could pull me down and leave me renting videos to the privileged crowd for the rest of my life. I let the warm shower calm my nerves and wash away my sadness and images of the dreamy pool boy.

With my head tilted down, I watched the water swirl down the drain taking part of me and my thoughts with it. Swirling, swirling, swirling. I watched long strands of my hair swirl down. I saw textbooks waiting for me on a dusty bookstore shelf, down. I saw unpaid tuition bills, down. I saw studious study groups with an empty chair where I should be, down. I saw relaxing evenings hanging out with friends, down. I saw dreams for my future, down, down…"No! You're not flushing my dreams," I yelled into the shower head, my voice gurgling with the water filling up my mouth. *I am stronger than this*! *I am not watching my dreams swirl down the drain*

with hair and used suds. I began to sob. Tears. Down. Down. Down. A five-minute shower sob led me to a place I have never been. A place I did not know existed. Inside of me, I found myself.

Drained of tears, I felt a quiet rage well up in me, starting in my core, then shooting like one thousand firecrackers through my veins. The pulsating energy left me shaking under the shower head. I turned off the water and leaned against the tiled shower wall. I looked up at the bathroom mirror and noticed my reflection was clouded over. I was naked and barely visible. I kept staring as the mirror revealed its secrets. First, the outline of my curves appeared. Then my light brown pubic hair, made darker by wetness, revealed itself, then the details of my breasts began to appear—soft beige with light rose areolas— then my eyes began to emerge. They were more intense than ever before. The circle of sparkling green now looked like an intense raging sea.

Suddenly, my entire womanly image stared back at me. I no longer felt like an awkward child. Either the shower had transformed me, or she had been there all along, waiting to be seen. I did not look away. I met her. I stared into her raging eyes. I looked at my body, my bare skin, and wondered if the men saw what I saw. Did they see the entire me, the whole person, or did their eyes see only body parts? "Oh, she has a nice ass." "Did you see her sexy stomach?" My percolating rage was now simmering. Easier to get burned when you can't see the hot bubbles. Simmering is where I would stay. A fitting temperature. I was in control. *For now.*

My body appeared soft and smooth in the mirror. The mirror was a liar. My body now held a secret. A secret I would share with no one. My body contained the energy of one thousand bombs that could ignite at my will, or maybe without my will. I would keep the explosive key locked away. I would do no harm to myself or others. I would use this burning energy to fuel me. I stepped out of that shower, smoldering, and cleansed of my former self.

Chapter 26
demons, drama, and angels

The water on my skin had dried, but my body was still vibrating. My awakening was not visible to anyone else. I was just another solo driver caught up in rush hour traffic, except most other drivers were driving from work; I was driving to work. The drive across town gave me time to think. *Too much time*. Being stuck at a red light behind a Colorado license plate caused my mind to wonder off to my time in Denver. A time and place that could cause me to boil over if I thought too much. I thought about how much had changed in my life since I left that mile-high city during the summer of 1986, just before the start of my senior year in high school. I barely made it out of there alive. Three years ago. A lifetime ago.

Eighteen months there. Months that were my equivalent to my brother's army boot camp, only his boot camp was much shorter and his experience did not leave him wanting to end his life. *Not to my knowledge*. Wanting to leave this body and this life is a heavy feeling that I frequently flirted with, but in Colorado, I was dancing with death. Already on shaky ground from my parents' divorce and their individual decisions to remarry the wrong person—again—I was tossed out like the trash when my stepmom decided that I should go live with my mom and stepdad, three weeks shy of my sophomore year. My brother, who was already living with my mom and stepdad in Denver, and I disturbed our stepmom's angelic family photo: the one with her, my dad, and her three little angels. A house of cards. A photo sham. A polaroid that had barely dried and yet the edges were already disintegrating.

Being typical teenagers, my brother and I had lost our angelic halos, and she made sure to let our dad know about any questionable glance or failure to live up to her expectations—ever changing expectations that shifted daily along with her borderline personality. A personality that unleashed explosive anger toward us when our dad wasn't around. *Her word against ours*. We did not have a chance with a pussy-whipped man.

As a minor, I had no choice but to pack my two bags and do as the evil stepmom said. I was devastated. I was carved out. I left the sunshine with a shattered soul and a straight-A, stellar transcript and suddenly found myself alone in a high school counselor's office with a receptionist and counselor who were confused by my presence. They didn't know what to do with me. I grew up in an area that always had an influx of people, coming and going. Neither scenario brought too much attention. It was different in this new place, a rich school in the suburbs of Denver. An affluent area with established people and traditions. People who were organized and prepared and who cared about the future of their children—people who would go to great lengths to protect the future of their children. People who would kiss the ground to have a child like me. And yet, here I was—alone, broken, barely respondent, with professionals who weren't sure where to send me. Scrambling and whispering behind a desk ultimately led to placing me in classes that "best" matched my transcripts.

With only a few weeks left of school, classrooms were preparing for final exams, students were presenting final projects, and cliques were well-established. I was required to take final exams in classes I had just entered. *No exceptions*. No one was in my corner fighting against the unfairness of this situation. Just me. A broken bird who got plenty of curious looks and some not-so-nice looks from girls. I know The Look. The same harsh looks that met me in the dressing room under bright lights. I hate that look. I was a ghost girl swept up in the crowd, moving from class to class, doing my best to hold on and end the year with a salvageable transcript. A transcript that was my ticket to a better life. Dreams of which I had been working on since I started school as a hope-filled curious child.

Eleven years later, I found myself on the edge of a cliff, watching my years of hard work tumble over the edge. One A after another, tumble, tumble. One "top of the class" project, tumble. One "best student of the year," tumble. Down, down, down...my hopes and dreams tumbled. *Would I tumble, too?* I was holding on, but I could feel my stepmom's heartless decision, and my dad's indecision, kick me closer to the edge with each completed end-of-the-year exam. Even the teachers did not know what to do with me. "A new student? Now? Have a seat here," they said, in a tone that did not try to hide the frustration they felt inside. I did as I was told. I sat in the chair that wasn't a desk like everyone else's. Bodies seated in their own desks; at me, they did stare. I sat in the outcast's chair. I did as I was told.

The finish line that marked the end of my sophomore year was not a celebration; it was a crawl, a scream, a million tears and one thousand shattered dreams. For the first time in my life, I saw Ds on my transcript. "This will go down in your permanent record," a voice boomed in my head. *I did not earn these Ds!* Those marks were a cruel joke, a punishment for being the daughter of two, now four self-absorbed people. Adult decisions that propelled my downward spiral.

As torturous as school was during those high school days, it was better than being at home. Another house of cards. Would I be the gentle wind that would blow it all down? No, not me, but I once again found myself on shaky ground. The summer between my sophomore and junior year was a blur. A blur of withdrawing to my room, a blur of going for long walks alone, a blur of buried anger and rage, a blur of fighting with my mom and ignoring my ridiculous stepfather—another grown-up ill-equipped to handle the needs of an emotionally despondent teenager whose life had just been ripped out from under her. My turmoil became their weapon to use against me. "Get along." "Be happy." "Be grateful." "Don't you know how good you have it?" *Fuck off!* None of us living under that roof had it good. My brother was being sucked into the army by an aggressive recruiter—who also tried to recruit me—my mom was *not* headed toward "happily ever after," and my stepdad was building a doomed construction business. Another house of cards. Money was spent to lease a white Porsche instead of buying furniture for the living room. *Fucking douche bag.*

My junior year began where my sophomore year ended. In a sinking pit. I once again found myself alone. This time I was in a gym, registering for classes, and once again there was confusion as to where I "best belonged." A different school in a different state meant different options and paths. Having already taken their equivalent of junior math, I was placed in a senior math class—this promised to be interesting. Additional classes were secured (French II, gym, history) and textbooks were purchased. I was an official student, starting school properly. Everything was ready, except me. Just like being sent there, no one asked or seemed to care. Most mornings I did not want to get out of bed, a feeling I had never experienced. My stepmom's actions, not redirected by the other adults in my life, had planted a seed of depression and discontent, and it was now fully rooted in my soul.

Toward the end of my junior year, the fully rooted, dark seed had sprouted limbs that wrapped around me tighter and tighter. I was suffocating. The ghost girl had given up. I stopped eating. I spent more time in my room. I began taking pills. Whatever I could find around the house. More than the "recommended dosage," but not enough to cause noticeable concern or irreversible damage. I was testing my internal boundaries. I stopped caring about everything, including my future—the greatest tragedy of all. The rising sun that once held promise now meant nothing to me. Days no longer held significance. Pale, weak, hopeless, and restless, I had been awake for hours one night, tossing, turning, and staring at the ceiling when something called me out of bed. Not a person. Not a voice. A pull that persisted. I listened.

I ventured down the steps into our sunken living room. A place I did not care to go, especially in the middle of the night. A place that dragged me down and made my skin crawl, with its dark suffocating energy. As strong as my feelings were, I could not fight the pull to go—to sink into the dark space. *I had no fight left in me.* I sat on the couch, alone in the middle of the night. I turned the television on and what transpired over the next thirty minutes may have saved my life—even if it was a made-up TV drama. The first scene was that of violence; horrid demons were grabbing and pulling and screaming. People were being tortured by fire but never consumed by it. Contained in a large brown box in our sunken living room, I sat watching scenes from Hell.

One after another, people told stories that had traces of my story. I drew myself closer to the television. I became fixated on their stories of desperation. Stories of people not wanting to go on. Different people, but they all had one thing in common: every single person told a story of taking their own life. Not just testing the waters, like me, but people who committed suicide, died, then were resuscitated. Different people and different methods of suicide, but similarities in their life-after-death scenarios. *Their hell after death.* The end.

I watched static for a few minutes. I was shaking. I couldn't move. Had I fallen asleep hours ago to find myself in a television-induced dream? Somewhere between sleepwalking and enlightenment, I walked up the steps, back to my room where I eventually fell asleep. When I woke a few hours later, I was not awash in hope, but I made a vow to myself that I would change my course and not push the limits of living to the point of no longer living. I was not saved, but I was going to choose life. *However fucked up it is.*

I have always felt protected by guardian angels, but that televised scene during the darkest night of my soul offered proof. I hope I am right, because I sure could use some protection. We all can.

Chapter 27
pink-toned hope

Memories of my deep desperation in Denver kept my mind preoccupied through green and red lights, through lane changes, and through freeway exchanges, bringing me to the parking lot in the shadow of two intersecting freeways. A few minutes early for my second shift, I parked far from the entrance and spent the next few minutes breathing and watching. Watching men come and go, watching girls get dropped off, some by yellow cabs. At least I had a car—one that I had purchased on my own.

I had stalled long enough. It was time to leave the safety of my driver's seat and head into the lion's den. I closed my eyes and asked for protection from my guardian angels, then I opened the door and stepped on the black tar. One foot in front of the other. *I can do this. One more shift. More money for my college fund. I can do this.* I was missing my Alaskan tribe, but eating pancakes with Cat and her friends the night before gave me faith in a possible friendship.

As the sun descended, the exterior of the club began to change from a harsh mustard tone to a soothing sandy-beach shade. The dripping gold tone changed to an angelic pink, layering the side of the building with its breathtaking hush. The sight of the blasé building turning into a heavenly canvas took my breath away. I wanted to run into the club and tell everyone to come outside. "Do you see what I see?" I would exclaim.

I turned my attention from the building to the sky, searching for the source of the light. No longer seen beyond the congested freeway overhead, the disappearing sun was painting the sky the color of hope. I risked being slapped with a late fine on my second night of dancing. I thought it was worth it as I needed to bathe in the warm pink glow for a few more minutes. I lifted my head and closed my eyes. A small dose of inspiration to get me through another night of the skin circus.

Seeing Doug at the door calmed my nerves. He looked at his watch, gave me a fatherly look, then told me I had two minutes to spare. *I needed that.* "Thank you, Doug," I said, meeting his eyes with a smile. My face felt warm.

I rushed past the bar, not without being noticed by Omar who teased me about being late. He made me laugh. *I needed that, too.* I also needed a deep breath before I pushed the swinging door leading into the dressing room. I did not need the secondhand smoke that hitched a ride on my inhaled breath, but there wasn't a damn thing I could do about it if I planned on working in a topless bar. The dressing room, with its swirling perfume and hair spray, was no reprieve. Just part of the show—smoky air blending with the golden vapors of beauty adorned. If it weren't so toxic, it would have been mesmerizing. I didn't use hairspray or wear perfume, but there was no avoiding either of them in the confines of the dressing room, a constant cloud of fabricated scents and visible "firm hold" swirling around me.

Wearing the choices of others was unavoidable after walking through the heavy cloud hovering in the dressing room. Hairspray does nothing for my hair, except make it sticky, and perfume gives me a headache and sometimes a rash if it is of cheap drugstore quality. I am not fussy, but if I am going to wear perfume it needs to be actual perfume squeezed from petals, not a potion made of chemicals. I did not choose the natural look: it chose me.

I could feel my body and face begin to grow tense as I passed each primped prima donna on my way to an empty chair. Their intimidating stares seemed set on making me shrivel and shrink. They would not win because this was not a competition with *them*. This was survival for each of us. I lifted my head a little higher and kept walking. They didn't know that an awakened beast was lurking beneath my soft skin, ready to strike them down and smear their nasty glares. I was beginning to feel the wakening of my own power. My extra time soaking up the sunset left me without a seat. The golden rule may not be practiced by everyone, but the unspoken chair rule was—the chair grabbed early is yours for the night. On this night, I was out of luck. Oh well, I could stand and primp, and I had what those seated dancers didn't have—a dose of pink-toned hope.

I was so focused on holding my head and hopes high, I almost missed Cat. Seeing her and hearing her say, "Hey, Jade," caused my body to relax. For her, I would smile. For her, I would offer a hug, one she would be happy to receive and return.

"It's a full house tonight. Tomorrow is the first. Rent is due," Cat explained with her sarcastic slant.

"Yeah, I know. My roommates left me a reminder note."

"You can put your stuff with mine and get ready here," she offered.

"Thank you." I was prepared to go it alone in the corner, but I was grateful for her kindness.

Cat may not have been the supreme prima donna in the place, but I noticed everyone seemed to respect her. At the very least, they left her alone. Maybe it was her age, a few years older than most of the girls, or maybe it was her calm demeanor. She was also gorgeous, a pinup doll with her long chestnut hair, blue eyes, and accentuated womanly curves. I had skipped a few steps on the "earn your respect" ladder by having her take me under her wings. Two "students" doing what they needed to do to survive.

She reminded me to check in with the DJ, which I did after changing and quickly applying my glittery pasties. Applying glue to my areola then attaching a sparkly circular "bandage" to the sticky area, is an experience that I may never stop laughing at. Gluing and attaching also reminds me of being in kindergarten. I suppose this scenario is different. It looks and feels dumb, but it puts a barrier between dancers and the dumb men, making us feel a little less exposed. They see enough of us.

Cat and I chatted for a few minutes, talking about our day. I told her about the cute boy at the pool. I didn't mention a damn thing about the book I read. She probably would have appreciated hearing about that more than my lifeguard fantasy, being the mature student she was. The night was young. I would share my book highlights when we rested our dancing feet. Just as I was getting comfortable, enjoying the moment as if I were on a casual lunch date with a friend, I heard my name through the staticky speaker.

"Next up, to Stage One, welcome sexy Jade who will be getting it Hot, Hot, Hot."

My body immediately tensed up hearing his announcement—and a little happy, too, knowing his "hot" reference meant that I would be dancing to the Cure. My warm-up song would be a hot one. *No rest for the wicked*, I supposed. I grabbed my small purse, gave Cat another hug, then it was showtime.

My steps to the stage were encouraged by clapping and a few whistles. Not a thunderous applause and the same whistles could have been used to call a lost puppy, but the sound of hands together was something to move me along. Better than a "boooo" from the mouth. As much as I didn't give a rat's ass, I hoped to never hear that. The music started before I reached the stage. *Fashionably late. Perfect!* The music was drawing me in, away from the bodies below my thighs. My "warm-up" began before the first words of "Hot, Hot, Hot" were heard:

Deeper and deeper, I did descend into the notes, into the beats, into Robert Smith's voice. I lost sight and feel for where I was and let my body do what it did best: move and become one with the music. My body was outward and free, but to protect myself, I retreated within. I was on a stage, dancing with Robert, from the Cure, not a room full of drunk and horny men. I was reminded of all the man drunkenness I had witnessed as a young girl, during my dad's many fishing tournaments. The men fished all day trying to catch a "prize" while downing cold Coors from ice-packed coolers. By the campfire, they would slur their stale beer breath and carry on about the big one that got away. I needed to get away from those fish tales and dance my way back to Robert. Just me and him—dancing and spinning. Both of us wearing our makeup and costumes—entertainers, not clowns, we were.

So lost to the "Hot" song, I did not notice the scattering of dollars growing near my high-heeled, fast-moving feet. A bed of dirty green flowers multiplying beneath me. The song reached its final note. Then came the applause and more whistles. Genuine and enthusiastic this time. It took my body a few seconds to catch up with the moment. My shadow kept spinning while the "rent-paying me" bent down to scoop up the sweaty dollars. My landlord would not mind the sweat.

While gathering the bills and putting them in my purse—not a shove, but a fold and tuck—I noticed a man across from me, smiling and waiting. I smiled back, grabbed my top, then sauntered over to him. The default walk when one is wearing heels and a tiny costume.

"When you're done, will you give my friend a table dance?" he asked, handing me a twenty and pointing to his friend, who looked like he wanted to hide under the table. "It's his birthday today and you are definitely his type."

"Yes, I'll find you," I replied with a plastic smile before quick-stepping it to Stage Two.

The hot, fast pace that started my second night did not stop. There was no resting until the last call and last song of the night, and there had been not a single minute to talk to Cat. It wasn't until we were eating pancakes at her—*now our*—favorite all-night diner that I was able to tell her about the "life-changing" book I began reading poolside while drowning in a cute boy's look. As I had suspected, she was more interested in the book than a cute boy. *Smart woman*. I hoped she'd be smart enough to go back to school. *Me too*. I drove home with two hundred fifty more dollars in my expanding purse. I would need to use some of that money to buy a bigger purse.

And so began the spending justifications and the attachments to the world of dancing. A makeshift welcoming family, enough cash to pay rent, made in one night, not five days, small purchases made here and there. Small decisions and details that would reveal themselves over time. On that night, I was driving the happy train to my apartment on the other side of town, where my pillow was, but not my heart.

I arrived home just before 4 a.m., making sure to jingle my keys over the full shitty litter box. I counted out my portion of the rent and utilities, then I left the cash bundle on the counter, along with their stupid note, crumpled with care.

A hot shower washed away the smoke, the sweat, the perfume, the hairspray, and most importantly, the lingering smell of the patrons' alcoholic breath. The water was beginning to wash away the shivers and shame, interrupted by noticing the note I had left taped to the toilet paper dispenser before going to work. "Bring your own!" the note read. I laughed out loud in the shower.

I fell into bed with a sense of satisfaction and a trace of hope—remnants of a falling star I saw during my drive home was my last thought before falling asleep.

Chapter 28

sparkling snake charmer

I would still have been on probation if I had been working at a normal job, but this was not a normal job. Time speeds up under the neon canopy. Other things speed up too. Lines grow deeper and pink lungs age faster. Strong backs start the shift flexible and young, then wake up the next day old and stiff. Bending over backwards, for scattered dollars. The flexible ones, like me, made their way upside down, down the stairs—arms leading the way. I was also a pole dancer—climbing to the top of the smudged brass poles—no bell to announce my victory once there, just the freedom of soaring above the crowd.

A bird, I pretended to be. For just a moment, a needed free-flight fantasy. There I would stay for just a moment, breathing in the top layer of the smoky room, slightly less toxic with each rising inch—at least that is what I led myself to believe. What goes up must come down, so I did. Never the same spiral descent—leaning back, spinning around, holding on tight with arms bent, while my legs became the dance. Landing gently on the ground below while dollar bills were scattered to and fro.

I needed the cash. There was no doubt about that. I wanted to attend university. There was no separating that desire from my pulsing blood. However, after four weeks of driving, arriving, primping, dancing, and counting, my singular motivation for *just the money* was gaining some competition. Other things were catching up: the increasing desire to earn more than the night before; the growing need to acquire new costumes and new moves; and a developing connection to a place that was beginning to feel like home. Easy for a wayward soul to fall into an alluring trap of belonging somewhere, whatever the cost.

One must have thick skin to bear so much bare skin in a place that has its share of pricks. Those standout assholes never became regulars—our guardian angel doorman, Doug, made sure of that, but those men did leave an impression before their asses were kicked to the curb. A mark that may have humiliated and angered them, but in their drunken state, I doubted the lessons were ever permanent. As for the effect their crude behavior and words had on us dancers, it seemed nothing that couldn't be removed with prayers and a good cleanse. I relied on the power of this remedy. If having my heart break into tiny shards and fall on the frozen cement in a faraway land had not taught me how tough I was, I was learning it then. Unwelcomed touches and vulgar comments that easily slipped from city lips did not reduce me to a puddle or weaken my core—a shield of invisible armor I wore. I had passed the one-month test.

Omar, behind the bar, reminded me of this when he handed me a soda topped with two floating cherries, for "good luck," he added. I offered him a thank you and a "cheers," then took a sip. Always in a rush, I had not noticed, except for those rare slow moments, when he polished his bar glasses to perfection. He seemed to enjoy this ritual, and the sparkling glasses lined across the entirety of the bar made a beautiful reflective display, enchanting me and hypnotizing me with their brilliance. A shine pure and true—a contrast to the neon, glitter, and glam. A shine that was needed in a place that would reveal its ugly dinginess if all the lights were turned on. Truthful grime endured by only the cleaning crew, if ever there was one. Like my life,

I tried to not look too closely at the soil and stains. Best to step on them or dance around them. Omar's spotless perfection revealed a certain pride in his craft, and I suppose that gave his idle hands and active mind something to do while he watched the skin parade, always on display.

"You are still here," Omar went on to say as I enjoyed my soda-sipping moment beneath a hanging row of sparkling, upside down glasses that gave the appearance of a chandelier. "I did not think you would last one night, and you are still here. Enjoy your cherry prize. Now go take off your clothes," he ordered with a laugh and a smile. I laughed with him and thanked him for the soda before rushing off to do as I was told by the black bow tie-wearing man.

One month in this place meant I had achieved lifetime member status of the three-stage circus. The brass poles were high; the retention rate and the standards were low. I should have disregarded this accomplishment. I should have stopped becoming emotionally invested in a place that would lead to only one destination: a long walk to my car one last time before driving away toward the pink sunset to wake up the next day to a golden sunrise, only to realize that nights of dancing might be filling my purse, but that cash earned would be quickly spent and leave me with a sore back, and with no security or future on which to fall back. *Concerns for another day.* I was green. I was getting caught up in the scene.

It was at the start of my cherry-munching celebratory shift that I met a favorite of the dancers—one who made them sparkle, at least on top of their skin. When at least ten girls rushed out of the dressing room, I knew something was up, I just didn't know what. A fire? A bomb threat? A wealthy patron? Who or what could it be? I followed the ladies out of the club and into the parking lot. I was still in my street clothes; most of them were not. I would follow these ladies over a cliff, it seemed. I caught up with the women standing behind a gold-colored Nova with its trunk propped open. Next to the car was a lady I did not recognize. She was not the dancer type. She was a sliver of a woman with a baby on her hip. A brief conversation with her revealed that she made costumes all day and sold them out of her trunk at night. A traveling entrepreneur selling her own form of snake oil, for the snake charmers to hypnotize the snakes, who crawled from the gutters and slithered in, low-bellied.

I did not have the vantage point of other dancers closest to the car to see what they saw, but I did notice a few garments strewn along the left side of an opened trunk: brightly colored fabric adorned with glitter and delicate stitching. Into the enchanted trunk, I was called. *Sell me some snake oil, then add some more.* I resisted my urge to push through and grab my share. I was still new here. I couldn't really afford a new costume anyway, I reminded myself. While I waited for my turn, I noticed her dry and cracked digits holding a bouncy babe. Her prematurely aged fingers were a contrast to the soft pink baby skin that kicked and twisted and fidgeted under their squeeze. Aged hands that looked too rough for a gentle motherly touch, but who was I to judge? I wondered how she managed, being so frail and thin.

Her laboring fingers revealed she was also doing what she needed to do to survive.

Fingers dry and cracked from managing material and sparkly additions during her sewing day. Tiny holes and scabs in her skin from too many pokes from a needle. Needle pokes that must hurt and annoy, but that did not alter her mind, skin, and soul, like the evident needle pokes felt by some of the dancers who wore her costumes. Tiny costumes that did not cover up their choices. Thick makeup also did little to hide their scabs and late-night picks from their mind-altering trips. Talented seamstress hands that also fed and tended to her baby throughout her sewing shift. A shift that probably never ended from the looks of it. A baby gently bounced on the sewing momma's jutted straight hip as she told each girl to go try on her latest fashions. "Oh, that would look so good on you!" she exclaimed through her nervous grin, with her costume-peddling mannerisms. "That is your color! Try it on!"

Momma, baby, and a gathering of dancers were losing light as the sun began to dip below the freeway overpass. An industrial reminder that we were not in Kansas, and our sparkling shoes, regardless of how many clicks, would not get us one step closer to paradise. The fading light made the rusty car glow as the glittery sequins reflected their hope for a better day into the eyes of each girl needed on stage. Maybe the baby would grow up to be a dancer. *That is where the real money is, baby.*

Finally, my turn after all but two dancer chicks had left the parking lot scene. I picked up a costume that seemed to be tailor-made for me: a tiny fitted emerald dress with just a few crystal beads, perfectly placed to lay close to cleavage, and a matching bikini set that I could also wear to the beach. If that should ever happen, I was set. I paid Momma forty-five dollars. Hard to let go of those bills neatly folded in my purse, securely on my side. I told myself the just-right costume was a needed investment for the business I was in—the one of teasing, then sharing skin. Looking into her tired eyes with my extended cash made me feel better about my choice. She did not have to say thank you; her eyes said enough. Fuel for her car, a roof over their heads, and food for her baby's hungry mouth—before and sometimes in place of her own, was my guess.

I was the last one to leave the lady and her chubby baby, taking my time as I walked back in. Not worried about being late. I had passed probation. All would be forgiven when they saw me shimmy and shake my emerald charm—charming the sense out of their cash and snakes, if they had any before they stepped in.

Chapter 29

flying high on the pole

With all the tricks and spinning acrobatics, my time at the Phoenix club was making my muscles tighter than my time on the easy-stepping stages in Fairbanks. The Phoenix club was also making my skin thicker. The other option was to cave and give in. Leaving Fairbanks had torn away my raw emotions and shredded what I had failed to protect: my heart. Emptied of pain or heavily masked from it, under the brights of the sprawling city, I danced, collected my earnings, slept it off, then did it again and again. In the desert, I did not have whispering trees trying to tempt me to the dark side. Nor did I have emerald skies, shimmering above the crystal white, offering a glimmer of heaven and hope. I was surrounded by concrete and asphalt. I was turning into a dancing robot who no longer heard late-night cries urging me to end my life. They did not need to; I was dying inside.

I made it to the end of another month. Almost. It was the last Thursday of March. A few more days then a new month would start. Thursdays were payday for some, which sometimes made Friday eve just as busy as a Friday night. Staring into the club's warped bathroom mirror, I noticed my piercing eyes. So intense, they took my breath away. I stared deep and lost myself in the deepest green. I stepped out of the restroom and made my way to the third stage, rushing because I was late. I noticed a few men close to the stage begin to look around for their missing dancer. Where is she? Where did she go? Keep the circus going, is what their stretchy necks were saying. I was headed to the stage when the unexpected happened.

A fat stubby finger jammed its way into my mouth, rubbing its calloused nub, coated with a grainy substance, against my gums. I grabbed the hairy leathered arm attached to the fat finger and nearly yanked it off before spinning around to see what asshole was attached to the appendage. His short and squatty body was an extension of his stubby finger. A stubby finger covered with wiry bristles. Like a cleaning brush for small spaces, except his brush made me feel dirty. I didn't know what the asshole rubbed across my gums, but it was starting to tingle and burn. I spit out what I could on his shoes and then freed my right hand from his forearm and tried to wipe off whatever he had wiped on.

My left hand held his arm with the might of ten warriors. A force that was growing stronger with each step toward my protector, my muscular angel at the door. The fat little prick didn't resist too much. I think he enjoyed being pulled by me and from the glossy, lost look on his face, he didn't seem too concerned about anything. Doug jumped from his stool and rushed to my defense. I told Doug what happened, not that I had any details beyond the finger ram. I let Doug handle the rest; he became the man's judge and jury. The gum-rubbing man would not leave here the same man as when he came in, not that he would remember any of it.

I rushed to the bar and asked Omar for a drink of water, quickly. I told Omar what happened. I could feel my heart begin to race and my mouth became parched. I began to sweat and shake. Omar came around the bar with a glass of water and a clean towel. He then gently took my arm and escorted me into his office and asked me to sit down. I did. I didn't want to sit though. I wanted to sprint around the club, or run down the street, or fly through the air on my flying trapeze. Omar asked me if I had ever done cocaine. "No," is what I said.

"That is probably what he gave you, little fucker." I had never heard Omar cuss and hearing those words from him made me laugh. He laughed too. A nervous laugh as he looked closely at me.

"Your pupils are huge," he observed.

"I'm supposed to be on Stage Three right now," I said, in a voice that did not sound like my own, while sitting on the edge of his fake leather office chair.

"It's OK, they will live. You will too, you are just going to be flying high for a while. Longer if he gave you meth."

"Oh, fuck! How long will that last?" I asked.

"It depends. Through the night for sure."

I was trying to stay calm and focus on Omar, but the small office was getting smaller. My skin began to crawl, and my body began to shake.

"How long will this feeling last?" I asked Omar.

"An hour or two, it depends on how much he gave you and how strong it is."

My mind began to race, thinking about what exactly might be racing through my veins and brain. I was a mixture of raw anger and elation. A soaring feeling was beginning to take over. I felt like I could boldly ask every man in this club if he wanted a table dance and not one would say no. I began to exhale worry and inhale courage at a rapid pace. I told Omar I could not sit in his office for an hour. "There is no way." I was panicking. "I would be better off dancing, I think. At least I could burn off this energy racing through my body."

"Okay," he conceded, "but drink that glass of water first and you should have a snack. I will be right back." He returned with half a sandwich. "Eat," he said, thrusting the two white triangles held together with egg salad at me. The sight and smell of it made me want to vomit in his black trashcan.

"I'm not hungry."

"I know, but eat anyway. When you are done, then you can dance. I am going to watch you, even more than I normally do," he confessed with his playful signature smile.

"I bet you will!" I responded, smiling back.

Omar left and shut the door behind him. I did as I was told, forcing myself to eat half his dinner, quickly, so that I could get the hell out of that claustrophobic space. I imagined his wife making his "dinner" for him before he drove himself to work that day. Assuming he had a wife. I had never asked and I hadn't noticed a wedding ring, nor had I looked. If not her, then he made it. I wondered if he had kids. I had never thought to ask. When would I have time to ask, rushing by his bar every night? I looked around his dimly lit dusty office for signs of life—his life. I saw nothing. Not exactly the type of place to display holiday family photos. In a thousand directions, my mind was spinning. *Fuck* was all I could muster, and if I didn't leave that office soon, I was going to find a rabbit hole to fall into and never be seen again. Not a bad idea, I thought.

I checked my face in a small, dirty mirror resting on a shelf. I gave myself a fright. My distinguishable sparkly irises were barely visible. Intense black was staring back. I did not recognize myself. The mystery substance was changing me—my voice, my eyes, my inhibitions, my skin. My thoughts were racing, and my face was morphing. Looking at my reflection was a mistake. I turned and pushed open the door like a submerged diver returning to the surface just after running out of air. I left his office, smelling like eggs and with legs that felt like they had been scrambled. My brain felt less scrambled, but also unrecognizable. I was losing control.

I was terrified. I was headed back to the restroom when Doug's hand stopped me. *Please don't talk to me, not now,* I wanted to shout.

"Hey, are you okay, Jade?" he asked, fast-stepping to catch up.

"I'm high, but I'll be fine. Omar made me eat and he said he would keep an eye on me."

"Yes, I'm sure he will," Doug said, looking down at his shoes. "Hey, I roughed that guy up, then kicked him out. Not before asking the little prick what he rubbed in your mouth. He said cocaine. He said he thought you would like it. I'm sorry that happened to you, Jade."

"Thank you, Doug. It won't happen again," I told him. "I'll be alright. I'm going to dance it off." Truth was, I did not feel alright. The heavy coating his stubby finger had smeared across the top of my gums had quickly mixed with my saliva and was now soaring through my veins.

"You missed your last stage set, but you'll have a few more chances before the night is over. It's only eight."

"Great! So not only did the asshole get me high, he also cost me!" My simmering anger, now a thousand bombs unleashed. "Why did you have to tell me that? Five more hours in here! I won't survive!"

"You'll be alright," he encouraged. "You're strong!"

"Thanks. I feel like I could climb ten brass poles right now."

"Get to it then!" he said, patting my shoulder.

This place had its share of asshole customers, but the people who ran it were alright. I felt protected, even though my shield was lowered for a few minutes. Never again. I would be on my guard from that night forward.

I did zip around that club, asking every patron who wasn't already being entertained by a dancer if they wanted a table dance. I had never had reason to consider who might be as high as me on cocaine—or anything else—but once feeling the effects of coursing courage, it made sense that everyone else must be, too. My flying-high state of mind put a hundred more dollars in my purse before the next stage set. I was invincible. My mind was rebelling against the feeling of spinning in a thousand directions: of paranoia, of jitters, of a racing heart, and of not being in control, but there wasn't a damn thing I could do about my state of mind except enjoy the ride. There was no joy, just turbulence, and the view sucked.

When I made it back to Stage Three a few guys from over two hours before were still sitting there. *Get a fucking life!*

"Nice of you to show up this time," one of them teased.

"Yes, isn't it?" I smiled my "eat shit" grin at him. I froze for a second and imagined thrusting my heel into his jugular. It was very tempting and the darkness racing through me, revealed through my pupils, would have no remorse. Three things stopped me: the thought of Omar having to clean up the bloody mess—ruining a pair of heels—and having enough sense left to not throw my freedom away on another clueless prick. I spun away from his creepy, drunk eyes before the darkness inside changed my mind.

I didn't mind being on stage in my normal state—a sober state. On stage, I could escape.

I could rise above the crowd and my worries. I could get lost in the music. I was rising much higher in this state, but I felt awkward, like I had little control over my limbs. I was angry about someone forcing *their* addiction into my mouth. My normal rhythm had been replaced with the shakiness of a wobbly washing machine. Like the one in our apartment that would rock itself out of the closet when it was out of balance. That was funny; this was a violation. A dangerous one, too. I kept breathing and trying to sink deeper into the song, but like a helium balloon, my head floated aimlessly above my body. I was either one beat ahead or one beat behind, it seemed. Or I imagined it all. Fuck, maybe I was writing the song perfectly with every muscle in my body. *Dream on, Jade.* The men gathered around the stage did not seem to notice or mind my jittery dance. They did not come to watch a ballet, just a stuck ballerina.

Dirty dollars were tossed onto the stage. I watched one soiled bill, mesmerized by the brief float it took before slowly drifting to the ground like a gentle butterfly, merging with the other paper wings. Dirty butterflies that I would fold neatly and tuck in my purse. They were all filthy and smelled of a thousand sweaty palms, but beyond the disgust I saw their potential to help me build a better future. For a moment, I caught myself trying to count the dirty butterflies, then I realized what I was doing. I looked up and spun my body a few times, trying to snap out of my fascination with the floating and falling paper. *Dizzy spinning.* The brass pole did more than give the customers a different point of view, it also gave dancers something to hold on to when they needed support or when they were bored. I grabbed hold. The ride was moving fast, and at any moment, it could come to a crashing halt. I held on.

"Climb the pole!" someone yelled. *I'd like to snap your pole in half,* is what I thought. I scanned the ground looking for who may have asked for a circus act, but I could not pick him out. Maybe I imagined it. Then I heard it again. "Climb the pole!" This time I caught his lips forming the request. I stared for a moment while he stared back. I would honor his request but not for free. The "bold me" gestured for a tip by rubbing my fingers across my thumb, smiling a placid ballerina grin the entire time. He was either an idiot or rude. Probably both because I did not see either hand reach for a wallet.

"No tip, no trick," I mouthed slowly. He got the message. He reached into his tight pocket and pulled out his wallet, saving himself from looking like a bigger asshole in front of his friends, or whoever they were. Whatever he first reached for got a reaction out of the guy sitting to his left who slugged him on the shoulder. Easily persuaded it seemed, he pulled out another bill, which seemed to please his friend, who smiled and lifted his beer in approval. The pole-request man, who now had more eyes on him, thanks to me not removing mine, held a twenty in my direction. He was going to hang onto that precious twenty, so he could tease every penny out of me in return. He couldn't just toss the twenty on the stage and let me get on with my trick, he was going to make me work even harder for it. *Fine. I know the game.* I bent down and let him slide the crisp twenty into the side of my G-string, then me and my newly acquired superwoman strength stepped our way to the brass pole.

Let the games begin. I grabbed hold with both hands, then wrapped my legs around the dirty pole, a thigh on each side. My shoes fell to the ground with little effort. I should have put more effort into their drop and given them a little kick and thrust. Right into someone's unsuspecting forehead. *Next time.* I began the climb. Hands reaching, arms pulling, body following, thighs lifting and thrusting me upward. Repeated until I reached the top.

My cocaine-induced climb gave me a few cheers and a few more falling butterflies to scoop up later. I held on a few seconds longer before making my descent. Letting the music carry me away. "Feel like making love…" Swaying my upper body with the rhythm of the song, while I held on with my legs, strong.

It was time. Securing my grip, I extended my legs out then spun both around the pole, a little faster than normal. Spinning wildly, I engaged my core strength to slow my spin. Gracefully, this time. A spinning ballerina stuck on her pole. Round and round she goes. I imagined that the pole was a beautiful bronze dancer, holding me, supporting me, smiling at me. It was my own reflection staring back at me, and she was not smiling. I had already earned my twenty, but now I was just entertaining myself. With the pole tucked securely in the crevice of my left arm while my right hand held on tightly, I pushed my body away from the pole and stretched my legs out and pointed my toes like a proper ballerina. More cheers and more floating butterflies. I pulled my legs back then wrapped them around the pole—like a lover I did not want to release. With my back arched and my head tilted back, I spun my way back down. Twirling down faster than normal. Like a firefighter headed for a call, I was spinning down the pole to save a life. My own.

My trick was spun. The song was done. So was I. When I bent down to collect my butterflies, I felt nauseous and saw falling stars from the corners of my eyes. *Let me make it off this stage without passing out,* I begged of my guardian angels. An angel, by the name of Cat, was waiting in the wings. Quiet like a cat, she appeared next to me. She scooped up the rest of the money and, with her right hand on the small of my back and her left hand holding my left elbow, she escorted me to the dressing room. I felt safe with her, the family I didn't have outside of the club.

Chapter 30

angels in the hazy gray

Safely back in the dressing room, even with Cat's help, I was still wound up. She started laughing at me. "I have never heard you talk so much or so fast," she admitted through laughter.

"Yeah, well, I have never been high on cocaine before, so that makes it a first for both of us."

"Do you like it?" she asked me.

"Do I like what?"

"The feeling? The high?"

"No, I'm jittery, and I don't like the feeling of not being in control," the words were rushing out of my mouth. "Oh, and I don't like feeling paranoid," I added. It felt like every dancer seated to the right of me was talking about me. I turned my back to their phantom whispers.

"It will wear off," she explained.

"Do *you* like it? I assume you've tried it."

"Yeah. I like it too much. More than studying. I rarely go a day without it. That's probably why I'm here and not working on my counseling hours," she confessed flatly, while firmly holding my gaze in the mirror. A confession and an indirect warning to me. "Don't do it, by choice, Jade, and don't think you will ever see me do it. I don't want to be a bad influence on you. I think you have potential. I want to lift you up, not drag you down. If you make it out of this place, maybe I will too."

"Oh," was the only response I could give her. I did not look away from her pleading eyes. In that moment, I felt both connected to her and terrified for how the euphoric high might change me. What I did not admit to her was that I did like feeling courageous and invincible. A feeling I was already craving more of.

"I wager most of the girls in here—and the men, too—enjoy the high, in any way they can get it," she added. "This place is full of outcasts and risk takers and people who have given up on the notion, or never had it to begin with, that life alone, pure unaltered life, can give them the high they can get from a substance or from a pretty girl stroking their ego—the only thing they own that she will ever stroke, and own it they do. Inflated. In here, they can demand the attention life outside these walls would never give them, if their wallet is padded, too."

"You *should* be a counselor, Cat. You're so wise."

"Yeah, because I'm one of the oldest dancers in here," she laughed.

"How old are you?"

"I'm going to be twenty-eight next month, on the fifteenth. An Aries. Aries people are said to be good organizers. I need to organize my life a little better." Her eyes changed from play to sadness.

"Let's make a pact," I told her. "Let's both enroll back in school this fall—even if it is only one class."

She smiled, then turned directly toward me instead of speaking to my reflection in the mirror. "Sure, kid, let's."

We looked at each other for a few more seconds. Both of us wanting to believe we would, and wanting to believe more, that we could go the distance and make something of our lives beyond the smoky walls. At least, that is what I believed. I had moments of self-doubt, but my belief in a better future was strong. It was what kept me moving forward and what motivated me to drive there every day. *It was only costing me my soul.* Cat's belief seemed less solid. I hoped to be a positive influence on her.

"Well, it's time to go earn some money for school," she announced, patting me on my left thigh.

"Yes, yes, it is."

She stood up slowly in her catlike manner. I sprang from the chair like an overwound Jack-in-the-box. Both of us, side by side, stepped back into the circus to get our share of the pot of gold at the end of the rainbow. A rainbow that shattered into a million fragments before reaching us, the dancers dancing under the freeway overpass. Like splattered paint, the rainbow scattered and dropped on the dirty parking lot and on the flat roof above. The rainbow effect dissolved when it hit the stained and littered black. The beautiful pastels were instantly transformed to a hazy gray, the color of pollution and smoke exiting a smoker after his body writhed in coughing pain.

I lost sight of Cat for the next several hours as I danced, smiled, forced flirtations, and danced some more. My small side purse was beginning to bulge. The stitches were beginning to stretch. Talking, walking, or dancing, I kept touching the clasp, making sure my future was secure. Sometime before midnight, it felt like my body moved through a revolving door. The door spun me around a few times before dumping me into what felt like another room. In that room my brain was lucid, and my body was fluid. I enjoyed the sensation and wanted to experience it again. I wanted to further explore. I pushed this truth out of my mind and said a brief prayer that I would wake tomorrow with no lasting effects or desire for more.

The intense effects of the cocaine were beginning to fade and my body was searching for the familiar rhythm of a slower hum. It was like returning home after an unplanned but exciting trip.

Only fifteen minutes until I heard the first few beats and the first few words…"You show us everything you've got…"

A song that I already had enough of, yet every night I could not wait to hear it. *Play that fucking song.* My brain hummed on. I could not wait to jump onto the stage with the other sweaty ballerinas then leap the fuck out of that place. A place that had changed me in a matter of moments and that was continuing to change me, in other, less obvious ways. Every night, a sigh of relief when the DJ dropped that "last call" needle. That meant we were one step closer to rocking and rolling home. We were on our way to counting our dollars, putting on our street clothes and stepping back out into a world that was also changing. A world that looked different for each dancer, but one that probably did not encourage spinning and snorting like that circus freak show. If it did, may God protect their souls.

Trying to make myself small in the corner of the dressing room, I began counting my dirty butterflies, tucked in front of my folded thighs. I had made three hundred thirty-three dollars that night. Not bad for a Thursday and my best night so far, I concluded. A voice inside whispered the words, "Cocaine is good for your little purse. You should do more." I squashed the greedy voice and quickly divvied up my sweaty butterfly pie. Three piles—the DJ, Omar, and Doug. I gave Omar and Doug a few extra bills. I took the fall—or the stubby finger rub—but they caught me. I wasn't sure if all the dancers tipped out. I knew the smart ones did.

"Do you want to join us for pancakes?" Cat asked.

"No, I think I'm going to head home," I responded with a voice that affirmed my decision.

"I understand. Drive safe." Her tone was nurturing and comforting.

"I will. Hey, Cat," I said as she was walking away.

"Yeah?"

"Thanks for helping me tonight and for sitting with me when I was on the ledge, ready to fall."

"Thank you for doing the same," she said with a wink and a smile. Then she stepped into the night.

I wasn't far behind. I paid the DJ, who thanked me with a bow then I gave Omar his deserved share.

"You made it," he acknowledged, teasing me with his devilish grin.

"Yeah, I survived," I said, both relieved and a little embarrassed. "Thanks for sharing your dinner with me. Next time, make it turkey, please." We both laughed.

"You are alright, kid. Drive safe," he said as I smiled and turned toward Doug, who was standing guard in the parking lot.

"Thanks for being my hero tonight, Doug. I don't know what you did to that guy, but I hope he never comes back or does that to another girl," I said in the most grateful tone I could muster. I handed him his piece of the pie then gave him a quick hug before dashing to my car which took me into the calm streets. Too quiet for a mind that was still spinning and twirling. The fresh air blowing through my window would help calm my nerves and guide me to a soft landing. My pillow and bed.

Chapter 31

two months later

Summer was approaching, and the days were stretching. When I first started working at Desert Rose I had been able to watch the sun set as I drove across town, heading west. By the time I had reached the club, only a few lingering rays remained in the sky. Two months had passed since then. A move brought me closer to the club, only a few minutes away, and changed my travel direction from west to east. I had moved away from the university students and away from my former roommates. My departure from college row was not a friendly one, nor was it a hostile one. My roommates, Alena and Christina, were not thrilled with my departure because it meant they would need to find another roommate, nor were they broken up about saying goodbye to their topless-dancing dweller who came home in the early morning hours, sometimes dangling her keys loudly, and who was still sleeping when they darted off to a 7 a.m. class. Although I worked all night, they treated my "sleeping in" with malcontent, commenting more than once about "how nice it must be to sleep in." The last time I heard those words, "Fuck off!" was my retorted defense.

The hours I kept made me the perfect roommate, in my opinion. My late-night hours meant my roomies didn't have to deal with me. They also didn't have to deal with an obnoxious boyfriend, or any boyfriend, or other friends. It was just me, coming and going to the rhythm of odd hours. My time on college row and longer commute were done. I was glad to leave, but I hated saying goodbye to my poolside lifeguard, who I had stared at a few more times before moving across town. I also hated saying goodbye to my bagel boyfriend. Those were the fantasies that Sean had stirred in me. Hope too, though they were just cute boys who didn't even know my name. I had to take care of myself. Cutting my commute down and being around women who supported me was a better arrangement. That was the plan.

I moved into a five-bedroom home with four other dancers. When Cheryl, Omar's right-hand girl, told several of us that her mom's home, "with a pool and not far from the club," was up for rent, five of us decided that we liked each other enough to become roommates. We signed her lease and moved in without hesitation and with little discussion about anything else. What was there to discuss? When you need a place to sleep at night, roommate rules and expectations seem inconsequential. I chose the smallest room, which suited me just fine. I came with few personal belongings, and I was so thrilled to have moved out of Cat Shit Hotel that I would have slept in the pool house, if there had been one.

Four weeks had passed since I had moved into the "dancer" house. Living with four other dancers was an entirely different experience than being the third wheel in an apartment along college row. *The grass isn't always greener.* In only four weeks, I had seen things in the west-side house that made me miss my outcast living arrangement. Things not discussed, like the amount of drugs that would be consumed by dancer chicks and their sketchy friends, and the late-night parties that never seemed to end. Or the number of men who would come calling, or slithering, hoping to crawl into bed with a dancer chick.

I did not sign up for this dancer lifestyle to "party all night" or date casually or do drugs frequently. I started dancing to pay for school. I had dreams and plans. Two things that were never discussed in these new west side digs.

"No," was my standard response. No, I don't want to go out. No, I don't want to do a line.

No, I don't want to meet your boyfriend's "cute" friend. I did not miss the cat shit or the bitchiness I had left behind on college row, but I did miss flying solo. I was no longer the odd one out, but mostly, I wanted to be left alone, an attitude and way of being that did not blend well with party girls. Party girls who were doing more than what they needed to do to survive.

A few weeks into this new housing arrangement, I started riding to work with Farrah, the loudest woman in the house. Everything about her seemed bigger than life: large eyes, large breasts, big red lips, big blond hair that seemed to grow before my eyes, curves that took up space and pushed at the seams, and a big personality that was prone to extremes. We were opposites in more ways than one, Farrah and I. Our unlikely friendship began in her car, and we grew closer with each passing day. Her small sports car had room for only one passenger, and I was the chosen rider. I offered to drive many times. Except when she was low on gas, *her* standard response was, "no." My car was not up to her big standards.

It had only been a few weeks since we had begun riding together, but we had already learned a lot about each other. I told her about my college dreams. She told me she had struggled in school and was constantly in trouble for being too loud in the classroom or for fighting with girls outside of the classroom. She told me her mom skipped out when she was seven— "drugs and drinking—she was mental," Farrah said. She told me about her truck-driving dad and how he never remarried, and how his single sister and mom helped raise her, an only child, when he was on the road, which was most of the time. I told her about my dad's drinking, his three DUIs, my parents' divorce, and my brother's decision to join the military. Farrah and I were sharing stories and building trust in each other.

Upon that bed of trust, I caved. My weeks of relentless "nos" become one "yes" just before a shift. We were sitting in her car, parked at the edge of the club parking lot. Farrah was about to do a line, like I had seen her do several times. With her head tilted down and the tightly rolled dirty dollar close to her nose, she paused and offered it to me.

"Do you want some?" I didn't say, "no." I didn't say anything. I just looked at her.

"Just one line. It won't kill ya. It'll wake you up," she persuaded. "You were just talking about how tired you are. Come on, don't be a baby." She pushed the dollar and the small mirror with the white line on it closer to my face. I got a whiff of sweet and metallic. A switch flipped in my brain and a stored memory of feeling invincible was released. My mouth began to salivate. I became very aware of how hot it was in the car.

"Okay. Just one line. Just this one time." I took the dollar from her. She held the mirror. I inserted the bill in my right nostril while closing my left nostril with my left pointer finger. I inhaled. I felt the burn. I saw sparks. I felt euphoric. I felt no worries. I liked how I felt.

Farrah and I were bonding over shared rides, secrets, and lines but we weren't the only dancer chicks in the dancer rental house.

Two of our three other roommates were sisters, and they each had a Rottweiler. Two large, black dogs that often deposited huge turds in the living room. The turds would sit there until one or both sisters picked up the piles— never in a rush. A smelly kitty litter box was one thing, but steamy shits on the carpet were disgusting. Finally fed up, three of us strung caution tape across the archway to the living room where the turd bombs were dropped. A toxic smell that was beginning to float through the house. A bold move, considering how hot-tempered our dog-owning roommates could be. We did not care. We were sick of the shit and their lack of consideration. We laughed hysterically at the sight of the strung tape. Why Farrah, the owner of the tape, had it in the first place, I failed to ask. It was probably best that I did not know. Farrah, Crystal, and I laughed until we had to flee to the fresh air outside. The three of us, poolside, gasping, laughing, and clutching our bellies in the joy we had found in yellow caution tape.

Tammy, one of the dog owners, did not appreciate our humor when she returned home an hour later. Another hour for the putrid poop to turn the entire house into a foul toilet. She ripped the tape off, then she ripped each of us new assholes. "Why didn't you just pick up the shit?" she yelled at each of us as she crammed the yellow tape into the overflowing trashcan. The shit should have been the first to go in the trash.

"It's not our job to pick up your dog's shit!" Farrah screamed back before slamming her bedroom door.

Smiling to myself and holding in my outburst, I quietly disappeared into my room. Smiling smugly may have sent Tammy's head spinning. My head was already spinning from laughing and breathing in the toxic turd fumes. I lay on the twin bed that faced the garden-themed mural on my bedroom wall, the main reason I was drawn to the room. A faded fairytale scene, just for me. Choosing the smaller room with a washer and dryer in it also meant not competing for one of the larger rooms with an adjoining bathroom. I wasn't up for that competition, with those women. Just after moving in, I was already enjoying my garden escape while they squabbled.

The small alarm clock on my milk-crate bedside table told me we had two more hours until we were needed for the night shift. "We" included everyone under that roof. *Maybe it wasn't such a good idea to live and work together.* I didn't have enough time to venture out of the house. I couldn't just lie on my bed and pine for a painted garden to grow. I rummaged through my small stack of books and found one to reread. I read ten pages, then I drifted off to sleep.

"Jade, we're leaving. Do you want to ride with me?" Farrah called from outside my door. "Jade! I'm leaving," she yelled again, banging on my door. I heard her words, but I was lost in a dream. I was resting in a garden, surrounded by large sunflowers, their golden faces lifted toward the sun. I felt the warmth on my skin. I did not want to leave. "Jade! Are you okay?" she asked, now approaching my bed. *Third time was a charm.* Her not-so-gentle push of my arm interrupted my sleep and yanked me from my sunflower dream. "It's time to go to work. Let's go!" she ordered, as she turned to leave. I had a House Mom at work and at home.

Disoriented and weak, I lifted my sleepy head, and fought to lift the rest of my body, including my desire to join the living and breathing. My left leg was numb, my brain was dizzy, and my back was sore, but the show must go on. I stumbled toward the door, where my dancer bag had been dropped the night before. Like a stray puppy following a new owner, I followed Farrah's path down the dark carpeted hallway, where the stench of brick-sized dog shit had become trapped. A smell that slapped my face and burned my tired eyes. I held my breath, nearly collapsing by the time I reached the safety of the polluted outdoors, before plopping myself into the shotgun side of Farrah's yellow sportscar.

My yellow chariot was being driven by a woman who was loud, yellow-haired and well-endowed. Not exactly how I imagined my Cinderella dream, and my chariot driver was escorting me toward dozens of less-than-princes who were not-so-charming. Maybe one of them would offer me dinner, or at least a snack, because my oversleeping had caused me to miss a meal. A toothbrush and combed hair would have been luxury items, and I wasn't sure until I smelled myself, but deodorant was needed, too. Fortunately, I had everything I needed in my dancer bag, and if not there, I would find it in my black trunk, locked and tucked under the long shelf that served as a flat surface for makeup, hairspray, sweaty foreheads, dry elbows, and for the bold who risked the wrath of our House Mom if caught, a place to snort lines.

I was officially living on the West Side with four other dancers, drowning in high heels, sequins, and estrogen, and making more money. I was unofficially doing drugs and losing sight of the reasons that had brought me there.

Chapter 32

traveling dancers

Desert Rose Cabaret had become my new dancing home, but it wasn't the only strip joint in the state. I found a change of scenery in other clubs as a traveling dancer. I also found other customers, but their beer-bloated faces all looked the same to me. The venue change was never the change I needed most: a vacation by the shore. When the hours became too long, my heels too tall, the room too small, and the smoke and the stench of beer-drinking men too thick, I dreamed of the ocean—a soothing and peaceful scene, if only in my dreams. A salty smell entirely different from the men's sweaty skin. Strip clubs flowed with music and testosterone, keeping everyone humming one octave above a mindless drone. During moments that threatened to turn me into a brainless, barely dressed doll, I learned to dive into the deep of myself. Sometimes crashing, sometimes calm, the ocean, buried within, was my escape when the walls were closing in. My beating heart slowed to match the pace of the waves, lapping. I reminded myself to breathe. *This too shall pass. This too shall fade away.*

With my bank account at almost seven thousand dollars, and growing every Friday when I deposited more, I did not throw caution or dollars to the wind, nor did I grab a friend and drive to the shore. I found a sidekick who agreed to travel to other Arizona topless clubs with me, and with our absence approved by Omar, Sabrina and I ventured to a club in Tucson the second weekend of June. We had to make the two-hour drive down south and dance a shift. In turn, the club owner let us stay in his apartment, reserved for traveling dancers. We were searching for more.

My appetite for drugs was also growing. What started as a horrible violation forced into my mouth had morphed from occasional lines to more frequent thoughts of leaving reality in a way that only drugs could deliver. I only got high when others offered me a ride on the white powder train—I never spent my own money or searched for it. *I was just being social*. I told myself that it gave me and my purse a little lift. After all, it was hard working the night shift.

Getting harder with each powdery dip. Nothing like the virgin snow I loved to ski on as a kid. This snow was tainted. This powder did not send my spirit soaring high like snow skiing did. This snow shot me to the moon, then dropped me hard to my knees. A crash landing every time. Each time praying a little harder for my pulsing heart to find its natural rhythm, for my mind to find its original mold, and for the crawling on my skin to end. Prayers were easier to say than the truth. I was in control, I told myself. I told myself that the final weeks of being a teenager were the perfect time to live wild and carefree. When doubt of that decision crept in, cocaine's persuasive power told me everything would be fine.

Sabrina and I could have passed for sisters, or at least cousins. She was taller, tanner, and more talkative, and her hair was a shade darker, depending on the week, and saving for college was the last thing on her mind. She was saving to move away from the desert. Somewhere along the East Coast was her dream. She could not tell me where, specifically, other than "somewhere far away from here." I told her she should pick a place and focus on being there—really see herself there. She just laughed at me, then she told me she wanted to go and explore, let the wind carry her to the place she was meant to be. She wanted to meet a guy, fall in love, have a family, then live happily ever after. I laughed at her. That path was the last thing on my ambitious mind. I told her I would visit her and her family after I graduated from college. We both laughed. Sometimes we even laughed all the way to the bank.

Traveling to Tucson gave us a change of scenery and the money was decent, but we decided to try again, this time north of the valley, in Flagstaff. We chose this dance destination because I learned, after making a quick call to the club, that it was a popular spot for the professional football players who were in town for training camp, just down the road. The smaller club did not have the apartment perk, but we could stay in a nearby youth hostel for only ten dollars a night. We could afford that rate, and we would blend in with the traveling hippies. We were used to sharing a dressing room with dozens of divas, so sharing a bathroom with a few strangers was easy. We were also used to sharing our bare skin, so it would not bother us if a stranger walked in.

After making the two-hour drive from Phoenix to Flagstaff during the second Friday of July, Sabrina and I left my car parked at the hostel and walked the two blocks to the club.

Wearing shorts, tank tops, and backpacks, we looked like every other young woman in this college town. From the exterior, anyway. If one were to search through our bags, they would find items not found in a typical book bag: heels, pasties and pasty glue, tiny costumes adorned with sequins, and a tiny baggie filled with white powder. A tiny baggie with white powder might be the only common item found between our bags and the college crowd's. For two blocks, the walking distance from the youth hostile to the topless club, we could just blend. Just be. For a moment, we weren't "dancers," and we weren't walking toward higher education or a dream life along the East Coast; we were just enjoying some normalcy found along a sunny sidewalk.

Because we had time, we stopped in a few antique shops. We were just looking and having fun. Neither of us had the living space or cash flow for trinkets or vintage clothes. Sabrina took a photo of me next to a cardboard cutout of Marilyn Monroe. She laughed at me when I tried to pose like Marilyn. We weren't splashing in the ocean, but we were laughing and forgetting that we would soon be taking our clothes off for professional football players.

Stepping into the Northern Arizona club was a contrast to entering the one we had left behind in Phoenix. This club had only one square stage along the center of the back wall. It was raised about eight inches from the ground, and it did not have a pole in the center. No stairs to climb or to descend, hands-first, while in a backbend. I felt a mixture of relief and dread. How could I entertain customers for an entire song, without props to spin and lean on? The walls were devoid of neon and floor-to-ceiling mirrors. How could I entertain for an entire song while having to stare only at them?

The small square room felt closed-in with walls painted black. Four-tops with banquet-style chairs, pushed in tightly, filled most of the floor. *I wondered how we'd be able to dance in such cramped quarters.* There was one waitress, who ran herself harder than any dancer, serving every man in the joint. Not with a fake smile like dancer chick's. She did not have to smile. The customers weren't there to see her smile or to see her breasts. Well, maybe they were, but with the cocktail waitress it would require more imagination. Too much thinking for some men, it seemed. If their beer was icy and she kept them coming, her tips were guaranteed. Unlike our tips or expectations. We were expected to serve it up hot. If we met those expectations, we were rewarded. *Most of the time.*

Except for a few locals, the men had muscles that puffed out of their expensive and professionally pressed shirts. They smelled of the finest cologne and they held one-hundred-dollar bills in the air, waving them occasionally. What did the hold and wave mean? A table dance? More? Rushing past the lifted crisp bills, we darted into the dressing room. We were told to be on time, and we almost weren't. Quickly changing out of our street clothes and into our dancer costumes, we were soon breezing in and around the waving wads. Their crisp bills, not bulging parts of them. Those bulges were evident too, but those were zipped up. Our make-me-go-go drugs stayed zipped up too.

The men were intimidating. An awkward first date would be an understatement. With shaking knees, I asked a player seated at a corner-of-the-room table if he wanted a table dance. He looked me up and down while I looked down and noticed three fanned one-hundreds on the table.

"Sure, show me what you got," he said coolly.

This was a whole new level of callous confidence. My entire body could have squeezed into one of his thundering thighs. It would have been a tight fit, like the shirt he was wearing, but with my flexibility, I could have done it. Any muscles I had acquired dancing for over six months were lost in his bulging shadow. I smiled nervously and asked him his name.

"It's not important," he said. "The only thing that matters is your sexy body and if you turn me on."

I swallowed behind my shocked expression and frozen eyes. This player was not there to charm. He was there to satisfy his lust and to show off his athletic earnings and muscles. The song "Push It" began playing and I began dancing…

My petite pale body was "pushing it" in every direction in front of his dark, bulging frame. We became Salt-N-Pepa, he and I. He must have liked the show because he kept me busy until I was called to the stage, almost thirty minutes after I started pushing it. When I left the stage, I noticed he had already moved on to another dancer. That was fine by me; he had lined my purse with one of his fresh hundreds. I did not want to get too cozy with any of these men. Best to keep circulating, I thought.

When the DJ announced, "Last call for alcohol," at twelve forty-five, I could not believe it. The night had been a whirlwind of table dancing and stage sets. The stage was not a lucrative business in the club. Also fine by me. I would rather have a purse full of crisp hundreds than a wad of dirty ones. For being in a small club, I barely caught eyes with my friend, Sabrina, the entire night. The "cousins" were a hit. She and I and every other dancer in the tiny club—fewer than ten of us. Odds were on our side that night.

Choosing to dance for professional football players was a lucrative business decision. After tipping the bartender, doorman, DJ, and waitress, Sabrina and I still had over five hundred dollars. Some of the football players' coolness must have rubbed off on us while we were rubbing on them, but beneath our sweaty skin, we were little girls dancing and skipping. I didn't know what the men were hiding under their skin, but after a night of staring into their intense eyes, I would guess it to be lust and unbridled sin. I buried those thoughts along with my smile and my tempered excitement. Drunk on a night of abundant tips and pleased by our well-planned trip, we stepped into the dark and quiet of the night.

"Look," Sabrina said, pointing toward the sky. "The stars are so bright and beautiful tonight!" I stopped and looked in the direction her hand was pointing.

"Wow," I said softly, with reverence. Like being in church, the moment called for a whisper. "I can't remember the last time I looked up at the stars." No sooner had those words left my lips when an emerald sky flooded my memory, and warm thoughts of Sean's embrace warmed my body. I felt dizzy. The love I had felt standing next to him washed over me, too, only I no longer felt safe. I felt abandoned. I wanted to leave my body. I wanted to fly from the stained sidewalk in front of a strip club, and soar among the stars, never to be seen again. Maybe there, I could find Sean. I closed my eyes and tried to hurl thoughts of him into the deep, vast sky, but my efforts were useless. Images of him flashed through my mind: our last dinner together; the white candles flickering next to the virgin snow; his strong body on top of mine; our last kiss next to my dorm-style digs. Memories flooding my mind and taking all my remaining strength. Memories that streamed down my cheeks, each drop representing a moment with Sean.

Drop, drop, drop, on the sidewalk, they did plop. Walking away from the club with five hundred extra dollars in my purse felt great and gave me a sense of security, but the cash could not hold me or make me feel safe, like Sean's arms had.

"Are you okay?" Sabrina asked in a concerned tone, a first from her. Genuine concern for her friend who had never cried in front of her or expressed weakness or vulnerability.

"Yeah, I'm alright, just remembering a boy," I admitted.

"Oh, I understand. Boys are dumb," she laughed. I laughed with her. I was still crying but laughing too. For the next two blocks, we made our way toward two twin beds reserved for us, while I wiped my tears with hands that smelled like dollar bills lightly scented with the finest cologne.

After our flush night we could easily afford those ten-dollar twin beds. We would probably be the wealthiest people sleeping in the youth hostel on that night. That information would stay zipped tight. Our busy night left no time for doing a line in the dressing room. We were tempted to open the tiny zipped-up bag while walking down an alley on the way back to the youth hostel; then we decided to save it for the next day. Not because we were responsible—the night's adrenaline was wearing off and the need for sleep was settling in. I washed my tired body in the lukewarm water in a humid bathroom, dimly lit. Sabrina did the same, in the shower stall next to me. My purse was hanging on the hook inside. I wasn't about to let my hard-earned cash walk away while I was washing away the night. The entire night—the men, the sweat, the stares, and thoughts of Sean. I tried.

Sabrina and I did not say a word to each other in the bathroom. We just smiled at each other in between brushing our teeth and hair. Smiles, flushed cheeks, and eye sparkles that reflected a five-hundred-dollar night, and a look from her that acknowledged the heart pain I was hiding under my glistening skin. With my purse tucked under my pillow, I fell into a deep sleep on the crinkly twin bed. I experienced the kind of magical falling that comes when the mind feels secure enough to let go of every worrisome thought. My mind was releasing, and my body was falling deeper into the nothingness, where bills, college degrees, bulging biceps, bitchy roommates, and white lines in the dressing room did not exist. Letting go that comes less often than a full moon and the closest substitute to the letting go that came with a real escape, oceanside. The drive to the shore was too far and the need for cash and drugs was more pressing.

Chapter 33
football camp

After our profitable evening, Sabrina and I wanted to spend one more night in the college town. A quaint place filled with stars in the sky and professional football stars with raw lust in their eyes. We wanted to stay, but we had to drive down the mountain back to our dancing home. We had promised Omar we would return for the Saturday night shift. The small northern club, a few blocks down the road from our twin mattresses, held the promise of another rich night, but the club back home was the long-term bet. The players were in town for only a few weeks before they would need to make their own drive down the mountain to prepare for the start of the season. No doubt, their lodging and travel accommodations were vastly different from ours.

Any dreams we had of moving up north and sucking on their puffed pecs and bloated wallets were pointless. At least we had tasted a sample of the riches, unlike missing out on the money that flowed for the Alaskan dancers during the heyday of the pipeline. Those cash-rich days were legends that I had only heard about—whether I wanted to or not. Stories that were probably exaggerated with each passing year as the men from that era became more nostalgic for "the good ol' days" and wanted to impress young women with their affiliation with anything successful. It did not work. It only frustrated young dancers like me, who felt like our time dancing in Alaska was a letdown compared to how it could have been. "What could have been" was not included—nor needed—in the fine print.

Reluctant to leave the town that had boosted our earnings for the week, we tossed our bags in the trunk of my car, locked it, then ventured out in search of breakfast. Lunch for most everyone else. We found a diner that would fill us up without expecting too much in return, and where our tired faces and tousled hair would be overlooked. Sabrina and I talked about our night, whispering to each other about the players and how they had waved their money around and how neither of us were sure what that meant.

"Maybe next time we should ask," Sabrina asserted. I laughed at her. She might have the courage to ask, but I did not.

"Yeah, sure. Go ahead and ask," I told her. "Do you want to come back before they leave? We should be able to get away one more time before training camp ends."

"We should go by there!" Sabrina shrieked. "A couple of the players invited me. They sign autographs and talk to fans."

"Let's do it!" I exclaimed, unsure of where my enthusiasm or desire came from.

We rushed through the rest of our breakfast—a hamburger, fries, and a soda. The most filling option for the least amount of money. Dancers burn calories, and we were starving. We paid the waitress, leaving her a generous tip, then we hustled to the bathroom to freshen up. We did the best we could, but our hair and lack of makeup bore no resemblance to the women we were the night before. Nighttime and neon lights can create an illusion that cannot be duplicated in the bright light of the day, especially in a cheap diner. We laughed at our attempts to look sexy, then we ran out of there, like two high school girls late for class. Away from gawking customers, we ran to my car. Slightly out of breath, more from laughing than running, we made our way to the football field.

My nerves caused me to almost trip over a concrete block in the parking lot. If not for my dancer's grace, into the gravel I would have fallen on my face. Sabrina and I had a good laugh then we walked toward the field that contained players and cameras. Seeing a few reporters and their cameramen sent my nerves into overdrive. I did not want to appear on T.V. *Not here, not anywhere!* We arrived during a time when the players were lined up to greet fans and sign autographs. Sabrina and I talked about hanging back and watching the players from behind, but we decided to be bold and join the line of fans. We were fans too, for reasons beyond football. Green reasons. Other than our breasts, that were now covered, we had nothing for the players to sign. We would not be taking our tops off in that scene. We found a table to the left of the players that had merchandise for sale, including team photos. We each bought one. We agreed it was the least we could do after a night of generous tips. Every dollar earned from our blood, sweat, and few encore tears, under the stars after the dancing ended.

With our glossy prints in hand, we inched our way toward the long line of muscular men. Wearing tight uniforms instead of tight shirts and writing with pens instead of waving crisp bills, they also looked different in the light of day. As we got closer to the line of men, I began searching faces, looking for any that looked familiar. My heart began racing. From stress, not drugs— those we had yet to touch. Our little stash was in Sabrina's bag. I couldn't see it, but I had not stopped thinking about it. I was craving the euphoric high that followed the inhale and burn. The high that accompanied the racing heart and spiraling mind was worth it.

I was still in the honeymoon phase.

It was almost our turn to get an autograph. *Thump thump thump*…faster and louder my heart beat with each step. My hands began shaking. Good thing I would not be the one signing autographs. We paused in front of each player, said hello, and thank you, looked closely at each face, then watched for a reaction when they looked at ours. Nothing happened until we nearly reached the end. There, in front of me, with a table now between us, sat the first man I had danced for. My nerves sent a radioactive blast through my body and seized my voice. The source of my nerves was not infatuation or lust. Nothing like that. My shaking was the result of embarrassment and shame. I suddenly regretted being there. *What the hell are we doing this for?* I thought, regretting our decision. We could have been halfway home, but the only way to get there was to finish the business at hand and drive on. The nameless player, whose bills were now nestled in my purse, resting on my hip, asked, "Who should I sign this to?"

"Jade," I said. My name was a trigger that froze his pen and face, except for his eyes, that looked up at mine.

"Well, well. Venturing out into the light of the day." His voice had lost its callous tone. His eyes and his voice were less intense. Almost playful. "Nice of you to show up here. Do you like football?" he asked.

"No, just the perks," I teased. He laughed and I saw what I had not seen the night before: a beautiful smile that calmed my nerves and made angels sing in the end zone. He signed my photo and handed it back to me, holding onto it a second longer than necessary. The man who had been insensitive and assertive was now flirting with me. I smiled back—a real smile this time. I took the photo from him, then moved on to the next player. I didn't care about more signatures but leaving the line felt rude, so I stayed, filling up my glossy print with names I didn't recognize. Reaching the end of the line meant I was free to politely leave. The only player I did "know" kept looking in my direction with each autograph exchange, stealing glances in my direction as he greeted other fans, even twisting his neck to watch me walk toward the parking lot. I couldn't flee fast enough. He was not my Prince Charming, and this was not a romantic comedy scene, unless I tripped in the parking lot this time.

Once safely in the confines of my car, Sabrina and I burst out laughing and spent the next ten minutes laughing our asses off. Then I noticed what I had not noticed at the signing table. My knight in shining one-hundreds had written his phone number on the back of the photo. I showed Sabrina, and our laughter turned into hysterics after she told me he and I would probably get married, and I would become a professional football player's wife. I laughed at the thought of it.

"Stop!" I told her. "I am going to pee my pants! We have to get out of here and find a bathroom." We did, laughing the entire time as I drove in search of the nearest toilet. We found a convenience store with gas pumps. Perfect! We emptied our bladders and filled up my gas tank, then made our way down the mountain toward Phoenix. Not exactly a vacation to the shore, but we had made some cash and laughed our asses off.

Chapter 34

the show must go on

Sabrina and I had just enough time to take a proper private shower and get dressed before rushing out of her apartment toward our everyday reality—another shift back home. A dysfunctional, loud, and obnoxious home with not one alcoholic father, but dozens. A home void of puffed muscles and crisp bills waving in the testosterone-infused wind, but with plenty of puffed egos blowing in the stale air. Our bare-skinned concrete reality deflated my motivation. I wanted to plop on Sabrina's secondhand couch and lose myself in a show—a romantic comedy would be perfect, as long as the leading male character was *not* a football player. Doubtful I would stumble across one with the leading female role as a topless dancer. There is nothing romantic or comedic about that, in the eyes of most, anyway.

Romance was rarely witnessed under the hissing neon bar lights, but I saw comedy everywhere. Those thoughts I kept to myself. Sarcastic and sometimes dark thoughts that helped me get through a shift. Thoughts I could not control. I just wanted to watch a show, not put on a show. What I really wanted, I contemplated while Sabrina finished in the bathroom, was to lose myself in studies, to earn a college degree, and create a better life. In that order. Not to become the ringleader of a traveling titty-flashing show. A circus complete with a peanut gallery, salivating animals, and a spinning brass trapeze. My wants felt like a luxurious dream that was not meant for people like me. Those dreams belonged to the ones who slept soundly at night because they knew their rent checks would not bounce.

Wants and dreams that had become buried under my needs, my daily cash pursuits. One dirty dollar at a time, released from calloused and sticky beer fingers, had covered the private place in my being where goals lie dormant, just waiting for their chance to grow. It felt like a place in my soul void of nutrients, suffocating any possible chance for fragile dreams to push through. Try as I might, I could not scoop up and shove the tainted bills into my purse fast enough. My purse and I were fraying at the seams. Even in my dreams, singles rained down on me. Sometimes the dollar bills covered my face with their dirty scent, waking me from sleep and stealing my breath.

The once-upon-a-time light needed to cultivate dreams was being covered by a powdery substance that made me feel grand. Temporarily, its false promises shone brighter than the sun, before darkness closed in—around everything, it did descend. Getting caught up in the lure of quick cash and the routine of skin flash, I was losing sight of what that "better life" might look like. The hedonistic world I had fallen into was destroying my quiet, studious nature. I wanted to find a quiet library corner to push myself into, escaping from the noise surrounding me. Instead, I was backing myself into a corner, pushed, pulled, and prodded along by a world that was closing in.

"Run now," a voice broke in. "Run away from here. You are better than this," the voice scolded. "You are not this girl," the voice screamed. "Use your brain, not your boobs." The voice brought shame.

The voice of the man on the infomercial playing on Sabrina's television had been droning along in the background of my mind chatter. I heard him speak, as I watched a tiny bird pick at the frayed chair on Sabrina's balcony. His hard sell twisted and turned toward me: "Get out while you can! And if you act fast," he declared, "I will throw in a blanket for you to sleep on when you are living on skid row along with the other could have, should have, has-beens."

"Are you ready?" Sabrina asked, standing next to the couch with wet hair and her bag in her hand. How long she had been standing there, I did not know. "Are you ok?"

"Yeah, I'm fine. Let's go," I replied without looking at her. I turned off the amped salesman on the television and tried to squelch the voices in my head while grabbing my bag and walking out her apartment door toward another night of the flashy show—plenty of flesh with little soul. Suddenly, a blanket along skid row sounded more appealing. Under the blanket, I could hide. "The show must go on," I said to Sabrina in a tone that did not reveal if we should stay or go.

With a few minutes to spare, we each snorted a chalky little line drawn on Sabrina's cloudy makeup mirror before getting out of my car. Instant gratification obtained. Sparks shot to my brain. I was transformed from the nerdy girl who wanted to hide in the library, reading and studying, to the sexy one who wanted to twirl and spin, and who wanted to forget about *everything*. Snorting and crossing lines became my new vocation. We were parked far away from Doug's observant eyes. Eyes that showed genuine compassion. I could disappoint myself, but I did not want to disappoint him. He will thank me eight hours from now when I hand him a generous tip, none the wiser to my preshow slip, I thought. Slipping further, I was, into a dead-end abyss.

That inevitable dead end and dancing and doing drugs was farther down the road, too far to see in my current reality. Higher than the lone hawk that circled above, I tried to hide in Sabrina's shadow as we walked into the building. I was careful not to look directly into the eyes of our gatekeeper. Looking away told him all he needed to know. He had seen it all before. He would not be surprised but he would be concerned. With my pupils and confidence growing, there was no stopping me; I would own the joint. Fire would fly from my stilettos. I would glow in the skin show.

Two hot wires, ready to singe anyone who got too close, Sabrina and I raced to the dressing room to change our clothes. Omar kept polishing and watched us race by. He didn't say a word to us. He just watched and smiled with a grin that said so much. Where Doug was the protector, Omar was the jester, not worrying too much about the shenanigans that took place under this two-bit circus top. He just watched and laughed—aloud, and with his eyes. Nothing was to be taken too seriously by him, unless you were a no-show, then we saw the fury within. Two extremes for the laughing bartender. Only one for the steadfast protector standing outside.

We grabbed the two dressing spots left near the less-than-desirable start of the row. Like sitting next to the teacher, dressing too close to the door meant you could not hide a thing from the House Mom, who popped in frequently to keep us all moving and to keep us all in line. I did not care. I had nothing to hide; our indiscretions took place outside. We took care of our appetites before stepping into the lionesses' den and under the hissing lights. I tore off my blouse and jeans, like they were on fire. Instantly, my bare skin grew sensitive to the floating scents and chill in the room. I slipped into a fire engine red dress that barely covered my tanned and tight dancer behind.

Underneath the fire that also spilled my cleavage, I wore a tiny black G-string and matching black triangle top. A fiery combination that would surely cause some heads to turn and hopefully turn a few men into believers. *Now that you have seen the light, open your wallets and give, give, give. Show me the money! Give till the giving becomes a sacrifice!*

"Hey, Jade," I heard a distant voice say. I turned and scanned the line of bare curves and tits, and tiny threads, all supported, or ready to topple, on tall stilettos.

"Cat! Where have you been?" I blurted out.

"Where have I been? Where have you been?" she inquired.

"Oh, we just got back from Flagstaff. We danced in a club up there," I responded, as she walked toward me, fully dressed and ready to go. Cat was the always prompt responsible adult in the room.

"How did that go?" Cat wondered, in a tone that was a mixture of interest and doubt.

"Really well," I admitted. That was as much as I would say. I was not about to reveal my extra earnings to a room full of pretending-not-to-listen ears that leaned in close while faces never looked away from makeup application. My gloating about one night's earnings might turn this place into a caravan of dancers traveling to the northern lights—not the beautiful Alaskan kind that sparkle in the sky while a sweet muscular young man holds your hand, but the kind that glimmer with gold chains and false promises. A long line of tasseled titties would march out of this place and become a traveling circus headed "up north." No, my personal Fort Knox would remain heavily guarded in the interior of my mind while dressing in a room of women who hid very little. Cat's wink told me she understood. Her maturity was my stability. Her prolonged gaze into my dilated pupils also told me she knew what had happened in the parking lot. She kept looking, causing me to look away. I might feel invincible, but she won that staring game.

She gave me a hug and whispered, "Be careful." The tone of her voice interrupted my high-flying party and my carefree attitude. *Damn her! Let me soar a little longer.* Next month I'll turn twenty. Then, like a responsible adult, I will stop this nonsense. As long as I don't fly too close to the sun, I will be fine. *That's what I told myself.*

"I will," I promised. Always the first to the floor, she left, but her words lingered. I tried to shake them off as I applied lipstick—a red that matched my fire within. I did not resent Cat's warning. I appreciated her concern. Even if I was not ready to receive it. The final fashion touch—I slipped into new black heels, a little taller than the pair I began my dancing career with. I was soaring.

Chapter 35
locked and unloaded

I counted my money in the car while Farrah drove us home from the club. I should have counted my blessings, too, while I still had the presence to do so.

My cocaine high that began the night had morphed into a full-fledged frenzy after doing another line in the dressing room sometime around midnight, away from watchful motherly eyes. I tried to say no to the tempting platinum devil wearing neon pink, with lips and fingernails a matching tint. A Barbie doll, offering me another rung on a descending staircase that was headed toward addiction. I tried to pivot and run toward the dressing room door, *just one line before work, not a single more, just one line before work, not a single more*...a chant that danced across my brain. Like my flirty curves that swayed and lured during a table dance, neither my best intentions nor their desires would be obtained. My promise to self and the lap owner's wishes of reaching enlightenment with the help of a dancing girl, would go unfulfilled. We were caught in a dance of empty promises. My heels remained planted, and my eyes remained fixed on another quick fix that would transform my wilting petals into a fake bouquet—the kind held by a drive-thru bride on the Vegas Strip. If anyone looked closely, they would notice I was fading plastic, not nature's magic.

I inhaled pink Barbie's temptations; I breathed them in without hesitation. Thoughts about consequences, I did not give. The trip from my left nostril to my ignited brain was a quick one. The ride was short, but the view was euphoric. Euphoria, the name of the rocket ship that would take me on an earth-bending ride before exploding into smithereens, scattering the bending horizon with my broken dreams. Barbie wiped off her mirror, tossed it in her bag, then looked at her pink plastic watch.

"It's just after midnight," pink Barbie said.

Plenty of time to dance off the electricity flowing through me before last call and before the DJ played that final KISS song—the one that made the men lament and made the girls sing "Hallelujah" as they offered sweet praises to Jesus for delivering them to this final stage. Gene sang the words, and we all danced along, giving the last of what we had left to give. I can't say the same for most of the men, who kept their wallets closed while we were corralled and exposed.

The song lingered in my buzzing body while I finished counting my ones, a third time. Hard to count dollars when you're trying to hold on tight to a rocket ship soaring high. The air is a little thin up there. Farrah's singing did not help my hopeless counting. My routine of counting discreetly at work went by the wayside at the end of my shift. I was too busy spewing dime-store philosophy to a new dancer about the life of a dancer. *What the hell did I know, less than a year in?* Someone needed to show her the ropes—or the poles. With my ride about to leave, I told the new girl I needed to go, then I gave our support staff decent tips, regardless of what my final dollar count was.

"Shhhhh, I am trying to count," I told Farrah, as calmly as I could.

"Fuck off!" was her response. "Let the teller at the bank count your dirty ones." We both started laughing. I counted my stack a fourth time.

"Three hundred and thirty-two dollars." I was prouder of my ability to count my cash pile than I was of the grit it took to earn it. More sweat had been pouring, as my internal churnings reshaped white powder to perspiration, covering my body in tiny clear beads that popped out of me with each twirl, spin, and eat-shit grin. "That's a good night, Jade," Farrah said as she raced through a yellow light, "I made barely half that." I wasn't sure what to say, so I just smiled at her before tucking my folded stash into my purse. My nightly earnings had been on the rise over the last few weeks, as I was gaining more regulars and keeping my body fueled with the energy to keep up with their demands, and the demands I placed on myself. Back bends down the stairs and more twirls in the air, more smiles, and more spins—a performing artist consuming more, more, more. I was losing more too.

As we approached the house, Farrah let her discontent spew from her lips. "Motherfuckers! There is nowhere to park! Annoying bitches!" The roommate honeymoon was over and done. I was, too. I just wanted to stash my cash under the mattress and go to sleep. We carried our bags and our tired selves down the sidewalk, lit by a flickering streetlight periodically popping with the sound of fried insects. We walked past six houses, making dogs bark when we clicked and stomped past each locked fence. *Beware of the Dog,* the hanging signs read. Farrah's cussing matched the rhythm of each step. Her animated anger made me laugh. I couldn't help myself. I was laughing so hard, I thought I might pee my pants—or my skirt. I wasn't sure which would be worse.

"Stop making me laugh," I pleaded with her. "I'm going to pee."

"You should wait until we get inside, then pee on the carpet, next to one of these annoying bitches," Farrah sneered. "Or better yet, pee on their leg."

"Stop! I really am going to pee my pants!" That was it. This was no longer a laughing matter. I began to sprint toward our front door, needing desperately to slip in and race to the bathroom. That would not happen. Two guys I had never seen before were standing near the front door, smoking cigarettes, and watching me run toward them. They showed little concern, and except for their inhaling, exhaling, and flicking, they did not move. I tried to avoid their eye contact, but I could not help but notice their eyes were scanning my body. No doubt trying to decide if I was one of "those dancer chicks" who lived inside. I did not say a word when I rushed past them. Even if my full bladder wasn't about to burst and flood their scattered ashes, I still would not have said a word. They made my skin crawl, which made holding my bladder that much harder.

"Jade!" a multitude of shouts were made from the hazy living room. There would be no slipping in or escaping from the smoke that seemed to have a permanent presence in my life. "Join us, Jade!" The party chorus sang. I said nothing. Just a blur, racing to the bathroom. *Yes, yes, yes, I was almost there. I could end this barely contained nightmare.* Or not. The bathroom was locked. *Fuck! That's it, I am moving out and living on my own.* I ran down the hall toward a bathroom in Farrah's bedroom—the bedroom I *could have* fought for if I had had that desire in me. I flung my bag on her bed, then clutched the knob like my life depended on it.

Fuck! I pounded on the locked door to let whoever was on the other side know there was a line forming. If I wasn't trying to avoid pissing all over Farrah's carpeted floor, I would have said a little prayer for them, too. As angry as she already was, I hoped, for their sake, they had permission from Jesus himself to be in her bathroom.

"Hold on!" the unfamiliar voice said. *Oh, this is going to get interesting.* My pee dance was morphing into a disturbing seizure when Farrah blew into her room. Her face and spilling chest were just as red as her candy apple miniskirt.

"Someone's in your bathroom," I warned. "Bad news for both of us." That was all she needed to hear. She began pounding on the door, telling whoever was in there to get the fuck out. "Now!" Whoever was on the other side took their time then the knob finally turned, and two girls stepped out. A few minutes that felt like an eternity to my stretched and screaming bladder.

"Who the fuck are you? Why are you in my room?" Farrah yelled at them. Her explosive personality and her body, with exaggerated curves, took up space. She owned every inch of it, too. The girls did not respond. They looked at her and burst into laughter. Farrah's face was inflamed, and her hair seemed to be charged with electricity. The kind that shoots violently out of monsoon storms. I wanted to pull up a chair and watch the unfolding scene, but I needed to pee! I pushed through the bathroom door, stepped over Farrah's tossed clothes, lifted my skirt, then pulled down my G-string. Relief finally came. I did not bother closing or locking the door behind me. I would have peed in front of an audience at that point. I also did not want to miss what was about to go down.

Amazed by the river flowing out of me, I heard Farrah slam her bedroom door then tell the girls to dump their purses on the bed. "You aren't leaving here with a single thing that belongs to me!" Her fury had taken on an impressive energy.

"You can't make us do that, crazy bitch!" I heard a squeaky voice say.

"Watch me, crazy little cokeheads! I am twice your size and what I can't handle, my gun will," Farrah exclaimed, in a controlled fierce tone that sent shivers down my spine. The giggles stopped. I pulled up my thong, lowered my skirt, then watched from the door. There stood Farrah with a pistol in her hand, pointed at the two girls, who were suddenly very accommodating to Farrah's demands. Out tumbled their stuffed purses, all over Farrah's new cream-colored silk comforter. *God, please don't let blood spill on her bed.* Standing firm in front of the door, with steady hands on her pistol, she asked them to spread out their shit. She scanned everything. "Hand me my lipstick, ring, and birth control pills. Now!" she demanded. The taller of the two did as she was told. Farrah took one more look at the purse piles, then told them to turn their pockets out. They did. Their pockets were empty. Farrah's breathing was calmer, but she was hesitating. *Oh God Farrah, what are you doing?* Making the two strangers suffer a little longer, it seemed. They were shaking. "Pick up your shit and don't ever step one foot in my bedroom again," she raged. They did as they were told, then they apologized to her. I kept watching from the bathroom doorway, praying this would end without bloodshed. "Leave your IDs on the bed, too," Farrah blurted out. They did. She lowered her gun, before stepping aside. "Unlock the door, and get the fuck out of my room," she snapped. "I will be your personal escort out of this house."

Farrah followed them down the hallway. I was a few steps behind. Once in the living room where our other roommates were laughing, smoking, drinking, and snorting, Farrah shouted, "Who belongs to these thieving bitches?" Emphasis *bitches*. Stoned faces froze and silence seized the room. "Who belongs to these thieving bitches?" she repeated.

"I think they came with the two guys out front," an unfamiliar voice said. Farrah was not about to retreat to her room without closing the door on this situation. Her fury was intense. She brushed past the trembling two and opened the front door where the two creepy guys still stood. "Are these yours?" Farrah sneered while pointing to the girls who had lost their laughs and their confidence.

"Yeah, what's it to you?" the greasier of the two muttered.

"What's it to me?" Their words became one thousand lit matches tossed on Farrah's red-hot coals. A fire exploded. "Your skanky girlfriends were in my bathroom stealing my shit. Take them and get the fuck out of here. Now!" Farrah stepped aside, letting the two pass, then she stood on the front steps until their car was out of sight. She wasn't done yet.

"Who the fuck invited those tweakers into our house and then let them into my *locked* bathroom?" No response. About twenty people in the room and not one said a word. Farrah waited then served up some memorable words, "If I ever see those bitches again, I will kill them. If anyone ever lets strangers in my room again, I will kill you, too!" Her words reverberated around the room while her body thundered down the long hallway. She slammed and locked her door. *No! My bag is in there.* Not wanting to disturb the beast breathing loudly inside, I knocked lightly.

"Hey, Samantha, it's me Jade," I said softly. "I left my bag on your bed." Without saying a word, she unlocked her bedroom door and handed me my bag. "Are you okay?" I asked. "You scared the shit out of me."

"My gun wasn't loaded. I just wanted to scare them. Guess I scared you, too," she responded in a tone I had never heard come out of her.

"Yeah, you did. It's not fucking funny. Don't ever do that again," I instructed without smiling. "Goodnight." I turned away from her and went to my garden room. I locked the door, shoved my purse under my mattress and fell on my twin bed. Too tired to wash my face or brush my teeth, I plunged into a haze of disturbed dreams.

Chapter 36
broken doll on blue carpet

The neon circus of my late night had morphed into the burning hell of the twilight. In my sleeping daze, there was no escaping the drug-fueled room that I had avoided the night before. During sleep, the twisted faces that Farrah had shocked into silence came alive in the dark corners of my mind. Smoke and evil laughing faces swirled around me. I tried to run from the room, but the stretched faces kept stopping me. They flew in, then vanished, only to repeat their taunts again and again.

I woke at noon. My body was drenched in sweat and my left arm had fallen asleep under the weight of my pounding head. My eyes were burning. My bladder was bursting. My legs weren't ready to stand. The second time in less than twenty-four hours that I had needed to pee, desperately. Only this time, the need to spring from my bed and rush down the hall felt less urgent than last night's sidewalk sprint. The lower half of my body was dangerously close to being soaked; a contrast to the Sahara that burned my throat. As I lay there, trying to ignore the impending flood, the previous night's memories washed over me. My overactive mind began to play the "what if" game. What if Farrah had shot someone? What if the thieving girls phoned the police? A dramatic scene would have followed, with at least one person sitting in a jail cell. I could not turn off these thoughts or calm my bladder. I had to get up from this twin bed that had room for only one. The effort was much greater than it needed to be for a nineteen-year-old. My spinning and back-bending profession was speeding up my aging.

I stumbled into the hallway toward the bathroom. I heard talking from the living room and from the silence that followed, they must have heard me say, "Damnit! Not again!" when I tried to turn the locked bathroom knob. No point in just standing there waiting for the knob to unlock itself. I walked around the corner to see what the silence was all about. I gasped when I saw what stared back at me. Four gray, strung-out faces, with dark shadows under glossy eyes, were fixated on me. Four terrifying tweakers left over from the night before. I could not tell if my own shaking was moving the strangers in front of me, or if they were shaking on their own. Maybe it was both. All I knew for certain was the sight of them sent shivers down my spine and made me taste bile.

"Do you know who's in the bathroom and how long they've been in there?" I asked the ashy shadows. The four shaky, gray people looked at each other, as if doing so would help them recall who had left. It seemed whoever might be in the bathroom wasn't noticed or missed. My request did not deliver Farrah's intensity from the night before. Maybe that was needed to get a response. "Let me ask you another, more important question," I said, each word adding frustration. "Who invited you?" More stares. These people probably could not have told me their own names, if I had asked.

On that silent note, I turned and stepped back toward the locked knob. This time I pounded on the door. No response. A pattern in this creepy place. I was ready to knock the knob off whoever was on the other side of this locked door. By the fifth pounding, I was becoming concerned about the silence coming from the other side and by my screaming bladder. I ran to my room and grabbed a bobby pin to pry open the locked door. A few failed attempts led to a successful click. One click was all I needed. I turned the knob and stepped in. My relief at seeing an unoccupied toilet was quickly replaced with horror. On the floor lay a crumpled body. My gasp fractured the sealed silence. I did not recognize the woman-child with her face buried under tangled blond hair. I would attend to her as soon as I took care of my own needs. It felt rude to pee in front of a stranger who was face down on the floor, but I didn't know what else to do.

After flushing the toilet, I bent down and searched for a pulse on the limp doll's wrist. I did not take the time to wash my hands. I figured my unwashed hands were the least of her concerns. I could not find her heartbeat. Panic escalated my own. My hands began to tremble. I rolled her over, swept her long blond hair from her doll face, gave her a gentle shake. Nothing. I leaned my left ear toward her mouth and listened for her breath. I listened and watched her chest, praying for a sign that this crumpled doll was alive. "Oh, please God," were the words I said aloud. Her chest did rise and fall, but it was slow. Much slower than mine. Too slow. I raced out of the bathroom and pounded on every bedroom door. All shut. The sleeping beauties were still sleeping.

"Wake up! There's a girl passed out in the bathroom!" I screamed and pounded. Light snoring and a fan blowing were the responses I heard. I gave it one more attempt before racing back down the hall to the kitchen where an avocado green phone was mounted to a wall. I called 911. I listened to the rings. *Come on, pick up!*

"911 operator. What is your emergency?" said the calm female voice. I needed that.

"There's a girl passed out in the bathroom; I need help. I don't know her or what she's on, but she's barely breathing, and she won't wake up." I was about to pass out after blurting out my words. *I just needed to pee, now I was dealing with this!*

"What is your address?" she asked.

"Oh, shit! Hold on." I sat the phone down and grabbed a bill from the pile of papers on the table. I barely knew my address during a calm moment;

trying to recall it during a life-and-death situation was impossible.

"4964 West Stella Lane, Glendale."

"OK, I'll dispatch a call for help. There's a fire station a few miles from you, so they should be arriving within a few minutes."

"Okay."

"Are you near the girl?"

"No, she's in the bathroom. I'm in the kitchen."

"All right, I'm going to stay on the line while you check on her."

"Okay." I sat the receiver down on the table, then screamed, "Get the fuck out!" as I ran past the weirdos in the living room. They flinched, but no one moved from the couch.

The nameless girl had not moved either. Neither had my roommates. Apparently, I was the only loser left to contend with a possible dead girl. *This is insane!* I checked for a pulse again, this time by putting two fingers against her neck. I did feel a beat, then another. The silent space in between the beats seemed stretched, I discovered this after checking my own neck artery which was about to burst all over the fucking bathroom. Hers was barely noticeable, but at least she had a pulse. I kept my two fingers on her neck while I watched for a breath. *Come on, rise chest. Come on!* Her little doll chest did rise, but the fragile doll was fading. I raced back to the phone, gave a report to the waiting dispatcher, who said help should be arriving shortly. She told me to stay with the girl and to administer CPR if needed.

"Do you know how to administer CPR?" she asked. I froze. I tried to recall learning it two years ago in high school, but that lesson was a blur. Like algebra, I did not think I would ever use it.

Noticing my hesitation, she began to give me instructions on how to save a life, should I need to in the next few minutes. "First, I want you to open the front door, so the paramedics can get in while you're helping her. Then I want you to—"

Ding-Dong!

"I think the paramedics are here," I told her. "Hold on, let me make sure." I ran to the door, unlocked it, then ushered the four-man crew down the hallway toward the barely conscious girl. One of the four muscular men in blue carried a stretcher. They were prepared professionals. I stood back and let them take care of her. I had nothing to offer them beyond, "I found her this way about twenty minutes ago," and "no, I do not know her name." There was no purse nearby to help with identification. It probably walked away with the thieving bitches. I did not forget about my helpful angel waiting on the other end of the phone. I sprinted to the kitchen and told the calm operator that the paramedics had arrived and that they were working on her now. "Thank you," were my last words to her.

"She's crashing," were the words I heard coming from the busy bathroom. I watched the nameless girl being rushed out of that house while one man thrust his hands inside her open shirt. I watched them load her into the ambulance and whirl away. I noticed a few neighbors were watching me watching them. I went back inside. There, the tweakers still sat and the ladies of the house still slept. I considered going back to sleep and forgetting about this horrible scene, but I was too amped to close my eyes, so I went into the empty bathroom, locked the door, and turned on the hot water. I sat on the toilet lid while I waited for the water to heat up. I stared at the imprint of the stranger's tiny body on the blue carpet while the small room filled with steam.

Chapter 37
rinsing off the stench

Standing under the hot water, I decided I was going to move out of this toxic, dog-shit smelling place and move into my own apartment. A studio apartment where I could have some peace. My own place, where I would not be bothered to go go go. Where I would not be tempted to snort snort snort. A place where I could lock the doors and keep out ghostly faces and thieving bitches. A place where I could kick off my heels and just be me. A place that did not smell of cat or dog shit. Once again, the raining shower gave me the strength to face my life—the one I was making a mess of. The life that was supposed to be a bridge to get me where I needed to be was dragging me down into the depths of despair and chaos. I needed a sanctuary to return to after each dance shift. I needed a dose of hope while walking this money-lined bridge. Moving forward was key. At the end of this bridge, presently too far to see, was my salvation: a college degree. If I let myself stand too long on this rickety bridge, I might be tempted to jump.

I pondered what my own apartment might look like. I became excited by the thought of it. It would be small, and it would cost more than my paper-garden bedroom, but I would have my own bathroom, and it would not have blue carpet with the imprint of a broken doll. I needed more time under the shower to ponder my life, but a knock on the bathroom door disturbed my planning dream-trance. I rinsed the conditioner out of my hair and turned off the hot water. *Sure, now they wake up.* "Just a minute," I yelled.

"I have to pee," was the response on the other side. A voice I did not recognize. Probably one of the shadow people on the couch. *They can wait or pee their pants.* I didn't care! Not enough to respond.

I took my time drying off my wet body, putting lotion and deodorant on, brushing my teeth, combing my hair…another knock. Without a word, I unlocked the door, then my towel-covered body walked past the ashy-faced pungent-smelling couch surfer. I held back unleashing all my frustrations on the pathetic person needing a toilet, not because I was empathetic to his right to take up space in this world, but because I was checking out of this place and officially not giving a fuck.

Back in the confines of my paper garden, I locked my door and fell onto my bed. The morning events, after a late night, left me spent. I fell into another deep sleep. This time, nightmares did not find me. Just a feeling of floating in nothingness. That is where I remained until the day's turbulent fragments were folded into the approaching dusk. Dusk delivered a promise of falling dollars, or at least a hopeful wish. I opened my eyes to a golden hue that flooded the room. Descending rays made dust particles dance. A glimpse of heaven that would vanish with the setting sun. For a moment I did not know where I was, or what day it was.

Life was better that way. A golden moment that would soon disappear and leave me with settled dust and the memories of a barely breathing girl lying on the bathroom floor. Who was she? Was she alive, or did she die during that ambulance ride? Did I help save her life, along with other strangers who did not even know her name? Would I ever know these things?

It was all too much: the nameless girl, this house, these roommates, my night-shift profession, my growing drug obsession. I was not even off the bed yet, and my mind and veins were craving the white powder that would get me going. I did not have my own stash, although I dreamed about having a large glass canister full of white powder. Not the kind to make cakes out of but another type of sugar that allowed me to soar with the gods. Dreaming about glass canisters full of cocaine did not seem like a normal craving. *I might have a problem*, I confessed to myself. I did not have a full glass canister, or even a full little baggie, but I did know where to find enough to give me a lift—a nudge toward the gods. Just a few steps down the hall and I would find my way. *Gods, get ready.*

I tried to talk myself out of my drug cravings, but without it I could not get through the night, or the next hour for that matter. The girl who had fought against the effects of an unknown substance in Omar's office a few months before now craved the energy, the uncertainty, the escape that drugs provided. I needed it. Once discerning about what I put into my body, I no longer cared. As long as the mystery powder lifted me out of my reality and into my own Queendom, where I ruled supreme, nothing else mattered to me. My garden room did not have a mirror for me to look into. Just as well. I would not recognize the woman staring back. Or worse, I might see traces of the one disappearing.

Still wearing only my bath towel, I knocked on Farrah's door, knowing she was never without nose candy. "Come in," she directed. I did as I was told and found a different vibe than that night before. Music blaring, clothes scattered on her bed. "Hey, Jade. What's up?"

"You, apparently," I said. "Can you spare a line for your favorite roommate? The one who saved this place from being a death scene last night, and I'm not talking about you, gun-flinging Annie Oakley."

Half interested, Farrah responded with a chuckle, then a question. "What happened?"

"It's a long story. I'll tell you on the way to work," I replied while my eyes focused on the top of her dresser where a small mirror covered in white dust rested next to a tightly rolled dollar bill.

"Suit yourself and yes, help yourself," she offered, waiving her hand toward the mirror. "My stash is in the top drawer. Do that, then hurry up. We need to leave in a few minutes."

"Yeah, I know." I helped myself to a line. I breathed in the powder filtered through the scent of a dirty bill. Traces of sweat and grime. I felt the burn. My senses, damaged, altered, and restored, I left her room. Each step down the hall brought me one step closer to the gods. Soon, I would be enveloped by them—maybe I would become one. This idea felt right. I did not refute it. My courage—and lies—were growing stronger by the minute. Back in my room, I scanned the contents of my dancer bag, making sure I had everything I needed, including my purse.

It was missing.

My racing heart stopped. *My money! Those thieves…* then I remembered, I had stashed my purse under my mattress before I fell asleep. I retrieved it and counted my cash again. Five hundred sixty-five dollars. Too much to take to work, but there was no way I was leaving it here. Maybe I could leave it with Omar. No, that felt risky, too. I would just need to take it and not let my purse out of my sight. *Easy enough.*

"Hey, what are you doing?" Farrah interrupted my deep-in-money thoughts. "We need to leave, and you're still in a towel. Hurry up!" Her little line had turned the impatient princess that she was into a spinning dust devil. Maybe it wasn't little and maybe she was more like a cyclone. In the doorway she stood, watching my every move. When I did not move fast enough, she tossed a wrinkled dress at me. "Here, put this on, we need to go." I did as I was told. Leaving my towel on the floor beside crumpled clothes, I grabbed my bag and followed her through the door. We were on our way toward another night at the carnival skin show.

No time to investigate beyond the smoky living room, but I noticed the four ashy people were gone. The stench of cigarette smoke and foul body odor remained. Who were they and who had invited them in? Maybe no one did. Maybe they were couch-surfing tweakers who follow the trail of other losers and let themselves in through unlocked doors and into places where they could easily blend. Places where no one said a damn thing to them. Maybe they had turned to ash and were now scattered across the carpet, mixed with remnants of dog shit and skin flakes.

On the way to the club, I told Farrah about the crumpled Barbie doll, the 911 call, and the paramedics. She asked if the paramedics were hot.

"You would know, if you hadn't slept through it," I piped.

"That's one way to get hot guys over," she joked. "Maybe someone else will pass out tonight and I'll make the call."

"Yeah, sure, maybe I'll pass out and they can give me mouth-to-mouth." We both laughed, then fell eerily silent. My body began to shiver. "Can you turn the heat on?"

"The heat? What the hell for? I am sweating."

"I just got really cold."

"Well, deal with it! I'm not turning the heat on. It's July! We're almost at work, then you can dance up a sweat." She was right. I would do that.

Thanks to Farrah's whip cracking and yellow-light running, we pulled into the parking lot with ten minutes to spare. I waved at Doug when we passed his perch.

"Wonder if he ever takes a day off?" I pondered.

"Not as long as I've been here."

"How long has that been?"

"About six months longer than you."

"Oh yeah, that's right. Well, he deserves a day off, anyway."

"Don't we all," Farrah said. She was right. This place had a way of speeding up time. The standard one-week-off-per-year holiday pay did not cut it in this cutthroat, cut-your-soul-out place. The only vacation days I had were spent working down south in the desert or north in the pines, being fanned, not by a cool breeze, but by crisp one-hundreds used to taunt and tease. The taunting and teasing were worth my time and effort, but a relaxing vacation, it was not. Farrah's car trapped our heavy sighs, and our shadows revealed our slumped shoulders when we stepped out into the fading sunlight. Any traces of hope left in me were disappearing beyond the horizon, where the sun's rays would either wrap them in warmth or burn them up. We breathed in the scent of diesel while our feet traced the tracks of dusty work boots as we walked along the greasy asphalt toward one more punch on the work clock.

Chapter 38

a dreamy dance

The little bump in Farrah's bedroom had worn off and I was feeling worn out. I did not want to do this anymore. I did not want to smile pretty. I did not want to be a stuck ballerina, spinning endlessly and getting nowhere. I wanted off this carnival ride. At the very least, I wanted to hide. So, I did.

I hid myself in a corner, away from Omar's watchful eyes. The dressing room would have offered the greatest escape from the gatekeepers and ringleaders in this place, and another lift out of this slump by an easily found bump, but I wasn't up for the efforts it would take to reach the powdery prize. I wasn't up for chatting it up with another dancer. I had become what I dreaded most: the sad little dancer who had allowed lifestyle choices to cast a smoky shadow over the hopeful naïve girl who had stepped into this place just a few months ago. A lifetime ago, it seemed. I sat in the corner, none the wiser, but I sure had grown. *I'm just having a bad night*, I told myself. I was worn out from trying to save a lifeless life. I needed to save my own. I just needed to get through the night, then start looking for an apartment.

How did I end up surrounded by strangers who saw too much, and yet with eyes closed didn't see enough? Even crunched in a corner, trying to make myself small, trying to hide, I was surrounded by mirrors reflecting my bare skin to too many men. Men who were too busy looking at my spilling breasts and barely covered ass to see the sadness in my eyes. The same sadness I rarely saw in theirs. In the strip joint, they lived like kings, as long as they kept sharing their dirty greens. The crown was theirs if they kept feeding the skin machine. In the club, they could escape from an oppressive boss, or the stack of bills on the kitchen counter, or a wife tending to the not-so-glamorous side of life. I had come to this place in hopes of dancing toward a dream that was now slipping from my reach. A dream that was never in my grip, but at least had felt like a possibility. I did have, in a drawer under t-shirts, a university letter that had accepted me—that was real. I just needed to take the next step, then the next then the next, until I was stepping across a graduation stage. Steps that were not free. So there I sat, surrounded by mirrors, making it impossible for me to escape...myself. The smoky air distorted my image, but there was no denying what I had become. Where I would end up, was anyone's guess.

"Can I get a table dance?" the young man asked. My rest was over.

"Sure. What's your name?"

"Alex."

"Hi, Alex," I said. He replied with a lift of his glass and an angelic smile. Back to the bump and grind and my forced grin. So good was I, he asked me to do it again and again and again. He must have liked my sad girl vibe. *Different strokes for different folks*. The only thing I stroked on him was his ego, while he paid for mine. Four songs gave me enough time to notice he was an attractive young man with soulful eyes. Why was he here, paying for a tease, when he could be running around college town, getting whoever he pleased? He did seem a bit shy though, and there is something alluring and voyeuristic about paying a girl to take her clothes off while others looked on. *Most of her clothes*. Some things were left to the imagination. An alluring rite of passage that sadly, for some, led to a life of delusion.

The DJ's call to the stage pulled me away from my hip-swaying ride on the money train. I gave angel Alex a kiss on his soft cheek, and he gave me four twenties. Seemed a fair exchange in the skin trade. Easy cash that did not even require my real name or a handshake. *How will I ever escape this easy street?* I leaned in and said thank you with a smile that was born from my awakening core. No longer forced. His sweet face turned red, but he did not look away. My parting gift seemed to do more to him than twenty minutes of swaying and gyrating. His reaction did more for me than the four twenties folded neatly in my purse. For a moment I was suspended in his charm, lingering too long in the attraction in his eyes and his manly smell. He held me there. For a moment I wasn't a stuck ballerina, I was a young woman running through a field of flowers warmed by the golden sun. It was a perfect moment. *Perfectly unreal.*

My dreamy moment was interrupted by the DJ's booming voice: "Jade to Stage One."

"Nooo!" was my reply. My soft-skinned lap angel sent to rescue me from my spiraling slump laughed too. He did save me. For twenty minutes anyway. What about the next and the next and the next? An endless chain of minutes, locking around me, tighter and tighter—heavier and heavier, the chains became. So heavy were they, I was sure the chains materialized before the crowd's astonished eyes. Metal forming and fitting snugly along my curves. What a trick that would be! Worthy of a few extra dollars.

"Come see the girl who turns her troubles into heavy chains! She wears them so well! A custom fit if I've ever seen one!"

I could hear the rusty metal thud against the stairs with each step. One thud became two then ten, then a jumbled melody of clanking chains drowned out my stage song, but not the voices in my head. It was just one song on a stage. I had been here before. But these chains felt so heavy. *How can I dance like this? How will I get through this?* Remembering to breathe was the first task and less alluring than spinning on a dirty pole. The penetrating stares of the patrons turned my breath into stone, choking my throat. With my legs and breath now turning from the usual fluid to rigid, it all became too much.

On the same stage where I had stood dozens of times, I became the young awkward dancer standing surrounded by professionals during an amateur night. A night I once ran away from and thought I would never return to. Yet, here I was, a few miles down the road, working at a club that demanded more of me than that first place ever would have. *Maybe that is why I have stayed. Here I can do more than shimmy and shake. Here, I can creep backwards down stairs and slither up poles like a snake.* My swirling thoughts turned the stagnant smoke into a tornado spinning around me. I could not stand here and let this moment swallow me up. I could not become another stunned beauty that would need to be quietly removed and shown the door. No, I would find my feet and dance my way to the center of myself, away from the stares, the drugs, the bills, and my elusive college dreams. I would retrieve the pieces of me that were scattered across this room, glue them together with my salty tears and a song and lay the mismatched quilt next to my broken heart. What a pair the two would be. None of it pretty, but all of it me.

I let myself float along the notes that carried me in a way that no one ever could. Except maybe Sean. Briefly, he had given me a taste of what it felt like to allow my body and soul to fall into a song. An enchanted song formed in the thickest part of the forest—a song that could only happen when two pure and passionate hearts matched rhythm and intention. Only then would the green lights above sparkle just so, stirring the frozen pine needles into a uniform angelic orchestra, audible only to the lovers loving in the virgin snow. Across my stage, a thousand singles could have lain, and it would not have compared to the joy of being held by strong arms and tender hands. I survived my tumble by stepping into my center, visible to no one. I would need to stay in that guarded place to survive the night. Whatever personal hell I was putting myself through would not stop the inevitable from happening—the ticking of the clock and another chance for every dancer still standing at 1 a.m. to "show us everything you've got." That KISS song would eventually spin, but in that moment, my greatest reward was reaching this song's end.

Feeling broken and bruised by my occupation's abuse, I made it to the end of the night, barely. I stepped off the rock and roll stage, but not without pausing and dropping all the weight the last twenty-four hours had piled on me. I was not taking that garbage home with me.

Home—what a strange thought. An idea I had given thought to in between the lap dances and my less than stellar stage presence. I needed to find that place. That nurturing escape that felt more appealing than a collage classroom.

"Do you want to join us for pancakes?" Cat asked on the way to the dressing room.

"It sounds delicious, but I need to get some sleep. It's been a long day, and I have some important business to take care of in the morning."

"What business?" she inquired.

"None of your business," I responded with a smile. "I will tell you all about it tomorrow night, when I have something to tell."

"I can't wait to hear more." I believe she really did care. Her response felt genuine. She felt like home.

I was surprised by my night's earnings. Three hundred sixty-five dollars, minus the house tips, was my prize for surviving another punch on the skin -circus time clock. My mind and body were too numb to celebrate cash earnings. I changed my clothes, tipped everyone then stepped into the warm summer night. So lost in my thoughts, I forgot that my own car was not parked outside. My ride was still inside.

I looked up at the stars while I waited for Farrah. I thought about my future while trying to push away my past. *Would I ever look at the stars and not think about Sean?* I could feel my heart tear and spill onto the mismatched quilt that lay near its dripping veins. Every drip caused pulsing pains. With my eyes on the sky and my mind floating in another universe, something brought me back to the grimy parking lot. A large gray sewer rat was scurrying toward an overflowing trash dumpster. I wasn't sure what it would find there…mostly empty bottles. The last traces of alcohol were dripping out.

Chapter 39

a room of my own

I had to sprint down the stairs and across the grounds of my new apartment complex to beat their 5 p.m. deadline. With five minutes to spare, I made it to the rental office to drop off my two-hundred seventy-five-dollar rent check. I did not save myself from sweating, but I saved myself a late fee. I should have taken my shower after dropping off my check, now due on the fifteenth, not the first like I was used to at the house. Because I had not planned my day well, I was in danger of being late for work. I had avoided a late fee at home to possibly receive one at work. I could already hear Omar lecturing me. I made the call before leaving my apartment.

"I know, I know, I'm sorry. I'm on my way." He was not happy with me. I wasn't happy with myself.

Where did my day go? I had been lounging around my studio apartment, enjoying my afternoon, then suddenly it was four thirty, and I found myself in a panic. I had lost the afternoon to my albums and my daydreams. I danced to too many songs. The hours were short, but my joy was long. No gawking eyes, while I swayed around my place. Just me and the records spinning. I spent too much time organizing my clothes in my closet that smelled of fresh paint. I got lost in my book on the sunny balcony. A day of too much pleasure left me stressed. Stolen moments I did not regret.

I pushed Omar's scolding voice aside during my drive. Rushing off without my sunglasses left me cursing at my forgetfulness. I was paying the price. Tears poured from my burning eyes. Despite the discomfort from the summer sun's harsh glare, I could not help but smile. I was pleased with my decision to leave the chaotic house and move into my own place a month prior. August, with all its heat, had arrived. A brutal month in Phoenix, especially without air conditioning in my car. After driving that hot metal box on wheels, I never arrived anywhere looking or smelling my best, but my VW did get me where I needed to go—which, last month, was away from a house full of dancers and their drama.

Finding a studio apartment had been easy, and leaving the party house was even easier. In a club full of dancers, someone is always looking for a place to live. I moved out of my faux garden bedroom, and a new dancer, who had just arrived from Texas, moved in. Farrah, the only one I was close to, seemed surprised and disappointed when I told her I found my own apartment, then she told me she was going to move to LA in a few months. I didn't know if she would or if she said that to avoid feeling abandoned, but for all the chaos in that house, leaving was quiet and painless.

I thought about what I had just been through and where I might be headed as I drove to work on a Tuesday, late afternoon. I had been so busy settling into my new place that my August 8th birthday had come and gone without any plans. No after-hours dancing with my underage friends. No family invites: I barely spoke to my parents and my brother was out of state, stationed in Texas. My family had learned about my dancing from an overtalkative cousin who had sold me a dresser. She told her mom, who told my mom, who blamed my dancing decision on my dad who called my brother to ask if he knew. The three of them were disappointed and disgusted with me and did not hold back telling me so. Our conversations were short and tense and always ended the same: with my growing feelings of abandonment and shame.

Other than receiving a call from my sweet Grandma Violet, the morning of my birthday, the only attention I got on my twentieth birthday happened at work. My makeshift family made the day special. Every time I went up on stage, the DJ mentioned it was my birthday. His birthday announcements doubled my tips. That was enough celebration for me. No longer a teenager. No longer living with roommates. I was officially an adult, living at the edge of campus life, not in the center of college row, like I had with Alena and Christina. My location kept me away from the bustle of college life, including the parties, and kept the costs down. I once again had a commute, traveling west, but it was a shorter distance than when I first began dancing. I found a middle between my dream college life and my real night life. I was doing it my way this time. Trying, anyway.

I may have been on the edge of the university's reach, but I could still feel its academic and social influence, and I saw glimpses of it here and there...a boy at a bus stop reading a book...a girl wearing an ASU t-shirt. I didn't know their stories, but they reminded me not to lose track of mine. My lifestyle of doing drugs and dancing all night had also left me on the edge, leaving me stretched and frayed. I had spent the last few weeks living alone for the first time in my life, trying to mend the tattered edges and find myself. I realized it wasn't possible to find who I once was, for that version of me no longer existed. Her way of being and doing I chose to dismiss. I was searching for a me I was yet to know. I could never again be who I had been less than a year before.

The path to a college degree was not easy for anyone, even if their tuition was paid in full, but my road seemed to be full of detours and potholes. Changing zip codes would not solve my problems or fulfill my dreams, but it offered me a life preserver, so desperately needed in the turbulent sea. I grabbed hold. I was kicking like a desperate swimmer losing sight of the shore. I was kicking away from the undertow, with a labored breath. It hadn't pulled me under yet. If I kept fighting, I believed that someday, I would find my place in the sun.

I held a belief that those attending college were living a life in complete contrast to my own and that I was "less than" because of my choices and background. Beliefs I ruminated over one afternoon while watching bustling students from the stillness of a chair in my favorite bagel shop. Their sidewalk images became a blur through my tears. I tried to hide my crying eyes from my favorite bagel boy—my reason for making the drive on a day off from the club. He served a delicious bagel with a smile and a side of pain. I had continued going to the bagel shop, not because the bagels were worth the torture, but because, through the smudged window and my tears I was learning how to be one of them: a college kid on the other side of the glass, rushing to get to class. I had done enough watching and had felt enough wanting; it was time for me to step beyond the glass and become one of them. I needed to take the big bold step of enrolling and joining. I didn't know where or how to begin and I was scared, but there was a tiny voice inside me that believed it was possible. A blurry belief that *anything was possible*. It might be just enough to get me out of the bagel shop chair and into a college classroom.

As hopeful as this voice may have been, there was another voice threatening to rob me of my dreams. It was not a loud voice. It whispered— not sweetly, like a lover wanting to cast a spell. It made my skin shiver and made the hair on my the back of my neck stand tall. A whisper that began as one sinister note quickly morphed into tangible tentacles that fractured a million times, spreading through my body, casting an evil spell, and taking over my soul. The tentacles were hungry. Never satisfied by laughter or a good night's sleep, they needed to be fed. Delicious food was not their quest. They craved the tang of toxic metal and strong chemicals. They did not care if their appetite was killing the host. Satisfying their cravings was their only goal.

I had turned into a drug-addicted spinning ballerina. I couldn't make it through a dancing shift without snorting a line spread across dirty pocket mirrors never used to apply lipstick. What began as resistance had turned into dependence, as reluctant as I was to admit this to myself. Leaving the party house also meant leaving Farrah's stash. All grown up and independent, I had my own. I had my own dealer, too. An attractive, blue-eyed, dark-haired, fit man, nine years my senior, who I met at the club. One table dance led to a conversation, then another and another, which led to a lunch date, then another and another. Laughs over lunch escalated to afternoon sex in my studio apartment. I didn't love him—not like I loved Sean, however fleeting that was, but I had fun with my boyfriend-dealer, Diego. We laughed and joked and had carefree sex after eating tacos. One thing we never did together was share blow. Our visits were during his workday, so sober, he needed to remain. We moaned in afternoon delight then I saw him a few hours later under the neon lights. No strings were attached, just lines.

A couple of times a week, he came to the club with his captivating smile and a small baggie of sugar, just for me. Free. *Lucky me*. There's no such thing as a free lunch though. I was paying for it with sleepless nights, paranoid thoughts, and depressing lows followed by excessive highs, and my fit dancer body and childlike cheeks were becoming too thin. Each of these effects were taking their toll and taking me further away from the girl I once was. Her memory now buried somewhere in a landfill.

My hidden stash was tucked under a takeout menu in my kitchen. No random late-night visitors to keep it from or roommates asking for some; it was all mine. Protected behind a locked door whenever I left my apartment. I would return in the middle of the night to find an empty couch and a quiet bedroom. No one to curse at or talk to. No one to hug me or kiss me at the door, either. Just my steady stash, tucked in a messy drawer. Out of sight, but never out of mind. The thought of running out of my get-up-and-go consumed me. Running on empty may have been the best thing for me, but I did not see it that way. The job that was keeping a roof over my head and keeping me and my gas tank fed was feeding on my body and soul and stealing my mind. One line at a time. Blow after blow.

Would there be any gray matter left to offer up to professors? That, I did not know. Questions and thoughts that filled my mind and helped pass the time as I drove to the club night after night. Always arriving with a few minutes to spare. Enough time for another line before saying hello to Doug, always waiting and watching.

One night, Farrah, who was talking to the DJ, saw me rush by. She caught my eye. We said, "Hi" to each other, like two people who barely knew each other. I wanted to tell her about my new place and invite her over, but there was no time for that. With her unpredictable moods, I wasn't sure if she would want that. Maybe it was just as well. Maybe I did not need the drama of her gun-pointing ways. I pushed open the dressing room door, and I saw Cat. I still had Cat. More like a loyal canine companion, but I would never tell her that.

"I saved you a chair, my sexy friend," she said as she lifted her bag from an empty chair next to hers. "By the way, your sexy is starting to look a little thin. Maybe cut back." We stared at each other in the mirror. I knew what she was thinking and what she meant. I nodded at the truth and attempted to smile. My head and lips said one thing but getting ready for the circus meant only one thing to my hungry brain: find my tiny vial swimming in my dancer bag and snort a little before the long night. I prepared my face and costume for the evening and stayed loosely engaged while my mind thought of only one thing: a line of cocaine. I would take care of that in the only place I would find myself alone for the next eight hours hunching over the back of a toilet.

"How do you like your new apartment?" Cat asked.

"I like it a lot. It's small and peaceful, and I've been decorating, so it's beginning to feel like home." I heard myself say the word home and thought how strange and beautiful it sounded. *Home*. I let the word float across my highjacked brain. *Home*. I thought about my new throw pillows and coffee table, purchased from the secondhand store and my food in the fridge— cottage cheese, orange juice, apples, and jelly. Not much, but everything in that rented space was mine. "You should come over soon," I urged.

"I would love that! What about tomorrow? It's Sunday."

"That sounds perfect."

"You make lunch, and I'll bring the wine."

"Let's make it an early dinner instead," I suggested with a wink. I was excited too. "Well, let's get our asses off these chairs and go make some money."

"Always the responsible one, Lioness." She smiled at me while she gave her long silky hair a final brush before we ventured into the unknown that was becoming all too familiar.

Chapter 40

mysterious guests

I read the red numbers on my small alarm clock. I questioned their truth. *Is it really two in the afternoon? That can't be right. How is that possible? How did I sleep so late?* My efforts to lift my head from my feathered pillow shot a pulsing pain through my neck. I felt like I had jumped out of an airplane without a parachute, smacking my head on the hard concrete. I let my bowling-ball head drop. I couldn't lift my arms, and every inch of my body ached. I traced my memories of the night before, which now felt like ten years ago. *What happened last night?* I began trying to put the pieces together. Painfully, my tortured and twisted brain tried to recreate each frame. Like looking through my childhood View-Master, highlights from the previous night flashed. *Click. Click. Click.* More like lowlights under a fluorescent hiss, than animated scenes from Disney's Cinderella.

I saw images of looking down at men, of twirling down the pole, only to climb back up and do it all again. Spinning, twirling, laughing, and grinning. The whirling memories made my throbbing head pulse more. I closed my eyes, but the images only became more vivid and grew louder. I remembered wearing a new costume—a brilliant sky blue—recently purchased from the one-stop-trunk-shop, baby-bouncing momma. I remembered handing the DJ my 45s, which I had recently purchased from the same secondhand store where I found my coffee table.

Individual images that should have created a cohesive memory of the previous night did not snap together. *What went wrong?* My mind kept searching, looking for a broken piece or pieces. I wasn't sure which scenario would complete the puzzle. I remembered a tinge of disappointment about not seeing Diego, but that wasn't the missing piece. I was not attached to Diego like I was Sean, and his absence did not break my heart. *What happened? Think.* I remembered happily counting bills, but the final amount, I could not recall. A scratchy gasp escaped my throat. My purse!

My mind was now solely focused on securing my cash stash. Adrenaline took care of the rest. I rolled over and pulled on the drawer that should have my purse inside. My twisted body had trouble prying open the stuck drawer. *Come on damn drawer.* It gave lose with an unexpected release that sent contents flying into the air and spilling onto the floor, almost taking me with it. Relief. With the other scattered objects were my dirty bills. I dropped the drawer on top of my green-butterfly pile and rolled back over, securely on the bed. While staring at the popcorn ceiling, I continued searching for the lost memory files from the night. I remembered saying no to pancakes, thinking if I go, what will Cat and I talk about tomorrow? *Shit! I remembered Cat was coming over soon.* I could hear the blood sloshing in my brain, pushing against my skull. A tsunami was building. I had driven myself home, that much I knew. *Think.* It was useless. The events between driving home and waking up in my bed were not retrievable. Just static. A black hole.

The red numbers now displayed 2:20. I needed to pull myself together before Cat's arrival. Whatever time that was, I could not recall. I needed to call Cat. I really needed to get a longer cord and move my phone next to my bed. *Why the hell doesn't my bedroom have a phone jack?* I could not find the will to climb out of bed or my mess. I found only a mucky sludge, trapping me, pulling me into the deep. If not for Cat visiting, I would have stayed in bed.

Stumbling through my tiny living room, just steps from my bed, I saw a scene that felt staged. More like a painting than real life. One I would need to clean up. Two empty wine bottles, three glasses, and my small mirror clouded with white residue were on the table. I felt nauseous. I needed to drink and eat and call Cat. I needed to sit down first. I sat on the couch and stared at the obvious signs of a small party, but my brain could not fill in the characters holding the glasses or snorting the lines. Maybe it was just me. Maybe I used all but one from my mismatched wine glass collection. Maybe I was celebrating my solo living. Maybe I was losing my fucking mind. I covered my face with my hands and focused on my breathing. Although my stale breath was unbearable, it seemed the only thing I could control. Ten raspy breaths did not help me remember or take away the state I was in, but they kept me alive. *No small miracle*. I thanked God that I had woken up in my own bed, alone.

I made it to the kitchen and poured myself a glass of orange juice. The last few drops. I tossed the empty container in the trash, on top of three empty beer bottles. Complete confusion set in. *Who was here last night? Think*. It seemed impossible to think my way out of this dark hole. I filled up my now-empty glass with water, choked down some aspirin, grabbed some crackers, and plopped back onto the couch. I could sit here all day and not solve this mystery, I concluded. I prayed no crimes were committed, other than the powdery transgression that I was going to commit again. I wanted to call Cat and cancel, but she meant too much to me. I gave her a call, and we agreed on five o'clock. I had just over two hours to clean up and head to the store for some real food. Considering my condition, I decided it would be takeout.

The aspirin, water, and crackers helped me feel slightly better than a rotting corpse. The line I snorted before my shower did more to lift me out of my shallow grave. It was just enough to dull the jagged edges before Cat showed up. Whatever normal was, I wasn't sure anymore. With my borrowed and temporary energy, I cleaned up the living room and kitchen, and before making my bed, I counted my cash and pushed the difficult drawer back into place. Seven hundred forty-two dollars. More than I would need for the store, so back into the drawer all but forty would go. Still more than I could afford for a friendly dinner, but I also needed to fill up my gas tank. I was setting myself up. A skipped trip to the bank and a night I couldn't explain. I was riding a long dark train. My pounding head and nauseated stomach reminded me it was all too much. Wearing a pair of jeans, a Pink Floyd concert t-shirt, and flip-flops, I grabbed the full trash, locked my apartment which held an unsolved mystery inside, and made my way down the stairs.

I threw my trash on top of the Saturday night heap. The putrid smells, swarming flies, and scorching sun were more than I could bear. I threw up and added my own disgust to the heap. No one else would notice. *So much for brushing my teeth.* Feeling slightly better, after losing a little I drove toward food. I decided on Mexican food from El Charro, my favorite place. I hoped Cat would agree. I had forgotten to ask her what she liked. With all my forgetting, at least I did not forget about her. The wait for my food almost cost me a lifetime ban from my favorite joint. The smells and the crowded place brought up another wave of bile that sent me running to the bathroom. Just in time. My sweat-covered, green-tinged face caught the attention of the lady who handed me my bag of food. She knows me; she will remember this look. *Guess I'll be taking a break from this place.* Last night's choices had lasting consequences.

"Gracias," I mumbled, before bolting out the exit. In my car I was a mixture of complete disgust and major accomplishment. One more task: get some gas. Then I could go home and play hostess. A pale and shaky one.

Cat being Cat, she arrived at 4:59. I had gone thirty minutes without throwing up, so I was hopeful I could pull this off without embarrassment or a lecture. I hugged Cat and thanked her for the bottle of red wine. *Shit.* Why didn't I get Italian?

"Take a look around and I'll pour the wine," I told Cat from the kitchen.

"It's so cute," she shouted from the bedroom. Her voice radiated warm enthusiasm for my choices. I knew Cat was special when I met her, but I had no idea just how much I would need her in my life, until that moment.

"Well, it isn't much, but it's all mine. Everything in here, including the monthly rent—all mine." It felt good to say that. For a moment, I forgot about the self-imposed sludge coursing through my veins pushing its way toward my cotton-coated tongue. My happy moment vanished when the dark red notes floated to my nose. I would not be able to hide my state from the all-knowing Cat.

I told her about my night, including the mysterious missing pieces. She was concerned and offered an explanation: neighbors. Other than aliens landing in the courtyard, that seemed the only plausible explanation. I let my mind rest on that possibility while we moved on to other subjects. We talked about dancing, and boyfriends, and laughed about some of the regulars at the club. What I loved most about our time together was talking about school and how we both wanted to go back. I only had a few college credits; she was on her way to a counseling degree. I didn't mind her practicing on me. Offering unconditional love, she was a good friend and the family I needed. We promised each other we would enroll in the fall. I hoped we would keep our promises, most importantly to ourselves.

Chapter 41
campus visit

The fall semester started, and I was not one of the students standing on the corner with a bulging bag of books and dreams, but I did visit campus and meet with a counselor, Tanya, to discuss enrollment and a course of study for the 1990 spring semester. Among other things, she told me my acceptance letter was still valid, but I would need to take placement tests to determine which math and English classes I should be placed in. My heart raced and I broke out in a sweat at the mention of being tested. A strange reaction for someone who did well with tests and who thrived on the feeling of completing a test. But that was me *before* dancer Jade and cocaine hijacked my brain.

Dancing Jade was too busy moving and catching dollars to sit long enough for a test, especially one that required me to stay in the lines. The thought of a test smacked against the traces of last night's lines and my own insecurities about how I fit into this higher learning world. Or how I did not fit in. At the end of our appointment, Tanya pointed me in the direction of the financial aid office. The missing link for me. Or the gaping hole. There, I learned I could apply for Pell grants and loans, given my independent status and low income. Being paid in cash had its perks, but even with my more-than-minimum nightly wages, I wasn't exactly in the high-income bracket.

Other than being transferred a few times on the phone, scheduling my appointment with the university counselor was a simple task. However, the thought of all the tasks that lay before me and walking across campus with thousands of hurried students and professors was overwhelming. So overwhelming I had to stop, sit, and just breathe. Stepping into a topless club was stressful, but it did not compare to the level of stress this potential path was creating in me. The topless clubs made me nervous and the thought of taking my top off made me nauseous, but I knew the club staff would welcome me and although I had to prove myself, dancing came naturally to me. The challenges of topless dancing did not tax me in ways that proving myself in a crowded classroom, led by an intelligent professor, would. I tried to tell myself I had been a stellar student in school, that I had brains—brains that had been identified when I was a young girl, invited into a gifted program. All this peppy self-talk did little to persuade me that I fit in, that I could succeed in this competitive environment on my own. I felt so alone. I reminded myself that I had Cat and Tanya. One on each side of me—supporting me.

I left the admissions office with a financial aid application, three brochures on different programs of study, and a renewed feeling of hope for my future. The papers were getting drenched by the sweat dripping from my head and body on a warm autumn day—and by my growing thirst for drugs. A glimmer of hope was there. A little less stressed leaving campus than when I arrived, I gave myself the gift of imagination. I imagined that I was one of the students, walking to class, thinking about an assignment or an upcoming test. For a moment, I felt it. I felt the possibilities—that this could be my reality. That somehow, I could figure out how to be a university student while also taking care of my needs, like eating and putting a roof over my head. Just thinking those thoughts made me feel lighter and made me forget about my drug demons, growing multiple hungry heads inside my small frame. As I walked along the sidewalk, trying to fit in and with no trees in sight, I felt a shadow come over me. It surrounded me, then it stretched well beyond the perimeters of my skin. Morphing into ghoulish shapes, the shadow laughed at me and began tearing at my hopeful vision. Tauntingly and painfully slow, it did tear.

"Oh, just rip it up, be done with it," I ordered the shadow. "If this life is not mine to have, then tear up these dreams with one violent swish."

The shadow responded with a mocking sneer, "No, that won't do. The one to kill your dreams will be you. I will just follow you around morning, noon, and night and remind you of all the reasons your dreams are not meant to take flight."

The shadow won. I felt defeated before the race began. I found comfort on a bench under the swaying leaves of a Palo Verde tree. I had nowhere to be until five o'clock, five hours away. I relaxed at the thought of this. A mind void of deadlines, projects, and demands. I was relieved by this gift as I sat under the tree, trying to keep the shadow at bay and wondering how and where I might fit in. I flipped through the programs of study. I became distracted by people rushing by. Quick paced and deep in thought, some were weighted down by the burdens of mankind. And there I was, watching them sort it all out.

From the sidelines, I silently cheered them on. Not once seeing that I too might have insights to share and solutions to problems that did not yet exist. My sense of self was shrinking when two men caught my attention. On them, I became transfixed. A small area of grass stretched between me and the two men, who seemed to control not only time itself but the pace of wind. If they needed to be somewhere, it did not show. Wrapped within their nonchalant air was a persona of importance that only those of significance could properly wear. Whoever might be expecting them would surely wait, without complaint. With relaxed shoulders, two men shared genuine laughter, amusing those passing by and pleasing the gods, from which they most surely had descended. I will never have shoulders unburdened by the worries of common men, nor will I know what it feels like to keep company with deities. I was fascinated by the men and I wondered if I could keep up, especially if they represented a collegiate army of superhumans.

A question I let linger. *Better that way*. To offer an answer would mean tossing my loose papers and brochures, now curved and reshaped by my sweaty hands, into the trash, on my way to my car, never to return. These thoughts pleased my shadow lurking nearby; I heard its satisfaction when it turned and smacked its taunting lips. It was not concerned about the presence or absence of gods; it was sent from the land of doubt, with the intention of making sure I continued to feel left out of success, reward, and fulfillment. I did not have the energy or the belief to battle this suffocating shadow. Not today anyway.

With a belly full of Spanish rice, I collapsed on my bed just after 2 p.m. I was completely spent. Two and a half hours later, I splashed cold water on my face and brushed my teeth. I needed a shower after my afternoon sweat, but my sleeping dreams had taken precedence. I grabbed my dancer bag and my now empty purse, having deposited my recent earnings in my growing savings account. I paused just long enough to glance over my university papers. They were no longer pristine, but they were real, and my campus visit, not a dream. I locked my apartment door, with my dreams and drugs inside, and in a trancelike state I found myself on the road again, driving toward another golden sunset and dollar bills, raining.

Chapter 42

a spinning goddess

Surprised by my sudden energy, I floated through the club, riding a currency of endless possibilities. I was a spinning ballerina, doing what I needed to do, but I wasn't weighted down by any of it. Eventually, I planned on telling Cat that I had officially enrolled for the 1990 spring semester at Arizona State University and that my financial aid application had been submitted. For the moment, I wanted to quietly celebrate my baby steps and keep my dreams private. My dreams were too fragile to stand tall against spoken words of doubt. Running and hiding from my dream-stealing shadow was more than I could contend with. Maybe my smile and joyful glow would be my greatest defense.

With my backside working another table dance, I did not see him come in. "You look beautiful," he mouthed to me as he walked by. My lover's words brought the hairs on my exposed skin to attention. Already riding a natural high, Diego's presence raised me to the next level of happiness. A smoky strip club seems an unlikely place to feel natural bliss, but the moods of my body and mind, on practicality did not always depend. Maybe it was intrusive to cut in on another man's table dance, but I did not mind and the paying customer's eyes were occupied, on my back side, not on the passing man.

My mind was disconnected from a body dancing on autopilot. I smiled at smiling Diego, and his sudden pause allowed us to hold eyes. Eyes that had seen each other in the quiet stillness of my cool, dark bedroom during stolen afternoons. A contrast to this place with its pulsing lights and throbbing music. A different place but our eyes were the same, and for just a moment we were there, far away from the club, kissing each other and falling asleep in each other's arms. When we were alone in my bedroom, we allowed ourselves to fall into the space where anything was possible. We remained in that space until our realities slapped us across our love-struck faces. The clock always told us what our longing hearts and lustful bodies wanted to deny. It was time to end our fairy tale escape and head back out into a world centered on money-making, not lovemaking. Fleeting scenes that had no expectations beyond my bed, but those moments lifted me out of my ongoing frustration and looming dread. My eyes told him more than a "thank you" ever would.

He found a chair next to his friends who were two drinks ahead of him. I finished my table dance and thanked the new customer, feeling Diego's eyes on me the entire time. Eyes that did not reveal jealousy, but a quiet pride. On my way to Stage One, I hugged the back of Diego's shoulders. The jealousy that he did not share now poured from his friends. Whether they knew about our love affair or not, I did not care. Let him tell or keep it to himself. I had nothing to hide. Except my daily habit and my dreams, of course.

I had experienced many emotions on Stage One. The first of the three sets were where my emotions were at their strongest: nervousness, anxiousness, embarrassment, a spinning euphoria, fear, frustration, celebration, and many other feelings along the spectrum of human emotions. At the start of my dance, I felt something grab hold that was newly acquired; it was big and bold. I became a goddess in control. A sensation that revealed itself in my strong shoulders, my calm smile, my ability to read the room while feeling the tunes, and the unleashed strength in my muscular arms and legs. I knew that I needed these men for the dollars they were willing to spend, but I did not need their approval. I felt myself stretch and expand beyond this place and beyond the shame and family blame. I saw my dark shadow shrink to the size of a smoke ring, before being blown to nothing.

Would it return? I did not know, nor did I care, for during this dance, I was a force, self-aware. Each spin and climb to the top fueled a confidence that was foreign and unrelenting. It did not matter if the growing goddess felt right or not, she had taken over and she steered the show; I just followed her lead. Maybe this was a hint of what it feels like to fall in sync with whispered dreams or maybe the goddess glowing within had fallen into the wrong frame. If so, I hoped she wouldn't figure out her mistake. I hoped she would stay. I would need her courage in the coming days.

A woman and room transformed by my cosmic possession. Magic flowed from my eyes, limbs, and fingertips. This electric energy lifted me to the heavens and put the crowd in a trance, growing stronger and stronger until the last note of this transcendent dance. The claps and cheers snapped me out of where I wished to stay—a spinning goddess, dancing on heaven's stage. My newly acquired boldness flowed without effort. I paused and breathed it in before scooping up the dirty dollars made effervescent by my radiance.

To my delight and surprise, the goddess was not a one-hit wonder, she had taken over my awkward core, molding me into someone I did not recognize but had always longed for. She did have one weakness, the fault of her human host: she did not intervene and blow to the wind the white line offered in the bathroom at a quarter past ten. What might happen to this body and brain already soaring through the heavens, riding shotgun in a chariot on fire, was anyone's guess.

A collision in my system is what occurred. Like gasoline doused on a fire, the drugs fueled my goddess flames and created an inferno inside that matched intensity with earth's nearest star. I became unstoppable during this night of cosmic crashes. I thought the goddess wise, but she was easily fooled and quickly trapped by an energy that allowed her to expand. Maybe she had just earned her goddess wings, and I was her first test. Could she redeem herself while saving me and her wings or would we burn together? I loved the power she gave me, but I was not her keeper, and I had little regard for her or my future when choosing cocaine. The part of my brain that allowed me to walk across campus and drop off my completed applications had been swallowed up by the raging flames. The intensity of their blue-white arms could reach the edge of the universe, and yet it would never be enough. Turn and devour themselves they would, consuming everything until they were left with nothing.

I stopped keeping score and rode the directionless rocket during my night of excess. No calm pilot to keep me on course, no guiding system to follow a star pulsing in the North, just an endless supply of fuel to keep this unpredictable ride alive. With a flip of my hair and a devilish grin, I left no pole unclimbed, no wallet unturned, and my strong back became an endless succession of back bends. We did not hold back, me and my newly found goddess friend. We unleashed our seductive sparks across the room. No one was spared. Into our fiery web, carefree men were snared. Once upon a time, to receive their dollar, I was honored; now the tables had turned. The beautiful goddess was morphing into a greedy creature of the night, who would stop at nothing to satisfy her appetite. "Oh, this is too easy," I heard my sidelined shadow say.

Maybe, buried under the shimmer and smiles, I was afraid of a future that held promise and hope, with its share of hard work. Maybe my insecurities were burning me up before I could become whatever it was I was destined to become. This doubt resuscitated my scattered shadow. Feeding on my charged negative thoughts, the shadow emerged from nothingness and began to take up space in the dark corner of this overstimulated place. I wasn't the only one to notice the shadow's presence; the goddess, folded within, began to ascend. A battle between my shadow and my goddess was about to begin. It was too early for me to know which force was going to win.

Chapter 43

my goddess vs. my shadow

I flipped the pages on my wall calendar three times while the battle between my dark shadow and radiant goddess raged on. December had arrived. Sometimes my inner struggle was noticeable to others through my impulsive actions, both good and bad, but mostly the epic war was hidden behind my sad eyes and under my thick skin. Some days the goddess lifted me from deep sleep and carried me into my waking dreams. On those days she fully displayed her magnificent wings after nighttime kissed our resting cheeks. On those days, she painted everything the color of possibilities. When I looked to the night sky and the memories of Sean began to blur my vision, leaving me broken and distant, the goddess would spin a healing magic. She transformed every sad starry tear into a tiny, brilliant crystal— enough to fill a gem museum. On the sparkle, I could have lived happily ever after.

I wanted to leap over the dirty dollars, scoop up those pristine jewels, then disappear. The goddess became my strength. Her sensual and powerful energy made everyone in our presence pause and watch, whether at work or in a crowded shop. She and I sailed through the guarded gates and when she owned the dance, our stage earnings were doubly blessed. When my lurking shadow tried to squash college plans, she was the voice that said, "You can do it." Before her presence reformed my way of knowing and being, my dreams seemed out of reach, but with her powerful hand, my chin was boldly lifting in the direction of my North Star.

If it were only her and me on my daily path, there would be no limits to what I could achieve, but in her new goddess status, she was not always the strongest force that inhabited me.

Sometimes, she would disappear, and one thousand screams from me fractured time but did nothing to draw her near. On her energy, I knew I should not rely, but we were unbeatable, she and I.

It never took long for the shadow to feel her absence; the suffocating haze was always nearby. A tiny opening in my shield of protection and the shadow pounced, quickly enveloping me, until I was left no option but to breathe in the shadow's dangerous edges. The jagged shards did cut and tear. They slashed my voice, then cut up my heart, leaving me voiceless, broken, and torn apart. Without my goddess, my strong stance and inner confidence vanished.

My shadow knew this. It swirled around me in delight, laughing at my descent into a dark abyss. Watching me fall, it laughed, knowing that as the light faded, so did the belief in my abilities—falling deeper and deeper into a well of doubt and misery. Shrinking to a point of nothingness. Smaller than the size of a pin's head. I was crushed by its metallic weight. My shadow, having consumed all my courage and goodness, grew larger than the universe. It was above, around, and below. It became the sky while breathing down my neck. I had lost hope. I was spent. I prayed for the return of my goddess spirit, believing that only she could lift me out of this personal hell and mind mess.

So went the days. An internal battle. It felt as though no end were in sight. I kept counting dirty dollars and sleepless nights. A body and mind too tired to do much of anything else. If there was to be a winner at the end of my internal war, the victor would own my future *and* my soul.

Brooding and sulking did not stop the table dance requests from coming. It seemed men liked the quiet mysterious type. That's how they chose to see me. Whatever version best fit their fantasy. I knew the truth: my fragile heart, protected by a firm frame, was falling apart. Sad eyes told more than my lips ever would, but looking too closely would distort their illusion of an angelic vixen sent by God just to please them. That's how they chose to see me. Worse than seeing my faults and sins, looking too close at my glossy, green eyes would require them to look at their own reflections: tarnished, twisted, and broken. *Some of them.* Some were just looking for a quick thrill or a place to celebrate life's grander moments. The kind of moments that shined in the light of day. Unlike this little midnight secret that they would keep hidden away. Some came with a friend and discovered it did not suit them. Others got sucked in. One glance at her exposed skin, swaying, just for them. They were forever lost in the skin circus illusion. Nowhere else could they control the strings of a being so desperate, contained in a body so perfect. A perfect pairing. A perfect storm.

I watched a dust devil quickly form and mysteriously spin in the dirty parking lot during my quick break. An appropriate place for a restless devil to conjure and play. I longed for it to sweep me up and carry me away with the trash and leaves, dropping me somewhere far from this club, surrounded by concrete and asphalt. My eyes followed the base of the swirling desert volcano to its wider top. Growing wider with each spin of the clock. I watched it rise higher and higher. Its strength, I was powerless to stop. The twirling mini tornado, orchestrated by a cruel conductor, succeeded at this game it came to play. On my vulnerability, it did prey. My eyes focused on the starry sky where my dreams crashed into distant moons. Memories of Sean blew in and burned the edges of my fragile heart, until a destructive fire reached my core. My goddess was nowhere to be found, and my shadow, though lurking nearby, left me alone. Alone I was. There was nothing more for my shadow to do. I was broken.

If only I could have seen a bright future for myself—without the help of a fickle goddess. If only I had been strong enough to rise above the shadow's darkness. If only I could have understood that beyond the vapor of those fallen stars resides an entire universe brimming with magnificence. For dreamers to cast dreams into. Not just one "star light, star bright," but an entire brilliant universe waiting to nurture fragile dreams.

Out there, farther than my teary eyes could see, infinite hope was forming in the shape of stars. If only I could believe that I too deserved to soar in the angelic realms and that the brightest light also shined in me, then I might have a chance to escape the dirty parking lot where, even during the sunniest of days, the freeway overpass cast a long shadow.

"Jade, you're starring on Stage One," Sabrina screamed from the door.

"I'll be right there."

Chapter 44

saved by a stranger

My heart was beating so fast, I was sure it would explode. My mind was racing. Neither my body nor my brain, could I control. Lying on my bed was like lying down in my coffin, only less peaceful. I went too far. I snorted too much. Or maybe it was cut with something dangerous. I wanted to run. I wanted to scream. I was scared. I began to pray…

Please God, I promise if I live through this, I will never do another line, ever. Please God, help me. Please. Please. Please.

I was begging. I was spinning. I was begging for an end to the spinning. I might die tonight, were my thoughts. My survival seemed hopeless. My living seemed pointless. Fighting to live in between moments of caring less and less. *Fuck it. It's time to put an end to this wasted existence.* How long will it take for someone to notice my absence? My twenty-year-old heart was pumping out the last of its days. Sixty years' worth of heartbeats used up during one night of overindulgence. My brain cells were dying. "Only the good die young." I heard the song in a disconnected mind that was burning its wiring and losing its grip. I am not good, and I stopped feeling young months ago. "Stop this tune!" I shouted, or maybe I thought it, loudly. I could no longer distinguish between the churning inside my brain and the wavy space beyond.

So much wasted potential, they will say. Wasted, yes. *She's so healthy in that fit body,* they will say when they find me stiff and lifeless, three days from now—two days after rent is due. That will bring them knocking.

Don't they see the truth? Don't they see by my shrinking frame? Can't they read my sketchy brain? Nobody cares! I'm paying my own way, that is good enough for them. Best not to ask too many questions. Too much truth spoils the meal and shifts the burden. I can't calm my pounding heart or switch off these scattered thoughts. *Please, God, make it stop!*

God answered in a way that was unexpected. Just like he had three years before when his prompting led my hollowed soul and frail frame to a sunken living room, during the early hour of 3 a.m. The disturbing images of a made-for-TV hell had flashed across the screen and saved my life when I was seventeen. Real or fabricated, it was enough to get my attention. I wrapped myself in the protection of that lesson, *for a time*. In my long-term memory, it did not settle in. I took what I needed from that lesson and twisted a path of redemption into a barely living hell.

Without clear direction on what I was being summoned to do, I walked from my apartment bedroom to the kitchen. There, on the counter, was a copy of *New Times*, lying backside up. My eyes scanned the tiny classified ads before resting on one: a drug hotline. What could a sober voice do to save me from my imprisoned disgrace? *Nothing*, was my thought, but at least someone would witness my plunge into nothingness. The same dark hour that had almost destroyed me as a suicidal teenager had once again fallen upon me. I made the call.

"Hello," she mumbled in a sleepy voice. "Hey, honey, we've got one," the lady yelled to someone else. "Make a pot of coffee."

She did not tell me her name, nor did I ask, but she learned mine. We talked for ten minutes—or was it an hour? I told her I did too many drugs at a nearby party with people I barely knew and now my heart was racing terribly. I thought I might die. I was so scared. I cried. She listened. She was patient and kind. Maybe at one time, she had been like me, making the same desperate call. I do not know. She could not remove the bad decisions from my pulsing veins, but she made me feel less alone during my night of torment. She learned about my job and my college dreams. She encouraged me in a gentle way. Three people, now on my side: Cat, Tanya, and this stranger on the other side of the receiver. She told me all that was possible if I stopped using drugs. I wanted to believe her. More than anything, I wanted to not feel this way, *ever again.*

"Are you going to be OK?" she asked before hanging up. "Should I call for medical help?"

"No," I blurted back. Maybe I did need help, but my mind flashed the scene of the passed-out girl in the bathroom at the house of horrors. I would not get carried out of here on a stretcher, at least not while the choice was still mine. "I will be fine," I reassured her. I wanted to believe that.

I thanked her. She told me to keep the number handy and call back if I needed to. I did not call back. I finally fell asleep with the rising sun.

I woke a few hours before my shift. One I would probably skip. My sheets were soaked in foul sweat and my head and body were a disconnected mess. My night of excess had almost taken everything from me. With my head throbbing and my stomach heaving, I wished it had. For whatever reason, I was saved. For a grander purpose, I could not conceive. The thought of anything grand seemed make-believe. My life was spared, but not the lessons or the pain. My brain felt like it had been scraped over a cheese grater a dozen times, and my body felt like it had been stretched, pounded, and twisted. I lifted my arms, then my legs, just to make sure everything was still connected. I needed water. I needed food. I needed an escape route from this life I had created.

I lay there for an hour, thinking about everything while trying to think about nothing.

More conflict I was powerless to control. My survival instincts kicked in once again. Water was my quest. A long and arduous journey it would be to the kitchen sink, not for the number of steps, those were few, but for the colossal weight each brought to bear on a body, spent, and on my shattered soul. How I would get myself from this low to a place of strong standing, in a university classroom, in just a few weeks, I did not know. More added stress that I could not process. On my way to the sink, I passed the *New Times* sitting on the table. Unsure if I should burn it or frame it, the sight of it made me nauseous. Maybe I dreamed the call. Maybe I dreamed her, the lady who had talked me off the edge. No, I knew it was real. It was all too fucking real. I drank the tap water, slowly. That would be my pace for the remainder of the day.

From the same phone that saved my life, I called in to the club and told Omar I would not make it in that night. He was disappointed but he spared me a lecture. I hung up the phone, then let my throbbing head fall into my left hand. I sat on my vinyl chair, facing the kitchen, knowing there was some white powder in a baggy in the drawer that would take all this pain away. So tempting, it was. So close, I could smell it. I would not give in to it. I could not. I grabbed two soda crackers instead and dragged my body to a hot shower. If I had learned anything during my night of flirting with death, I should have flushed the soul-sucking powder down the toilet, but I was weak and I wasn't ready. I would have willingly flushed myself down the toilet if I could. I was, after all, my worst abuser.

My hot shower washed away my dried sweat and the crust in my eyes, but it also made me shaky, and I gave myself a fright when I saw my reflection in the mirror. Staring back at me was the color of green that only looks good on the end of a toothpick, bobbing in a martini. Wearing my white terry robe, I lowered my weak body to the couch. I still belonged in the trash, stinking up the outside, but I was alive. No life in me, but I was alive. I turned on my small television and tried to lose myself in a comedy, a show I had only seen once before, *Seinfeld*. A quirky show and the only TV remedy for my barely functioning brain.

Ring Ring Ring. The sound of it startled me from the position I had been in for two hours. The unfamiliar sound rattled my brain and vibrated my apartment. It was my dad. He had called to tell me that my grandmother had been moved to hospice and that I should try to see her soon. I told him I would. He gave me the address, then we said goodbye. I struggled to move from my couch, but I promised myself I would see her within a week. I had a habit of breaking promises to myself, but I wanted to keep the one that I quietly made to her. *Have I even seen her this year? She called me on my birthday, but have I seen her since I started dancing?* I searched my brain for a memory that would silence my guilt. I came up empty. I was ashamed. My year of dancing toward a better life had not come without a price.

Chapter 45

hospice visit

I went to see my grandmother a few days after my night of extremes. I got high before leaving my apartment. One year before, I had landed in Fairbanks, Alaska, for my first dancing gig. So much had changed in my life since I stepped off that plane during that bitterly cold night.

At my grandmother's hospice, staring at death made me realize I was staring at me. A truth that was painful to see. I wanted to smash the mirror and run—away from my past *and* my future. This would not be possible unless I took matters into my own hands, ending it all. The consequences of suicidal choices shown to me—a despondent teenager on a late-night TV screen—revealed a horrific beginning, not the end of anything. My only option was to stop doing drugs and forge ahead. *I didn't know if I could live in this world without making myself numb to its painful effects*. I needed to turn toward my past and try to unravel every poor choice that had led me to this place of brokenness.

I thought I had more time to buy oranges for her. I thought I had more time to say, "I love you" and "thank you." I was wrong. My grandmother released her final breath on Christmas Eve, six days after my visit, without the scent of oranges in the air and without a basket of drying orange rinds near her bedside. Alone she was, as she inhaled her last scent of life. A scent that was sterile and strong, making visitors flinch and hurry their visits along— an attempt by well-intentioned and caring people to mask the sour smell of imminent death. A scent that is harsh and brutal, and painfully honest.

My grandmother, Violet, deserved more than her final exhale gave her. She deserved to be surrounded by more than a basket of drying orange rinds that I failed to deliver. She deserved to be surrounded by the aroma and vision of sun-ripened, sweet oranges in an orchard with boundaries well beyond her failing vision. Maybe she traveled to this place just after departing from a body no longer needed by her gentle soul. *I was comforted by that thought.* Maybe her last rush of adrenaline allowed her to brush the black fur of that purring and grinning black cat. *I shuddered at the thought of that.* I will never know who or what accompanied her spirit into a mysterious afterlife. The only truth I could admit is that I was not there holding her sticky, orange-covered hand when that took place.

As an oblivious twenty-year-old caught up in my own needs, death was not an imminent force to be dealt with hastily. Death was a distant concern. I thought I could bring her fruit during a Christmas visit. Death does not follow our misguided human schedule, I learned. I should have driven directly to the store, bought citrus, and immediately returned. I should have peeled an orange and shared it with her—laughing together when the released juices sprayed us. I should have stayed by her side, looked in her eyes, and told her I would be with her until the end. I should have thanked her for the many childhood memories. I should have thanked her for her kindness, her gentleness, her strong work ethic, and her willingness to relocate across the country with her husband and three of her children, so that her second-born, my father, could breathe easier in the Southwest. I should have hugged her and asked her how she coped with losing her third-born in a fiery car crash weeks after I was born.

So many things never discussed, so many things left unsaid. Father Time is rarely patient, nor does he grant many rainchecks.

I left my grandmother's hospice room that afternoon with sadness in my heart that turned into lasting regret due to my missed opportunity to share an orange with her one last time.

However, I did not leave without her giving *me* something. I would not deliver a basket of fruit to her, but perhaps her dying wish was more insightful, more profound. Perhaps during her final days, which they would reveal themselves to be, she sensed that I too was flirting with death. I needed a reminder of life's preciousness. Witnessing her struggle to live would become that reminder. Standing at the edge of what would become the place where she drew her last breath, an awareness punched me in the gut and then coursed through my entire body. A thought flooded my mind, a consuming thought that would change the direction of my life.

Although I did not return with a fruit basket or leave anything else to comfort her in her final moments, I did leave something behind. I left behind a part of myself that was attached to the life I was living. A life that highlighted dying more than it did living. Jolted by an insight of my own "dying" choices, my death shadow did not leap out of me and vanish, leaving me instantly whole and renewed. Rather, the separation was going to be noticeable and uncomfortable, and it was going to take more time than my afternoon bedside awakening had.

Like trying to peel away from a dense mud pit that had suctioned around my entire body, I would need to work through my attachment to a toxic life. I would need to release my body and my spirit one section at a time and then have the fortitude to stay released while I worked to free the next section of a seized body and soul. I would need to squirm my way out of the mess I had created of my life, and of my spirit. I might free myself only to be sucked back into a muddy death pit, and I might crawl away with a bloody, bruised, and exhausted body, but I was determined to change. The discomfort raging inside of me was not visible, like my grandmother's struggle to breathe, but inwardly, I could feel addicted cells begin to revolt at the thought of giving up drugs and the lifestyle I had fallen into.

I would not see my grandmother again until I said my final farewell to her while she was lying in a silk-lined coffin. Her final clothing request was honored; she was wearing a soft blue nightgown, matching robe, and slippers. Her choice in attire for an eternal sleep was unusual, but it did fit the easy-to-please, Midwestern woman. Her open coffin was placed near an entrance to the church chapel, perpendicular to an aisle that led to the altar.

I did not know when I walked into my grandmother's hospice room that hearing her say a faint goodbye would be the last time I would hear her say words—words that did not settle into an understanding heart. Her final goodbye echoed through my hijacked brain. Even with death, goodbyes rarely produce a clean break from what once was. This truth would ring true when attempting to say goodbye to the daily drugs that had become a part of my dancing life. Separating from the life I had been living and moving toward the life I wanted to live would not be as simple as deciding and doing. I already knew this. I wondered how messy it would get, breaking away from my toxic choices. A process that might take months, I thought. I didn't have months. Classes started in two weeks.

Chapter 46

sprint don't walk

I was disappointed by the absence of my bagel boy at my favorite bagel shop. I was too nervous to eat, but I knew I needed to, so I forced half a bagel down, hoping it would calm my butterfly nerves. Already wound too tight, I skipped coffee and sipped on water instead. A surge of emotions overloaded my circuits. I wanted to blurt my bundle of excitement, nervousness, and apprehension to the older couple sitting near me. Two gray-hairs who looked kind and receptive and who did not seem in a hurry. I wanted to tell them how I would soon be walking to my first class on the university campus. How I would be standing on the street corner waiting for the walk sign with the other students on their way to class. Routine for most of them. Life changing and overwhelming for me. Walking across the crosswalk would be the first challenge of my morning. Everything in my body wanted to sprint, skip, or do cartwheels. *Anything but walk.* I wanted to tell the older couple how, after a year of veering off course, I was able to turn myself around and land here, less than an hour away from my first university class.

My heart was beating so loudly, I thought they might start the conversation by asking me if I was okay. I was okay and I was not okay, and both were equally wonderful. My racing heart was pure adrenaline caused by excitement, not by a substance I snorted up my nose. A habit I flushed down the toilet two days before my grandmother's funeral. I was already distraught over losing her and carrying the burden of guilt about my failure to bring her oranges; I figured an added layer of emotional turmoil to my state of mind would not be noticeable to me or anyone else.

My family would just look at the dark circles under my bloodshot eyes, and say, "Oh, poor dear, she's taking her grandmother's death really hard." Anyone making eye contact with me would take pity on me for being so torn up over my loss. I was torn up over losing her, over losing time with her over the last year, over losing her on Christmas Eve, over losing sight of the urgency of my last moments with her, over losing the chance to eat an orange with her…yeah, I was torn up. I was also dealing with the overwhelming desire to do a line. The craving was unbearable.

Nothing could stop my craving or distract me from it, at least not for very long, not even a cute, dark-haired stranger at the funeral. He was definitely not a blood relative—I knew all of them. When I made the decision to stop doing drugs, I also told Diego goodbye. He made it too easy—to see him on a weekday afternoon and to take his drugs. I missed him, but I missed his drugs more.

My flood of tears during the service carried so much more than the loss of my grandmother. As I looked at her frail body, I thought her spirit might be the only one in the church who understood the absolute agony I was going through. I could feel her presence with me, and it was her I called on for help. Quietly.

The end of a life. The end of a decade. The day following my grandmother's funeral was New Year's Eve. A night to usher in nineteen -ninety. I would not be celebrating. Forty-eight hours of not doing drugs was enough celebration for me. My revolting body and drug-hungry mind saw nothing to celebrate. My brain kept asking me, *when can we get the fuck out of here and go do another line?* Whenever the thought arose, and it did at least one hundred times while I sat in the church pew, I pushed it down and replaced it with song lyrics, or thoughts of going to school. I needed to see a reward for my self-inflicted punishment.

That had been two weeks ago. They were two of the hardest weeks of my life, and I am no stranger to hard weeks. After tossing a clod of coffee-colored dirt on my grandmother's lowered coffin, I said goodbye to my family and drove myself away from the cemetery. I declined my dad's offer to join them for dinner at his house. I wasn't hungry, and I was in no mood for socializing with people who felt like strangers. I drove straight to my apartment, took off my clothes and fell onto my unmade bed. What began as a short nap turned into three days of sleeping, waking only to pee, taking sips of water, or having quick bites to eat. I had already told Omar that I would be taking the week off. Knowing about my personal loss, he was extraordinarily compassionate.

During one of my waking moments, I started to panic about money. That panic led to wanting a line to escape the stress-of-life stuff. I did not have any drugs to take. One smart decision that would hopefully lead to more smart decisions. I talked myself off the anxiety cliff by reminding myself that my rent was paid until February, my classes were paid for—thanks to a school loan and Pell Grant—my utilities were paid, and I had some groceries. I could not stay in bed forever, but I would be okay. So, in is where I stayed for three days.

Toward the end of my third day in bed, Cat called to check on me. She knew that I would be starting school soon; something she would not be doing. I was disappointed. Something I would not share with her. I did not need to—she was her own worst critic. As a *someday-maybe* counselor, she was also a supportive lifeline for me. She knew about my decision to stop doing drugs, something else she wasn't ready for. She asked about my classes, said sorry about my grandmother, and asked if I needed anything. "English 102 and Psych 101," "thank you," and "no," were my responses. I did tell her I would love a visit in a few days.

She said, "I can't wait."

"Me either. I could use a friend."

Then she said the words that helped me get out of bed, the words that have danced in my foggy head, the words that put a hint of hope in my step, "I'm proud of you, Jade. You can do this."

"Thank you. Talk to you soon."

"Talk to you soon."

I didn't ask Cat anything about the club. Thoughts of that place were more things I wanted to escape from. I wanted to escape completely, but financially I wasn't ready for that. I wasn't sure how I could manage everything in my life—avoiding drugs, working at a strip club, attending two university classes, and doing homework—but I was going to figure it out, one day at a time.

Lost in my thoughts, I missed seeing the older couple leave and I almost missed the changed streetlight. The crosswalk now said "Walk." I sprinted through the shop door and joined the other backpack-wearing, college kids, walking toward their dreams.

Acknowledgments

This project, in its final form, would not be without the organizational skill set, guidance, and gentle motivation of Kim Cecere, Principal of On Point Communications. She appeared in my life at a time when I realized I could not do *this writing business* alone. She has been a godsend and valued partner, bringing the right team and resources together. It's one thing to make the bold decision to publish a multilayered book on "your own," it is another to bring all the pieces together. I could not have accomplished this without her.

In the fall of 2019, I stepped into a writing workshop led by the author of *The Story You Need to Tell*, Sandra Marinella. In Sandra's class I learned about the helpful writing tool of reframing at the beginning of this book's journey, a short story at that time. An important and timely discovery that allowed me to see this story from a different perspective—a shift that gave me profound insight into details surrounding this story. An inspiring and dedicated teacher who leads with compassion, lifting every life she meets, Sandra's belief in me since our first meeting has been a blessing.

Author Ginger Scott stepped into my classroom a few years before I decided to leave. She graciously accepted my invitation to speak to my seniors about her books and successful writing career, and she was kind enough to make a return visit the following year. She was genuine, forthcoming, relatable, and—the greatest gift a speaker can give—she was inspiring. For my students and for me. She still is. Her prolific talents and compassionate nature are a beacon of light for me.

Publishing my first blog post on WordPress in summer of 2019 was terrifying to the point of almost *not publishing*. I pushed through the fear and did it. Almost six years later, I can state emphatically that I am glad I did. Writing, sharing, connecting, and learning from other bloggers across our planet has expanded my understanding of the world, my empathy toward others, my courage, and a belief in my abilities. I am grateful for the many fellow creatives I've met along the way—a creative family I am honored to be part of.

From elementary through graduate school and beyond, I've been blessed with knowledgeable and dedicated teachers who challenged me to do my best, by modeling admirable actions and sharing encouraging words, sometimes when life had brought me to my lowest. Angels for me whose kind presence and meaningful lessons continue to offer guidance.

To my dancing sisters, both near and far, who beautifully express with unique rhythms, I extend a sparkly thank you for sharing the dance floor, always full of challenges, accomplishments, grace, and feminine zeal.

To my family, both born of the same blood and chosen, thank you for being in my life, while boldly living your own. For your love and support in all its precious forms, I thank you with an ever-expanding appreciation and a heart eternally grateful.

About the Author

A writer of poetry and poetic prose, Michele Lee Sefton is a veteran English teacher who left the classroom in the fall 2019 to develop her writing voice. She has since been published in various anthologies and platforms, including *Piper Poetry Month Anthology* through the Virginia G. Piper Center for Creative Writing at Arizona State University. Collaborating with her artist daughter during the pandemic, she published a series of illustrated poetry chapbooks, *Being a Woman: Overcoming, Being a Woman: Becoming*, and *Being a Woman*: *Forthcoming*. In 2020, she published a collection of poems to celebrate her one-year blog anniversary, *My Inspired Life: A Poetic Journey*. Her titles, *Her Coastal Cottage: Where Truth & Love Rise* and *Honeysuckle Heat,* offer readers the author's vivid poetic prose in novella length.

    Jade's Broken Bridge (2025) is her debut novel. She continues to publish creative projects under her imprint, Tumbleweed Spirit Press. Michele Lee enjoys sharing and connecting on her writing and photography blog, Tumbleweed Spirit, dancing with other expressive women, and working with Sandra Marinella, the author of *The Story You Need to Tell,* co-facilitating narrative therapy workshops.

To learn more about the author and for contact information,
please visit **msefton.com**.

Author photo by Blue Orchard Photography